APRIL HARRIS VICK

AUGUST CAESAR'S GHOSTS

A NOVEL

CHAPTER 1

"**A**unt Lydia, if you've made it all the way to 60 without killing anyone, why do it now—and why with me on the phone?" my niece asks, suppressing a chuckle. *Sonya doubts my resolve. And she knows I am only 59—until next month.*

Determined to keep her focused on the issue at hand, I tell her, "The traffic light is stuck in all directions. If it ever changes, she'll cross Georgia Avenue right in front of my car. I could get away with the perfect crime."

Sonya warns, "You can't get away with anything. Don't let the traffic get on your nerves. Just like you always say, *two raindrops fall and DC traffic slows to a crawl.*"

Since traffic has nothing to do with my state of mind, I ignore my sister's daughter and continue in a whisper. "Yvette will be the first one off the curb." I do not mention to Sonya that Yvette is as gorgeous in real life as she is in my dreams.

"Who's Yvette?"

There is no time to explain, so I lie. "She's wants to marry August." Immediately I regret bringing up his name.

"August Caesar? You're willing to go to jail over August? I mean—can he even *do anything* anymore?"

"He's only 62, *Miss Millennial.* No one's going to jail, and believe me, he can still do plenty," I assure her. I have noticed that Sonya's references to male virility have increased ever since she and her husband finally conceived.

"I'm sure he can. But why haven't I heard his name lately?" she asks.

"He's laser focused on trying to sell his company. It's all he thinks about. I told you before. He employs guards, consultants, installers—mainly under government contracts. Now stay focused. If I time this just right, I could also kneecap a couple of perverts."

"What perverts? How do you know they're perverts?" Sonya asks, now with genuine concern in her voice. *Perhaps she does doubt my sanity.*

"Because—they're following her, hypnotized. Her ass swings like a pendulum when she wears heels." *That sounds like a very specific observation.* "Here we go, Sonya. I'll just rev my engine, line them all up, and lift my foot off the brake."

She yells, "Stop! The cops will know they were inside the crosswalk—with the green light."

Okay, now, you're being helpful. "Yes, but when *DC's finest* arrive, I'll be slumped over and crying inconsolably, oblivious to my hemline," I explain.

Sonya laughs, "*Your hemline?* You must be wearing your short leather *skanky hanky.* Ma calls that your *hussy* skirt."

Rather than quoting stats from her mother's own *skanky track-record,* I let that one slide. Instead, I remind her, "The mechanics still don't know why this high-priced lemon lurches forward sometimes without warning. But I won't bring that up right away. You'll tell them about that when you show up to bail me out."

"Why me? Aunt Lydia, I know you can't be serious. But this is getting strange—even for you."

I chide her, "It's just like you to chicken out when I need an accessory. Just tell them about the mechanic's work order in my glove box."

Sonya tries to negotiate. "Now you know the data in your car's onboard computer will rat you out, don't you?"

I do not tell her that a nearby bookstore's security camera probably has videotape showing me stalking Yvette on Fridays. I admit, "I hadn't thought about that. I also forgot about Yvette's daughter, *the detective.* She'll find August's calls on both our mobile phones. CSI will lift samples of our DNA off his unwashed sheets and scrape traces off his half-washed ass."

Sonya laughs and warns, "Geez, Aunt Lydia. That's *TMI*. Let's just say the evidence will paint a sad, incriminating portrait of a tragic senior citizens' love triangle. The trial will devastate your grandchildren and send your son out on a ledge."

That's not so funny. I add, "And don't forget that local perverts will rise up and demand justice for their collaterally damaged colleagues."

She has more. "The judge will sentence you to life—and then tell you to *just do as much as you can.* And you know you can't wear orange."

Now, that is a sobering image. The light finally changes. "Okay, that's enough of that, funny girl." I clamp down on the brake, blow into a wad of bubble gum and tighten my grip on the steering wheel. Yvette and the two unidentified pervs cross the street safely. "It's all over, Sonya. Get your young ass uptown. We've got a lot of work to do today. Goodbye."

After Sonya disconnects, I turn into the parking lot and pause a moment for reflection.

I do not really want to kill Yvette. I am neither jealous nor am I a woman scorned. I do, however, dislike bearing sole responsibility for managing *our situation.* I defer to her priority for quality time with August. If she really loves him, her love, while most certainly unrequited, easily trumps my lunar cravings for his signature phallic performances.

So, I agree to wear her girly perfume so August will always smell the same. I brush away strands of my hair, popcorn and other evidence that he will neglect to remove from his clothing. He's not careless, he just doesn't care.

Because I know August insists on *riding bareback*, I cherish the peace of mind that comes with Yvette's presumed monogamy. I cherish the micro-bacterial compatibility of our yeast. My fleeting homicidal fantasy stems from evidence that she is no longer carrying her share of the load. She has allowed our restless *hound dog* to wander off the front porch again.

I know this because my real dog busted him.

Two weeks ago, Canuck, my big Labrador retriever, planted his schnauzer firmly against August's crotch and took a long sniff. With Canuck's canines so close to his schlong, August froze in terror and pretended not to understand. Canuck, being of Inuit descent, does not speak fluent English. So, I translated for him.

"Canuck smells a cat in your underwear, August. No, he says it's not Yevette. He reluctantly tolerates her familiar scent. He says this is a new scent from some strange feral pussy. *What's that, boy?* Oh, and he also warns me that you—just like the seat of your red drawers—*are full of shit.*"

As I have been doing every Friday morning, I park in the reserved space outside my office window and follow Yvette into the same bookstore. She is obviously a creature of habit, killing time in here until 9 AM appointments with her psychoanalyst. I so wish that I could save her some time and money—help her sort through August's bullshit for free.

She probably wants to understand why she still loves such an asshole—a problem in and of itself. He is rakish and commitment-phobic. His 24-hour security business always provides limitless excuses to claim that he is *on-call.*

I believe that Yvette intuits the presence of another woman, but she has no sensory evidence of her competitor's existence. With no traditional signs of breadcrumbs, I suspect she has started seeing ghosts at every turn.

Of course, *I'm her elusive ghost*, invisibly serving both our best interests.

I want to spare her the agony her imagination could be manufacturing, but I do not know how to tell her about me and convince her to stay in this odd threesome. I want the three of us to sort this thing out. After all, she has been our unwitting participant for three years.

As usual, I spot her in the bookstore perusing paperbacks in the aisle reserved for Romance—the wrong genre for a woman who could be on the road to an unhappy ending. When I sneak up behind her, she is returning a paperback to the shelf, mumbling aloud, "I guess youth really is wasted on the young."

I whisper, "And retirement is wasted on the old."

Yvette almost jumps out of her skin. Then, appearing embarrassed that I have overheard, laughs nervously, "Oops. I didn't realize I was using my outside voice." I am so close that she brushes against me when she turns. However, I stand my ground in her personal space, staring at her over an opened book.

I reassure her, "Don't worry about it. At this point in our lives, we've earned the right to speak our minds. Who cares if no one's around to hear us? But you know what they say about *seasoned* women like us nowadays?"

"That fifty is the new forty?" she volunteers playfully, ringing her southern belle for emphasis.

"Oh, you must mean *sixty is the new fifty*, don't you?" I ask. I sense her indignation over my correction, but she remains silent, allowing the truth to prevail. She tries to widen the space between us, but I close the distance, slowly revealing my face. When I am certain that Yvette does not recognize me, I relax and add, "Just when we retire and have time to play, it's hard to find a man who can keep up."

She laughs, nervously flipping a shock of hair streaked with swaths of silver gray. While I know her age, only the most astute would challenge her undercount. She asks, "So, what do you do?"

Her question is vague, so I respond to my preferred interpretation. "Oh, they're all on the pill these days. The last time I invited a man over, I could hear him pouring a glass of water before he hung up the phone. I used to catch men looking at their watches when it was time to go home. Now, it means their erection windows are closing fast."

I laugh at my own joke and search Yvette's face for a reaction. However, I see only a slight frown as her eyes scan the aisles for possible eavesdroppers. She says, "That's funny. But I was asking how *you remain fulfilled* after retirement."

I smile knowingly, both at her awkward dodge and her reluctance to indulge my more entertaining topic. I answer her with a shrug, "Oh you mean that. My niece is taking over my real estate business—gradually. I still put in time while she transitions in and I transition out. Personally, I'm only interested in ventures I can afford to invest in."

As I speak, I look over her exceptional clothing, seamless colors and textures, accessorized by a double string of pearls. The last time I was this close to her, I almost fainted. But this time, I am in control. I take a deep whiff of her cologne—that is, *our cologne*. Her body chemistry ignites the fragrance, giving it depth and releasing an intoxicating aura. It seduces me.

The chemicals fill my nostrils, triggering a faint heartbeat that quickly gains intensity. When it spreads through my nether-region, I clinch my ass cheeks to muffle the pounding that must surely be audible. Victimized by my own ambush, I beat a hasty retreat from my aggressive stance. I step back to give both of us more space and try to remain reasonably dry. The emergency panties in my desk drawer are a block away.

Two young men rescue me on their way to the rear of the store. They wear traditional business attire. However, as they approach, their professional strides morph into urban rhythmic gaits. Yvette turns just in time to catch a pair of eyes locked on her butt.

Appearing annoyed, she glares at them and returns her focus to a paperback. When the wingman makes a lewd comment to me, I mark them as two professionals trying, inexplicably, to project a little *street cred*. I admonish them as I would kids coloring outside the lines. "We're blessed. But we know you can do better than that."

One remains in character. However, the much cuter man changes his tone markedly. "We don't mean any disrespect—just blowing off steam on a busy morning." His words are void of negative energy. After they have passed, I overhear him mutter, "I can't tell. No more than 45—tops. They might be sisters."

I expect to see Yvette smiling, enjoying a younger man's attention and a gross miscalculation of her age. Instead, she looks at me, astonished. She says, "All women in DC give me the same advice. *Ignore disrespectful greetings. Always return respectful greetings. But never, ever phrase anything in the form of a question.*"

Before I can debunk yet another urban myth, I overhear the guys discussing a real estate issue. As Yvette returns her attention to the bookshelves, I wade uninvited, with business cards in hand, into their conversation about an unresponsive broker and an absent loan officer. After offering a few suggestions, I walk away with another potential client for Sonya.

Yvette has wandered further down to the Senior's section of the Romance aisle. I look up at paperback book covers intending to project alluring images of older lovers, sex and intrigue. Instead, they remind me of glossy ads touting cures for occasional irregularity and erectile dysfunction.

I sneak in close to her again, this time our arms touch, startling me with a low-level electrical charge. When I pull my hand away it glances over her butt—*accidentally*. She does not react. Rather than stepping away, she apparently resigns herself to my intrusiveness.

I try to jumpstart what has so far passed for conversation. "You know, I'd love to see more romance novels about real people our age. I had no idea how amazing sex could be without the distractions. Though men suffer late-life crises, trying to make us share what's no longer there." Again, I think I have spoken too loudly, and graphically, for her tastes.

Looking at me as though her patience is exhausted, Yvette returns her remaining items to the shelf. "It's been fun talking to you. I'm late for a meeting."

You still have 15 minutes before your appointment with that quack. I block her egress and offer my hand. When she shakes it, I offer my business card with the other hand. "I'm Lydia Davenport. I've seen you here before. My office is just across the street." She appears relieved, nodding as though she has solved a mystery.

The young man's assessment was correct. We could be sisters. Even in heels, we are the same height and our eye contact is direct. Our mixed gray hair and complexions are almost identical though my hair is courser.

I try to establish a more respectful interval, trying to put her at ease. Yvette averts her eyes by looking down at my business card and my color photograph taken over ten years ago. The card provides only my name, toll-free number and email address—which, of course, also provides my business name.

She appears to be suppressing a smile. "I'm pleased to meet you, Lydia. I'm Yvette Saxton. My cards are being updated, but I'll send you my contact info." *So, August has taught you how to bullshit—you have no cards.* She assures me, "I promise I'll email you. I need to find space for an art gallery."

Now I am intrigued. "Or you can just text me—same number. It takes time to learn about the city. Washington is a collection of small neighborhoods—each with its own character."

She still pretends to be running late for a meeting that is only an elevator ride away. Talking fast, she says, "That's what I'm learning. I purchased a diamond in the rough. My boyfriend supervised the interior rehab work and is overseeing the exterior work in phases."

She catches me off guard with something I did not know. "Oh, that's nice." My response rings hollow, even to my own ears. I try to recover by asking, "So do you know where you want your gallery to be?"

Yvette looks down at her watch to emphasize that her time is short, and talks even faster. "Friends are planning a project near Logan Circle. They see some synergies between my gallery and their project and are helping me with acquisition and costs."

I know that her friends are the Sinclair's, a much older power couple who, I hear, introduced her to August. It is difficult to temper my excitement over the location, and its ongoing residential reconstruction projects. "Logan Circle, huh? I'd like to know more about that. I hope we get a chance to follow up soon."

Yvette is walking toward the door. "We will. I need to get a proposal to them quickly. But I really must go to my next meeting, Lydia."

You know it's your only meeting. Her concern is most likely getting out in time to catch August's radio interview with Reggie Thomas. I call out to her even as she hurries away, "I live right on Rock Creek Park. It's kind of a straight shot from here—with a few turns."

As I watch her slip out of the store unnoticed into the elevator lobby, a disappointed voice behind me asks, "Where's your twin sister, baby girl? Do y'all both do real estate?"

"No, we just have a lot in common—maybe more than I thought."

"Say what?"

"Nothing, man."

CHAPTER 2

When I step into Dr. Rousseau's waiting area, he calls out from his inner office, "Just give me a few minutes, Yvette. I'll be right with you. Please make yourself at home." I hear what sounds like a recording of one of his presentations.

My patients are single, divorced or widowed, all over fifty—part of the area's older dating scene. These healthy seniors are an active subset of the local social culture.

Some mature women expend their ample energy, resources and time to cultivate romantic relationships. Others simply take care of deferred and unfinished business. By far, most insist on monogamy—regardless of their perceived desirability. Many of them are determined to find and bond with a permanent soulmate while they can still negotiate.

The older men truly fascinate me. I tell my male seniors that these active, vibrant senior women are healthy alternatives to the destructive pathologies that often bring pre-geriatric men to my office—the frustrations of chasing women half their ages. Of course, many older men and women still insist on younger partners.

Dr. Rousseau focuses on active seniors with a special emphasis on African American men. His work influenced my decision to consult with him, a popular relationship therapist who has published a best-selling self-help book titled *The Hard Truths about Relationships and Aging.*

I have listened to him on local media, impressed by his answers to complex questions from studio audiences and callers. While debates over his approach have been fierce, I have been convinced that he could help me work through what I see as *my problem.*

However, after eight sessions, I have begun to doubt this confirmed bachelor's capacity to grasp the nuances of a grandmother's passionate relationship. Also, I ask myself once again why a self-actualized painter-sculptor is consulting with a relationship therapist. *Am I so emotionally challenged by August's questionable monogamy? Or, am I simply lost in my own bullshit?*

Precisely on the hour, I hear him turn off the audio device. He emerges from the back of his suite looking like a man ready to tackle the problems of the world. "Good morning, Yvette. Come in and sit down anywhere you'd like."

I think we are both clear about which is the patient's chair. Behind one of two facing upholstered chairs is a backdrop of framed wall-mounted degrees, awards and certificates with others upright on the desk. That is the *therapist's chair.* There is always a bowl of perpetually fresh fruit on the oval coffee table between the two chairs. We never eat nor do we ever drink from two large mugs.

As my one-hour session begins, I sit in the patient's chair wondering if my expression reveals the impatience I am starting to feel. His expression is always blank. Beginning five sessions ago he began transforming himself from a stimulating raconteur into a mind-numbing shrink asking me questions like my current homework assignment, *identifying home.* Though I have given the answer considerable thought, I would rather pretend I still do not understand the assignment's purpose.

As I begin the ninth week of molding my ample ass into this leather chair, I prefer that he deal with what I have clearly described to him as *my problem.* Instead, he spends precious time peering into my past, taking a guided tour through a childhood aborted much too soon and a marriage that lingered much too long—things I already know.

"Yvette?" he prompts me in his *therapist's voice.*

11

Despite his good looks and that impressive package that hovers in my line of sight, I have decided that I do not like him. I think he knows this but remains undaunted—perhaps energized by my disdain.

Before selecting him, I interviewed two other men—*a woman might have been judgmental*. But both men seemed to be bending under the weight of their own baggage. One began our journey on the coast of West Africa. The other analyzed the contents of my panties far more than the content of my character.

Dr. Rousseau stood head and shoulders above both—though I wondered if talking to such a handsome single man would be a distraction.

He asks that I pin images of anyone who is significant in my life to a poster board he has mounted on a tripod. Over time, I have brought in photographs of my daughter in her police uniform, my son's family—and David. Then there is the charcoal portrait I sketched of August.

Dr. Rousseau pins and unpins images from one session to the next. He occasionally repositions them on the board as we speak. Today there is only my sketch of August looming large over this ninth session as though we were holding a testimonial—*or a memorial*. I cannot decide.

I feel an urge to pin Lydia Davenport's business card to the board, and tell him she has been stalking me. When I began these therapy sessions, she began popping up in the bookstore downstairs and the café across the street.

Today I realized Lydia is the same woman who crashed a private reception a year ago honoring my work with young artists in underserved communities. Brazenly cutting into my receiving line, she reached for my hand and lost her balance. I caught her but she leaned against me—a *full bodied* lean—for several beats longer than rebalancing required.

After I glanced over her shoulder to remind her that others were waiting, she walked away and melted back into the crowd. Though the fragrance seemed heavier, with an earthier aroma on her, it was clearly *my cologne*. It was the so-called exclusive fragrance August bought for me overseas and insisted that I wear.

I would consider engaging Lydia as my real estate broker but I would need to reconcile her eccentricity—as well as her aggressive sexuality. I dismiss the notion of discussing her today, and leave her card in my purse.

I remember that August once told me he has *always attracted women who date other women*. It was the most bracing revelation I have ever heard a man share. It was also the most curiously suggestive. If I ever return to this office, I will raise these issues.

I suspect that Dr. Rousseau wants to request authorization from my health insurer to conduct additional sessions. If so, I will not concur. We have said everything there is to say. We have discussed my giving birth to twins as a high school junior and marrying David, only one year older but prompted by his father to *do the right thing*. I have said that we took turns working and attending school.

I have described raising my two children, teaching, encouraging gifted students and selling some of my own creations along the way. I have told him how everyone saw us as the quintessential modern couple though we struggled to hold our marriage together.

After 30 years, we grew so far apart that we could barely recognize in each other the people we once loved. After reaching an agreement on our remaining assets, I divorced David and moved from Pittsburgh to Washington.

I have never discussed my brief encounter with Ethel, the woman who offered to share her suburban apartment while I looked for a house in DC. We became fast friends until Ethel made some unfortunate assumptions. I am certain that our entanglement was no more than a dalliance, a manifestation of rebounding from David. It certainly has no relevance to the issues Dr. Rosseau and I need to explore.

"Home, Yvette?" His question annoys me since we both know that home is the happy place my ex-husband and I once knew.

"Haven't we covered that ground already, *doctor?* I say his title in the form of a question, but he does not react. I continue, "We've exhausted discussions about my youth, such as it was. I don't think we'll find any other place I'd call home. I get that it shaped the woman that I am. However, I certainly don't yearn for a do-over. It would help if you defined *home.*"

He is ready for the question and his response is immediate. "Yvette, home is the place you've felt safest, wherever that may be. The place that recurs repeatedly in your dreams. You return there periodically, to get recharged and reinforced. One of the greatest benefits to having a happy childhood home—for those fortunate to have that luxury—is that you can always return there, either physically or emotionally, to rediscover yourself."

I try to be difficult. "It's David's house now."

He ignores me again. "I don't know which home you will choose. I know you won't find what you are looking for or recognize it, unless you can associate it with your safe place. Think of it the way *African Americans,*" pronouncing the term like an anthropologist, "say we can't know where we're going without knowing where we've been. In your case, it's the place you've been that holds the most significance for you."

I think I get it, but still hear myself asking, "Who doesn't know where they've been?" His expression reminds me of the way I look at a precocious student during a teachable moment.

"Yvette, I've built my practice helping people who don't know where they've been or where they're going." He leans in hovering over the edge of the coffee table, his voice piercing softly, "on people afraid of where they've been, uncomfortable with where they are or terrified of where they're going."

I sense him studying me intensely, allowing an extended pause, in the space of which my thoughts race through my reasons for being in this pretentious little office with this pompous man. I think about how happy I should be about my independence, about shopping around for my own art gallery. Yet I am not. I sense his eyes following my gaze to the drawing of August.

I remind Dr. Rousseau that, even though my time with August has been exhilarating, I have discovered in this chair that I cannot be in a lasting relationship without also feeling secure.

"I don't feel secure with August. He easily groups the facets of his complex life into separate files. I cannot do that. I cannot separate the relationships I have with family and friends from my relationship with a man. In this chair, I have learned that this isn't a shortcoming. It is merely who I am."

I know that August is not my soul mate. I am thrilled by the sex—especially his intuitive responses to my needs. As though prompted by dialogue queues, his lines have great timing and phrasing. If he is only inventing this persona, he is either an anointed actor or a pimp. I cannot tell which. I am feeling less compelled to find out.

However, I remind Dr. Rousseau that, "August makes no promises to break or long-term plans to cancel. He has mentioned in passing that he may run for local office, making casual references to needing *the right woman by my side.*"

I could ask what that means, but August would never ask me without first being certain I will accept. I cannot imagine agreeing to anything so foolish. A seat on the city council would give the *Prince of Plausible Deniability* another excuse to be anywhere at any time.

I love August's redeeming qualities. He has overcome countless environmental obstacles on his journey. He knows exactly who he is and never tries to be anyone else—accept maybe the tough kid known as AC. "Sometimes he fails to act his age. Okay, he often fails to act his age. He genuinely wants the best for people and pushes them, including me, to pursue their greatest potential."

I look intensely into the doctor's eyes, saying, "But more than anything, I love the way he makes me feel—even when he crudely refers to it as *servicing me.* He touches me deeply, beyond David's emotional reach—*and well beyond David's physical reach.* Even when I know I should, I can never tell him *no.*" Dr. Rousseau is blushing, but I must go on. "To be honest, this is a slippery slope. If I slip and fall for him, I could *descend into a dark place from which I can't escape.*"

From my dark place, I hear the doctor's voice, but, annoyingly, he is not pointing me to the way out. "And so, then *home* Yvette?"

Although I find Dr. Rousseau to be an arrogant shit, I must concede that he is a capable therapist. I decide to indulge his game. "So, my relationship perspectives are framed both by my childhood and my years as a happy wife and mother." Without speaking, he sinks back into his chair. I muse about how narrow an ass print he must be leaving compared to that which would result from August's wooden apple.

I continue. "Since I know my perspective, I should know why I perceive my new relationship the way that I do. I may never be able to assess my feelings about August without comparing him to David—*to home.* I need to let August be August and Yvette be Yvette—separately. But no matter what, I do not want to grow old alone."

I hear Dr. Rousseau saying something else from far away. I can tell he intends it to be profound, but I cannot make it out. I am exhausted and sweat is forming on every inch of my body. *I cannot believe my hot surges continue long after other women my age are over this curse.* My eyes feel very warm. However, I will not cry in front of this man.

He sounds concerned. "Yvette. I don't know why I ask. I guess I'm just curious about something. Did anything substantially out of the ordinary happen to you today?"

I want him to focus on something else—anything else. I consider telling him about a conversation I had with JoAnne who says she has found something troubling about August. But before we could get the specifics, my son interrupted us. "We agreed to table it until our usual post session recap today. However, I do not want to discuss today with her. I would rather hear about the new mystery man in her life."

As fate would have it, I have forgotten to turn off my phone and the ringtone tells me it is a text from JoAnne. I am still not comfortable with text messages, online banking or social media of any kind.

The phone rings again playing a Coltrane riff. I scoot back in the big leather seat and suppress a smile. August swore I would feel his hands on my ass whenever I heard the ringtone he programmed in my phone.

"I'm sorry Doc. Let me turn this thing off." I fumble with my phone and shove it into my purse, but I have not successfully turned it off. We both hear the saxophone again. "He's just wants to make sure I remember to listen to his radio interview." I do not recognize my own voice.

When I look up again, the doctor is still waiting for a response to a question I no longer remember. My voice has a light, buoyant quality. "Doctor Rousseau, what were you asking me?"

"Yvette, how would you feel about continuing our sessions for a while longer?"

CHAPTER 3

"**T**his is it, Renee. You can see them through the glass and hear everything they say through the speakers." Just relax. Your boss should do fine."

I am relaxed, confident that Mr. Caesar is well prepared for this interview. Someone begins a countdown, "Ready in five, four, three, two, one and we are back."

"Good morning to all our listeners throughout the District and the Maryland and Virginia suburbs—that tri-state intersection of diverse cultures known as the DMV. I'm Reggie Thomas and this is Business Insider, where WDMV Radio presents the movers and the shakers in our local community. Our guest today is August J. Caesar, president of AJC Security. August, it's great to have you on our show today."

Predictably, Mr. C arrived a little later than planned, but in time to receive last minute instructions. However, his tardiness presents no problem. He can change his demeanor like a chameleon to adapt to changing scenarios.

I watch him take several deep breaths and exhale slowly. Composed, he morphs from harried late arrival to confident, focused guest. He responds instantly using what he calls his *money voice*, "And it's my pleasure to be here with you and your listeners, Reggie."

WDMV FM is one of the Washington Area's most popular radio stations and Reggie Thomas has been hosting the weekly *Business Insider* segment for 15 years. Appearing on the show is a rite of passage for local entrepreneurs, politicians and community leaders. It is a great marketing opportunity—thirty minutes of free radio time.

Reggie delivers his first question—which appears designed to help his guest relax—like a slow softball pitched right over the plate. "August, what products and services does AJC Security provide, and who are some of your customers?"

Mr. C begins to recite what he calls our *elevator speech*. "We have enjoyed some success as an emerging full-service provider of both physical and electronic security and surveillance services and equipment. Our primary customers are in state and local governments and we also now have our first federal customer."

I wish I could speak as well as he does. My delivery has improved over the past few years. However, my personal friendships require that I lapse into a more relaxed urban vernacular. Therefore, in professional settings I consciously form each word as I speak, limiting my ability to get my points across. Somehow, he can transition seamlessly.

Reggie continues, "I would imagine that security has become a booming business. I remember when I could walk into any government agency in town and go right upstairs to visit with anyone I wanted to see. Nowadays, I have to get past armed storm troopers and metal detectors just to get past the lobby."

"That's right, Reggie. Attitudes of people who inhabit the world we live in have changed. Over the last decade, we've come a long way from passive profiling and random ID checks to sophisticated detection, facial recognition and bio screening devices."

Reggie pretends to shudder—audibly. "Man, it all sounds like something out of a spy movie. So how did you get into this business, August? In fact, why don't you take a few minutes and tell us about your background and how you came to start AJC. In short, go ahead and give us a five-minute trailer of the *August Caesar Story*."

AJC's vice president, Jerry Lane, and I have already discussed this with the boss. He knows how specifically he wants to respond to this expected human-interest question. Jerry insists that guests who open-up on the show achieve a greater resonance with Reggie's audience.

"Well, Reggie, I was born in the city, the only son of a single teen mother. I grew up first, just east of the river and later, in Northeast, dropped out of school, and spent the next 22 years in the Army. I served four tours of duty in Vietnam, and while serving, finished high school and took college courses whenever I could. I eventually earned an MBA." Mr. Caesar says that people who knew him then have no idea he ever left.

"So, my quick math tells me you were in the Army from Vietnam to the Iraq War?"

"Yes. In fact, that was my last overseas assignment, Reggie. I worked in Army security and surveillance. After retiring, I worked in physical and electronic security for a large defense contractor until, well, I guess you would say I retired a second time."

"So, that's when you started AJC?"

"Exactly. I started it five years ago, sitting around a kitchen table with a compensation-deferred consultant and a part-time secretary." He looks out at me and winks. The boss continues to describe some of the challenges he faced in the first year and how hard we had to work to overcome them. I hear emotion in the boss's voice, but it comes off as passion.

I feel passion when I think about sitting with him at that kitchen table in Southeast. I had worked briefly as a temporary worker for the same defense contractor. After he left to form his own company, he hired me to answer phones, take messages and keep up with his schedule, leaving callers with the impression that he, Jerry and I were all at one location with additional staff.

However, Mr. C and Jerry were constantly visiting clients and buyers. They were tenacious. *Every buyer is a potential client.* I was never sure where working for these two rolling stones would lead me, but after five years, I have learned almost every facet of the business. My salary is too low for the level of work I perform. However, my salary has enabled me to purchase a three-bedroom townhouse in suburban Maryland.

"So, how many people do you employ now and where would you like to see AJC go, and what are the challenges you see on the road ahead?" Reggie asks.

"AJC currently employs 200 full-time employees, all working at customers' sites." I know he is ready for that question, which he and Jerry thoroughly discussed yesterday. "We have carefully established a footprint by performing subcontracts and state and local jobs. Now, we are looking at the federal space for avenues of expansion. Without getting more specific than that, I'd say our challenges are rooted in the growing number of new businesses in the marketplace, and the downsized government's tendency to make larger purchases from fewer contractors."

Despite AJC's relatively small size, I do not believe the boss ever intended for the company to grow as much as it has. I am convinced that if they could get away with it, he and Jerry would conduct all business exclusively from their homes and automobiles.

Mr. C tells me that, in this digital age, *rush-hour congestion is the nation's most asinine waste of time and resources.* However, the boss also says he functions within a culture where traditional behaviors, customer expectations and tax codes push many entrepreneurs toward brick and mortar business models.

Our plan was for Mr. C to respond within a few seconds to every question to avoid dead air and maintain continuity. The reporter in Reggie wants to cover all the bases. They spend the next several minutes expanding on a few points, and after short commercial break, Reggie reintroduces him and continues.

"August, I'm still amazed when I hear you guys refer to 200 employees as a small business. However, I must say that your explanations are as simplistic as any I've ever gotten from anyone, which makes them refreshingly clear. You'd make a great teacher—or perhaps a great politician." With about ten minutes remaining, Reggie tries to segue to politics. To his credit, the boss looks unfazed.

"I know we're here to talk about your company, and I know our listeners have already benefitted from some of the information you've shared. Three long-serving city council members have indicated they will not seek reelection next year—and two more are very vulnerable.

"I just can't let anyone on the show leave here, certainly not a DC resident and local employer, without weighing in on what this could mean for the city. What kind of candidates would you like to see in the race? More specifically, do you think businesspeople might make better city managers?"

It sounds like someone has leaked inside information to Reggie and I hope the boss does not take the bait. An announcement of his candidacy would be premature—perhaps fatally so.

The boss delivers a speech I have not yet heard. "It's interesting to hear you phrase the question that way, Reggie, because I think experience in business management could be essential to solving the problems that plague our city. Crime has affected every corner of the city—in fact, every corner of the DMV.

"The mayor and those council members from the wards most impacted have been bearing the brunt of criticism, but everyone, particularly the at-large city council members, has an obligation to work toward developing and implementing sound solutions. However, I believe that the key is job creation.

"Changing the way our police operate and changing the way our criminal justice system operates will help us crack down on people who commit crimes. Changing the way our prison, release and parole systems operate can reduce the gnawing problem of recidivism. But, as we seek solutions, we must remember that the issue is jobs, and the key to increasing job creation is effective leadership."

The boss sounds like he is on the stump—saying things that sound good without really saying anything at all. "Okay. Well stated, and thank you, August. You sound like a candidate yourself. I may have to start a *draft August Caesar movement.*"

Reggie allows a long pause, and I think the boss needs to say something here. He does, adding, "Well if ever that time comes, I would be honored to have you as a mentor and supporter." *That was spot on.*

"We'll have to take a break now and that's where you and I will have to leave it, August. But before we go, will you come back and declare your intentions on my show?"

"There is nothing to declare, Reg. But I'll come back anytime."

"Okay, but I may have to keep working on you. Also, since they say that behind every successful man is a woman; is there is a Mrs. Caesar—or a soon-to-be Mrs. Caesar?"

That question probably catches him off guard. None of us has anticipated it. "Well, no, Reggie. There isn't."

Reggie pushes the issue further. "Not even a significant other? No? Well now, folks. There you have it, August Caesar, President of AJC—and an eligible bachelor." *I know at least two women who are not going to like this.* "I'll be right back after a word from our sponsors. Don't move away from the number one station in the capital of the nation."

"And, we are off." They walk out of the sound studio. Reggie sounds upbeat. "Hey that was a great interview. Thank you so much for stopping by to talk to us."

Turning toward me, Reggie voice changes slightly. "And it was a pleasure to meet you also, Miss Renee Webster, right?" He holds my hand longer than necessary. The boss smiles, I shoot him a quick thumbs-up and head for the door. I am anxious to check for important messages before his *insignificant others* start looking for him.

As I walk through the radio station, I look back to see one of Reggie's female interns step out into the aisle in front of the boss holding out her business card just in case he *has any further questions.* Mr. C accepts the card. Then he and Reggie hurry toward the men's room. I laugh, thinking that they remind me of my older friend, Roscoe.

I met Roscoe the evening my mechanic called to say my car would have to remain in his garage overnight. Mr. C had insisted that I still attend an important business reception, and volunteered to give me a ride.

Nervous at the crowded event and unaccustomed to champagne, I allowed myself to be slightly over-served. In my agreeable state of mind, I found Roscoe to be a charming liar. Claiming he *was going my way*, he insisted that I allow him to take me home.

During the long ride, my tight-fitting garment—the *body sleeve* a salesperson convinced me to wear as my *cocktail dress*—shifted, giving Roscoe panoramic views. Once home, he got out and held open the passenger door.

Still slightly inebriated, I failed to make the dignified exit I had hoped to make from the low-riding sportscar. I stumbled, dress up to my ass, into the arms of a man who suddenly looked 20 years younger. A voice that sounded like mine asked if he was coming in.

I would later joke that what followed was semi-authorized entry. I remember that he moved with the dexterity of a cat burglar, bending me forward on my bed, ripping open my pantyhose. But surprisingly, he gently penetrated, rotated and sort of negotiated his way from different angles—exhibiting an uncanny accuracy for the bullseye. I closed my eyes, certain that I saw a light flash inside my head.

Eventually, he laid me down and made missionary love as though we had been intimate partners for years. When his body finally stiffened, he called out my name, *correctly*.

He collapsed, inhaling oxygen by the cubic yard. I was afraid he could not recover. Then, just before I dialed 911, he stirred. Roscoe calmly repackaged himself as though nothing out of the ordinary had occurred, drank cold water until his body temperature dropped, and strutted out of my place as smoothly as he had arrived.

My mobile phone rings, startling me. I recognize the number but, in my state of mind, allow Mr. C's forwarded personal call to go to my voice mail. I insist on answering the boss's business calls because I enjoy the insight doing so provides. But I do not enjoy taking his personal calls, of which he has too many.

Another call comes in forwarded from his mobile phone. I recognize the number of the vice president of UniverSec. "Hello again, Miss Webster, this is Peter Stanton. I'm calling to confirm our noon conference call with Mister Caesar today." I tell him that the call is firm on his schedule, and that he will take it on his way to the office if his earlier meeting runs long.

"Oh, he'll take it in his car again? I know I'm checking in early—and maybe unnecessarily. It's just that I'll have several very busy people on the call from multiple locations. So, it's a lot to coordinate. Yes, I understand that he was on the radio this morning. Okay then. We'll call him back as planned at 12:00 noon your time. Thank you, Miss Webster. Good bye."

Other than the fact that it is a large corporation, I know nothing about this company. UniverSec's interest in AJC is a mystery to me. We have standard practices for dealing with potential teaming partners, but Mr. C has chosen to keep this one close to his vest. I receive another call. "Hey Jerry, did you hear the interview? So how do you think it went?"

He quips his response. "Well. I would rather hear how you think it went." When I started working for AJC, I had perceived Jerry as Mr. C's *white alter ego*. While that is an accurate assessment, I have come to recognize that, at any position, Jerry is an exceptional team player. Wherever the issue involves management, marketing, money or one of our boss's unexplained absences, Jerry seamlessly shores up the problem or works around it.

I answer Jerry's question by saying what I think he would say. "I thought he punched all the issues, convinced listeners that he knows what he is doing and has a plan for continued growth and success." I immediately regret that my answer sounds canned.

Jerry responds predictably, "Now tell me what you think without trying to handle me."

I hesitate but decide to speak honestly. "I think he could have talked more about our commitment to customer needs and should have driven home our record for on-time delivery within budget." I can *hear* Jerry nodding, so I continue. "The only other things I would've liked were something about what a great place AJC is to work and our reputation for being a great teaming partner."

"Okay. Those are all excellent points. Don't be afraid to tell him. He needs to hear it and will respect you for saying it. Now, I don't suppose, with all the media glitz, you've had time to put together the morning rundown. No problem, just give me a call back when you have it, or send me your notes if I can't pick up."

"Okay, Jerry, will do."

"And oh, by chance, have you gotten any calls from Jefferson Sinclair? Okay, I was just curious." That question startles me. Jerry rarely asks me about the boss's personal calls—and I never divulge.

We follow with discussions about a few other items, including Jerry's vacation plans with his husband next week. When I start to hear the split-second breaks indicating that others are trying to call him, I wrap up. "Okay, Jerry. I'll tag up with you again soon."

It occurs to me that Jerry asked for mine, but did not give me his thoughts on the interview.

CHAPTER 4

"**S**mack, ain't that your old running-buddy on the radio—the one who used to boost for you and Pharaoh when y'all was kids?" Peaches still recognizes his name after the years that have passed since I pointed him out to her. Shantel answers her mother's question.

"Yeah, Peaches. That's August Caesar on the *Reggie Thomas Show*. Let Russell listen to the show, Ma."

Peaches sounds animated. "Now you know it's on the record that I can listen to a man with a deep voice like his all night long."

I look over at Shantel who laughs and turns around to face her mother seated in the back of my car. "As I recall Peaches, it was your voice I heard all night long."

They both laugh—loudly. Peaches stays on message, "Hey, what can I say? Girl, I like a man to *snatch* the pussy like they used to do—you know, way back when old school *niggas was real niggas*. Smack, I don't know whose voice I like more—your friend AC or my man Pharaoh." She begins to sing the chorus of an old song—all *night long*.

We are returning from taking Peaches' sister to the airport to catch her return flight to Louisiana. Dodging traffic, I cross the Wilson Bridge and follow South Capitol Street back to the gentrified former public housing neighborhood we call home.

The airport drop-off marks the end of a visit that began two weeks ago and lasted nearly two weeks too long. Shantel has taken a week off from work and the intensity of our household's interactions have been maddening. I have found salvation in driving the night shift for the airport limo service that employs me.

However, the ride home from the airport is nostalgic. I have watched DC transition through several phases of decay, redevelopment and gentrification. I welcome some of the changes, but note how some areas remain the same—even as swaths of adjacent real estate are reborn. I also note that, all too often, powerless people become displaced rather than relocated as promised.

When I stop at a red light, we glance back and moan while Peaches keeps singing. She still considers Pharaoh to be her man even though her one overnight date with him consisted of steamed crabs and steamy debauchery.

The circumstances surrounding some her other less substantiated conquests change with the retelling of each story. "Y'all can smile all y'all want. And Shantel, you know you was backstage with me that night my man from Motown called out my name."

"Yeah, Peaches. I remember. He got it right on the third try." Shantel is always willing to acknowledge the incident but, strangely, always insists on clarifying exactly what transpired.

Whenever Peaches' sister visits, it is only a matter of time and alcohol before they tell everyone *the story*. Before Shantel was born, two famous headliners invited them to a private party after a show at the Howard Theater. As local legend has it, both singers went missing for two weeks.

"And you saw how he looked at me when he sang my song." She continues with the inevitable, "Girl, I told you that man might be your daddy."

However, the logical candidate for that title is dead. Peaches' longtime boyfriend, Checkers, got drunk and beat her every weekend until the Coast Guard found him adrift out on the water, shot to death. His bloated corpse might have floated out to sea if they had not sighted it near the confluence of the Potomac and Patuxent Rivers.

"Please don't sing Ma, please. Let Russell listen to rest of the show. You know that's his boy," she adds sarcastically. Her mother stops singing but bobs to the melody she hears in her head.

As I listen to August talk about his childhood, I hear no regrets or remorse, but rather recollections of those days when we ran away from our respective foster homes. Luckily, we found Pharaoh—a careful hustler who taught us to survive in the shadows. I am not surprised when August does not provide specifics.

Shantel always asks me how he escaped our surroundings and enjoyed a successful life while I served ten years of hard time. Fortunately, I do not have to remind her on those occasions that I have been her reliable life partner and provider for her three daughters—*unlike their absent fathers.*

She also knows that my time in the Lorton Penitentiary has always limited my options. She is obsessed with understanding the contrasts between my life and that of the younger kid I protected—the kid who walked into that liquor store with me and left me hanging out to dry. I know this interview will prompt her to ask me about it again.

When the show's host asks August about the woman in his life, Peaches yells, "What did he just say? *No significant other*—do you believe that?"

Mother and daughter laugh aloud, speculating that August has merely played it safe—unwilling to encourage some or discourage others. I wonder why August didn't easily dodge the question by electing to *protect her right to privacy*—whoever *she* is.

Shantel encourages her incorrigible mother. "I believe there might be a mighty upset woman or two out there somewhere. There ain't no way AC ain't got one in DC who think he belong to her." Shantel knows just what to say to rile her mother, especially when she wants to stir something up. My life partner still surprises me with her capacity for instigating trouble.

Predictably, Peaches becomes introspective. I roll my eyes at Shantel. "You only saw the man once, Peaches."

However, my words have come too late. She remains quiet after the interview ends. At the next commercial break, her request comes as no surprise—certainly not to Shantel. "I know, but you didn't hear what he said to me, with his hand on my ass. Why don't you call him, Smack? Just tell him *Peaches asked about him.*"

"Yeah Russell, bring him over for my mother so we can all break bread and talk—you know, about the good old days." I do not like the look on her face.

I try once more to resist. "Come on now. It has been years since I saw him. AC must be over sixty years old. Plus, what about your boyfriend?"

"*My what kind of friend?* Who you talking about?"

"You know. Lump."

They both laugh. When I get a chance to turn around, Peaches is looking at me quizzically. "Oh, you serious, Smack? No, Lump ain't never been my *boyfriend*. He comes around and that's fine, but he knows when to leave."

"Don't get the shit all off track here. As I was about to say, you older than AC is, with my young assed daughter sitting up there next to you—laughing at people like a little child. You say y'all used to be boys. I don't care how long ago. Invite that high roller to the house. We can cook up some gumbo."

"Oh, in that case, I'll try, Peaches, but I can't promise anything."

CHAPTER 5

"Jefferson, that boy could sell ice to Eskimos."

I agree with Councilman Spencer's assessment. At the conclusion of August's interview, I turn off my radio and face my two guests who joined me to listen in.

Except for a little pain from arthritis in my knees and an occasional heart palpitation, I feel particularly strong today. I feel energized because I can still summon two of the city's political elite to my home on a weekday morning. *Not bad for a reclusive octogenarian.*

"Well, Mister Sinclair, you know it's easier for a black man to sell ice to Eskimos. Black people would complain that his ice ain't cold enough." Adele Wilkes cannot resist interjecting a play on the punch line from an old joke I hear at every black business conference.

As the story goes, at the turn of the last century, a black-owned ice company sought unsuccessfully to challenge an established white company for sales in a black community. The black seller went the extra mile to provide larger blocks, faster service and a lower price. Still, he failed and went out of business. Asked later why they continued to buy ice from the white supplier, customers replied that *the white man's ice just seemed so much colder.*

We all laugh good-naturedly at the painful old joke. I try again for their thoughts about August's performance. "So, just give it to me, straight with no chaser. What do you think?"

As expected, Jay Spencer is the first to speak in earnest. "Jeff, you have to remember that we're talking about running him citywide, not in just a single ward."

"But sometimes that can be easier." I immediately realize I have not only interrupted my powerful friend, but also insulted his intelligence with a fact he already knows. I wave off my own comment. "I'm sorry Jay. Please continue."

"No problem, old friend. Maybe I was stating the obvious. We're talking about a virtual unknown winning an at-large council seat. Y'all both know a dozen people have had their eyes on my seat for the past decade—people who've been working their entire adult lives in the political trenches, often with me."

Jay allows a moment for his point to sink in before expanding. With it, he has implied what I believe is his biggest concern—some of the people to whom he refers are his friends and protégés. However, they all have collected too much political baggage—filled with Jay's dirty laundry. They could never clean up all the bodies they have helped him bury along the way.

Jay continues, "Some started out as neighborhood commissioners and community organizers. Some have been church leaders, NAACP chapter presidents—hell, even a high school principal would be light years ahead of your boy. He's already sixty. People will wonder why he wants to do this, why *we want him* to do this. I know the Congressman will."

I have anticipated Jay's uneasiness about backing the politically unknown August and the threat he and a few others could eventually pose to his friend, the city's vulnerable fourth-term Congressional Delegate. Any wise politician would be concerned, and Jay, though past 80 now, is the most astute person on the city council.

I do not comment on his questioning August's age, considering his own. I merely add, "But all those candidates you mentioned fall light years behind August—if he's endorsed by Jay Spencer. And by-the-way, August looks like he's only fifty."

"I hear he behaves like he's only twenty-five." The interjection comes from Adele Wilkes, whose greatest strength is the difficulty people have trying to figure out her greatest strength.

She is a no-nonsense manager and organizer—grass roots, corporate, intergovernmental, a unique combination of skills, strengths and contacts. She is tireless in her pursuit of a goal, with a resume that includes managing several successful campaigns for mayor, suburban county council and city council seats.

My strategy hinges heavily on Adele's support. Jay's endorsement will be critical, but his top supporters have aged with him. He rode in on the coattails of a previous mayor now deceased, and has no one in his sphere with the influence in the neighborhoods that Adele brings.

If asked, she could have arrived today with at least one effective grass-roots organizer from every neighborhood east of the park. If necessary, my wife can still mobilize support west of the park.

I could not have anyone better than Adele Wilkes to do the hard work required to get August elected. I stare back at her in silence, not thrilled by her remark about my protégé but still encouraged that she has already begun the thorough sandpapering that is her normal vetting process.

She clarifies, "I don't want to work hard only to lose because he can't keep it in his pants, Jeff." Her candid—and graphic—remark does not solicit a comment and I offer none.

"I will say that he can certainly talk a good game. I'll give him that. And he's agile on his feet. He was smart enough to get in a few sound bites today without falling into the trap that you and Reggie obviously set for him on the radio today. I liked that. Now, is he clean?"

"Yes." Jay and I have already discussed privately the one issue that could have presented a problem, but Jay has assured me that it is no longer an issue. I am impressed but not surprised that Adele guessed that someone planted Reggie's political question. Of course, any astute person might suspect August's sponsor and longtime member of the station's board.

Now that Adele has raised the issue, Jay stays on the topic of August's past. "Jeff, we know some solid people who grew up in foster homes." Adele raises her hand to signify her membership in that club—and probably also to signify that membership is no excuse for self-destructive behavior.

Jay continues, "But I understand August grew up *in no home*, running with hustlers—one of whom we know all too well. There's always a chance that he may have gotten into something else somewhere along the way—something he ain't even told you, Jeff."

"Yes. I recognize that's always possible, Jay. But I'm confident that he hasn't kept anything from me. But I have no problem grilling him again face-to-face."

I know my promise will appease Jay but I try to read Adele. We seem always to be on opposite sides of issues, but have always shown one another a healthy mutual respect. Moreover, I have always responded to her fund-raising appeals. If she agrees, this will be the first time we have joined forces.

However, I have not yet identified any kind of carrot, something she needs but cannot obtain for herself. One of the purposes of this morning's meeting is to give her the opportunity to ask me for something. I cannot imagine that she has not come here without a condition, and it will be awkward for long-time hustlers like us to adjourn without airing it.

Adele's presence here and her posture, though guarded, suggests that she is at least seriously considering managing August's campaign.

"I like him, Jefferson. I had an extended conversation with him recently at a business conference. I honestly couldn't tell whether he's a good listener or just gifted with the ability to bullshit people. But that doesn't matter because either will work."

She is still talking—a good sign. "He'll hit home runs in the churches—a very strong double-bass voice yet with a mellow soothing quality. It has just enough of an edge to sell him east of the river. It has enough—how should I put it—*congeniality* to sell him west of the park. He's a decorated vet and a twice-wounded warrior to boot. I prefer that he was a sergeant-major rather than an officer. How do we package and sell the voters on his family ties?"

Therein is his weakness. I fill her in on the key points, but wonder how much she and August exchanged in that business conference conversation, considering her remark about *keeping it in his pants.* August has always struggled in that area but by now, he should be showing signs of slowing down. I tick off the essential facts.

"He divorced a wife from a very early marriage. His son from that marriage, from a good family, is a successful franchisee out west. The second son is here in community college—his local mother got into drugs briefly after his birth, but has been sober now for at least 20 years.

"As you know, August was a foster child, dead no-account father *and* foster father, no brothers or sisters—not even one long lost cousin. He does have a childhood best friend, almost like an older brother, who did some hard time way back in the 1970s but appears to have flown straight ever since."

"Any photos of August with either son will show very likable guys. Alone, he'll look good in print ads and TV spots." You heard how he sounds on radio. I look from one to the other, hearing an enthusiasm in my voice that belies my own lingering concerns. "His style is casual and folksy, but he's tireless, intelligent, focused, charming—one of those guys that people just like."

"Does he have any interest in getting married anytime in the foreseeable future? That would help. A long engagement would be better than running as a committed bachelor. Some women wouldn't trust him." Then, as though reading my mind, Adele restates Jay's point. "And are you absolutely certain he really wants to jump into this—at sixty? You know I'll need to hear that directly from him."

I respond immediately and candidly, "To answer your first question, he has a girlfriend whose looks and personality would blow everyone away—one of Edith's missionary women. But for some reason, he has still not yet proposed to her. Hell, don't ask me why not. I don't understand it. Like you say the man is over 60 now." Adele looks down at the table, barely able to suppress a knowing smile.

I understand how Adele feels about August's perceived promiscuity. While time has mellowed him, I am certain there are women who could come out of the woodwork and paint some very troubling pictures of his earlier years. Many here will recognize that the DMV is fertile ground for such exploits—by men and women alike. However, the Area hemorrhages bad blood from people who find that popular social hobby less than appealing.

I know that my wife shares Adele's concerns about some aspects of August's past and some of the images that might surface in print, digital media and on local television and radio. Edith has asked me on several occasions, *what do you intend to do with Sonny Boy, Smack, Doll Baby, Big Pharaoh, Little Pharaoh and Biscuit—hide them all in the witness protection program?*

My answer remains, *I do not know.* Edith has reminded me that, if August lets me down, I will have to eat a mile-long *shit sandwich—with extra shit.* But my wife of 60 years also reminds me on occasion of my own past transgressions with *ghosts* who live in what she calls *the shadows.*

Even if August's ghosts never take form, reporters could camp outside the row house in the H Street corridor where his son lives with mother and great-grandmother. Thus far, my strategy has been to pump a little money and a lot of expertise into the only thing that has ever kept Sonny's mother consistently engaged—food preparation.

She has tried working at least a dozen jobs and generally remained gainfully employed, but will look a lot more palatable to voters if she owns and operates a successful catering business. My best hope for Sonny is that he will stay in college and out of trouble.

However, it is strange, perhaps even disconcerting to hear Adele ask if August wants to run. While both Edith and I know he has not yet made up his mind, it strikes me as odd that others would question his intentions—given my support for him.

Although her ability to gather grass-roots intelligence is legendary, Adele should have no such information. August and I have discussed at length the need to appear energized and intrigued by the idea of running, even when privately suggesting disinterest.

"Perhaps you could share with me why you ask that. See, regardless of what he might say in public, we are here this morning because I know he's running. I would hope that you would debunk any rumors you might hear to the contrary. Mainly he's just thinking like the businessman he is. Right now, August wants a sense of the discriminators that will set him apart from the competition. That's where you guys—and a dozen or so others—come in.

"Neither he nor his business partner wants to run a larger business. As soon as they can value AJC high enough to pad their investment portfolios and retirement accounts, they'll sell. One large deal will give them the modest payoff they want. However, if prospective investors smell a fire sale, that could lower the value. I'll give you a sense of where they are next time we talk, but his decision will hinge a lot on what you tell me here today." They both know that I will not ask again.

Jay speaks up, "How can I say no to you after all we've been through Jeff? You ain't ever asked me for one damned favor in 50 years—now Edith is another story." We both laugh.

Adele reaches across the table to extend her handshake. "I guess I've got another one left in the tank for Jefferson Sinclair. It'll be nice to be openly on the same side—for a change. By the way, I meant to ask about Mrs. Sinclair. The last time I spoke with her, we talked about my son. Yes, my son the pastor. He's trying to work his way back here to get a church in the DMV. Sure, I think he would be thrilled to be out in Prince George's—or anywhere where the demographics were right, anywhere he can have the things that are important to him."

I am happy to find out about something that is important to Adele— something Edith can easily deliver. "He sounds like a solid guy. I know he comes from good stock. I wish you would bring him by the house—soon."

CHAPTER 6

"**L**ook mother, I could get into a lot of trouble if any of this ever got out, but there's something about August Caesar you need to know."

As usual, my mother picks me up in front of my precinct for our tag-up after her therapy session with Dr. Rousseau. Today I have something important I want to tell her but she appears to have other plans for the hour we will spend together.

"Oh JoAnne, let's not do that today. I'd hoped that after I brief you on my final therapy session, you might tell me more about your new boyfriend. You barely mentioned him before rambling on about cohabitation. What's going on? Is it that serious?"

My tenuous relationship with Kelly is the last thing I want to discuss with my strait-laced mother today. In addition, until I am certain that Kelly and I have permanently reconciled our differences, I will not tell her that Kelly, or *Kelisha*, is the *girlfriend* I hope to marry—not the big strapping son-in-law she has wanted.

How do I tell my mother that my sexual relationship with this woman has been so intense as to be transformative? How do I tell my mother I am a lesbian? Why does she not know? Mother has met most of the willing partners I dated during high school, college and beyond, a series of well-balanced women who marveled at Mother's capacity for delusion and denial.

First, Kelly and I must fix our problem. With me, trust is always the common ingredient in any winning formula for a successful relationship. However, there is something that limits the trust we can ever expect to share.

I love her inner strength as much as I love her talent for deep tissue stimulation. However, whenever her insecurity manifests as her impatience with *my insecurity*, we come to an impasse.

Kelly believes that our inability to connect is rooted in our different upbringings, and that our differing backgrounds should be the starting point for approaching our issues. That is a nonstarter. I have spoken with her at length about her absent father, emphasizing that paternal love is more important for a daughter than for a son.

The aunt who assumed the role of her caretaker shaped the woman Kelly is today. However, the support she provided Kelly was insufficient and bore no resemblance to motherhood.

Since my father has always known about my sexuality and—unlike Mother—has unconditionally embraced it, Kelly looks at me from light years away. To her I am a possessive gold-star femme whose stroll down easy street puts me at more of a disadvantage than her past struggles for emotional survival.

Now my simple request for the passcodes to her cell phone has sent us spiraling out of control toward *relationship Armageddon*. Unless we resolve our issues, I will not come out to Mother.

I know my mother can tell that I am upset. I lower my voice to a whisper. I am so distraught I imagine that someone has bugged her SUV. I begin to ramble, hoping that I will achieve coherency at some point. "A misdemeanor committed as a juvenile is not available for a routine background check or basic investigation. It remains in a confidential internal police database with limited access. Despite my concerns about your boyfriend, I only did this because you said an investigator showed up at your house asking about Caesar."

Mother seems impatient for me to get to the point. She begins, "Yes, that's right. The private investigator wanted to know if I had met anyone from August's distant past—his childhood. However, of course, I've only known August since Edith Sinclair introduced us three years ago."

My mother knows very little about August Caesar. I had all the information I needed the first time I saw him.

I had dropped by my mother's house unannounced one rainy night and noticed shadows moving inside her idling SUV. Several workers were inside the house performing rehab work. I crept up her driveway to her truck's rear window with my gun drawn. Her back seats were down. Peering inside I saw a man's naked ass piston-driving like a locomotive jackshaft.

My sweet innocent mother was absorbing far more than I would ever have imagined. I wanted to run away but could only stand there frozen, watching two senior citizens behave like equines in the wild. With workers just inside the house, my mother was almost naked. I believe August was wearing a hat.

I recall thinking that, if he could seduce her into joining him in semi-public displays, he could also control her. Just as I summoned the resolve to slip away, I heard my mother crying out Biblical references.

On the verge of intervening in a coerced assault, I was surprised to see her hands reach around to clench his ass. As her nails pushed into his skin, he drove harder and faster. Then I noted how wide she had spread her legs, bracing for every jarring thrust.

One of her feet propped in a window sill. Up until then, I had assumed that sex for my mother took place gently, under the covers with clothing largely intact. I was ashamed of my voyeurism but appalled by images I have never been able to erase.

I turn to glance at the back seats and wince, still able to see the two of them writhing like teenagers. I try to block out the vivid images and prepare her for what I am going to say next. "Mother, I know I should not have done it—but I could not help but search the database—on his name."

"JoAnne! You've got to stop this obsession. Tell me. Has he done anything to harm to me? No. Is he after anything material? No. What's wrong with you?" My mother perceives that I have been trespassing—but I do this work daily.

"Mother, listen to me. I saw something about a juvenile confession that was successfully plea-bargained to a misdemeanor." I allow that to sink in.

Mother suddenly is more intrigued than appalled. She did not know where this conversation was going, but surely, she never expected it to include a conviction—even as a juvenile. Still she appeals for calm. "How old was he at the time and exactly what did he do, JoAnne?"

"Sixteen. Mother, do not give me that look. I know what you're thinking. He was on his own in the streets as a child. Under those circumstances, I understand that no one would be surprised to find a juvie record. I didn't have time to read the whole file because someone walked in on me."

I doubt my findings will affect my mother's feelings about him—not under his life circumstances. I look around the street as though afraid someone might be watching us. "But that's not what concerns me now. Here's the kicker, Mother. When I went back a few days later—just a few days later, that same file along with its contents had vanished."

"Vanished?"

"Vanished, gone, poof—like it was never there." I expect her to be repulsed about the mysterious disappearance of a police file on a man who might run for public office. I am disappointed that what I see as good police work, she sees as compulsive obsessive behavior. Oddly enough, I sense that a part of her is impressed that August may have been able to accomplish such a feat. Involuntarily, I envision her in compromising sexual positions.

Finally, she relaxes and looks at me as though I am the one who has committed a transgression. "Why do you even care, Jo?"

I have found out something else. "There's more, Mother."

"Why do you even care so much about this?"

"I care because it concerns you. Anything he does to you—or makes you do—concerns me. The next morning my supervisor asked me, for no reason, to search his name in the very same database. Right, I couldn't believe it either. What do you think I did? I ran the search again as if I had never checked it before, and gave him my findings—that no such record existed. You don't get it, mother. It was inappropriate for him to ask me the way he did."

Even without knowing procedures, the sequence of events must sound more than coincidental to my mother's ears—though she would never say so aloud and risk adding fuel to my paranoia. "Second, I found out that if my supervisor suspects foul play, he can get a tech to provide a list of all log-ins that have accessed the database and the dates and times of their queries. That's right. I could be screwed."

Her instincts tell her I need protection. "You need to relax. You need to come up with a plausible excuse for having been in that database. Next, determine if a tech can tell him which file you specifically checked."

"Of course, I can invent a reason to be in the database, but your second point—the answer to which I do not know—is good. So, you're not concerned about the crime I uncovered?"

"What crime, Jo? You don't even know what he did—or if he did it. You need to focus on protecting yourself—now that an obsession has led you down this road."

She stuns me and I am glad I kept some evidence. "Mother, I just can't make you understand. You're in love with a man you don't even know. Oh yes you are. Admit it. If he asked you to marry him today, what would you say?

As I thought she would, she hesitates to answer, instead becoming pensive. "Funny, I thought about that in my session this morning. Honestly, I don't know what I'd say. Yesterday I would have said no. Then I heard him on the radio and felt a rush of excitement over the prospect of a run for office. Jefferson has such faith in him. Jeff's no fool Jo. He thinks August was born for this. So right now, I admit that I don't know."

"Careful, Mother, you don't know him."

"And you do because a homeless kid may have committed a crime? I know what he is. For a while, I've thought one of his crazy girlfriends might be following me. Just calm down—turns out she works near the doctor and spotted me. She was only being nosey."

I ask, "Are you sure it wasn't his baby mamma?"

Now my mother is intrigued. "Okay, young lady, now what else do you have to tell me?"

I struggle to suppress the glee I feel about sharing this information. "It appears that Caesar has a Cleopatra--and a young Caesarian."

I grasp the overhead strap as Mother veers off the street and stops next to a fire hydrant. Her expression has changed to a blank stare. She does not speak, too proud to ask me for the details. Therefore, I volunteer them. "He makes a home for them in Northeast. The kid is in his twenties, going to school. The mother appears to be chronically unemployed—and only in her late thirties.

The last comment about her age may have struck the most tightly wound chord. She steadies her voice. "Okay, super sleuth, you got me that time. August has never talked about family. I'm not surprised he has a child—just surprised he's never bothered to tell me. After the way I go on about my kids and grandkids. Private person or no, most people would've worked this into a conversation by now."

"Mother, a normal person would've worked that into the first detailed conversation you ever had." She knows she cannot argue the point, and remains silent. I need to say something else before she pulls back out into the street. "Mother..."

This time she braces herself. "Yes, Jo. What is it? I'm supposed to call August before I go into the restaurant."

"Good. You can ask him about his other son out in California, and from a marriage that time. No. I don't know anything about a divorce."

CHAPTER 7

I am anxious for feedback on my interview with Reggie Thomas, but first I walk the distance from the radio studio to my car. Following my doctor's orders, I have on comfortable shoes and have parked ten blocks from their location in Chinatown.

This morning, I found a two-hour metered parking space available next to a department store in Center City. On the street level, they have a fresh lilac-scented men's room that will be the perfect pit stop at the conclusion of this hike.

I will have plenty of time—no matter what I do in there—to go in and get back to my car before the meter runs out. Just one more parking citation and they will boot my car and tow it to some godforsaken place called White Plains.

Of course, I expect that different people have perceived and assessed my interview depending on their interest in its outcome. It will depend on how much skin they have in the game.

As the person—other than myself—with the most skin at risk, I am curious about Jerry's assessment. We are obsessed with becoming one of the government's ESP contractors. Only companies selected to receive orders through the Electronic Surveillance Protocol will compete for a pool of security contracts valued over a billion dollars.

While I do not want distractions, Jeff Sinclair has tasked a campaign committee to get me elected to an at-large council seat. I cannot decide if I should run. But until AJC win's one of the eight ESP contracts and hike the company's valuation, I have no interest in spending a million of anyone's dollars just to win a part-time government job that comes with a full-time suite of daily headaches. I simply do not want to work that hard anymore.

I would rather plan for an active retirement. We have invested heavily in AJC's pursuit of ESP. Jeff may have suspicions about my solvency but only Jerry really knows the extent to which I have leveraged myself. If we are not one of the firms selected, I will have to buy out Jerry and muscle through alone a few more years.

My quality of life and the lifestyles of the people closest to me will not diminish dramatically. However, I will not be happy—the most important goal I have set. Nevertheless, I want to get acceptable value for five years of my time and effort before I disappear on a slow voyage around the world.

I straighten my posture, hoping good form will delay the inevitable lower back pain. At least my breathing is relaxed. It occurs to me, belatedly, that I should have responded *yes* to Reggie's *significant other* question and then declined, for the sake of privacy, to reveal an identity. Instead, I dropped the kind of faux pa I would have artfully avoided in my prime.

I take my phone out of my pocket and the business card handed to me by Reggie's young assistant falls to the ground. I ignore it and continue walking. I remove my call forwarding from Renee's phone and mine rings instantly. Lydia's photograph flashes on the screen. "Hello."

She gets right into her favorite pastime—role playing. "Well August, it's a good thing I didn't have my radio turned up in the office. A little voice cautioned me against telling Sonya that my man was being interviewed today on the *Reggie Thomas Show*."

Though surely spoken in jest, I think I detect some irritation in her voice. *That damned dog of hers. Is she really offended? Is she merely using my gaffe to chide me?* I know I will regret indulging her. "What do you mean?"

She continues to tease—I think. "Well, I might be embarrassed to have anyone know that I'm late for my next meeting because, as your insignificant other, I was glued to your radio interview?"

There is no semblance of levity in her voice now so it is probably not the best time to remind her that we are not—nor have ever been—*a couple*. I play along anyway. "He caught me totally off guard with that last question. I know how I must have sounded." However, this is as far as I am willing to go. I need to use this time checking in with Renee.

However, Lydia is just starting to warm up. "What a coincidence, you caught me totally off-guard with your answer. However, I guess I should be thankful I didn't have to listen to you talk about your *First Lady*. You know whom I'm talking about. *Queen Oblivious*. I should have run over her ass when I had the chance."

"What are you talking about?" She does not tell me but I am certain I will find out. About once a month, Lydia craves my companionship and invites me over. That may be more time, energy and stamina than either of us has time to invest. After all, we share a common interest in women. She has never needed or asked for more attention—*until lately*.

Our conversation, such as it has been, has ended for me. "Look, I've got another call coming in. Goodbye Lydia."

She has a parting shot. "And tell that *little cookie* you hired to answer your phones to do her job. No one is calling to reach *the voicemail of Renee Webster*."

I disconnect. I have no real interest in her playful feedback, but thought that, after my thirty-minute interview, she would have made a helpful assessment—no matter how critical—to offer me.

As I walk the remaining blocks toward the Metro Center and my car, I try not to allow her call to cloud my concentration. I do not want to compound the effects of my trek with a tense posture, so when Lydia calls back, I allow her call to go to voicemail.

My lower back pain kicks in acutely and my calves begin to heat up. I need to get back in the gym. My 90-day sugar averages are teetering ominously up toward the tipping point for symptoms associated with onset diabetes. My PSA is climbing. My systolic pressure is flirting with 90. I must *cowboy up* and get this walking in whenever I can.

I am relieved to see my car up ahead and pleased no one has put a ticket on the windshield or towed it. Parking tickets, tows and speed cameras are the city's lucrative answer to budget deficits.

When I come back out of the department store, I open the car door and my phone rings again, this time pairing automatically with the cabin's speaker system. I have a call from Renee. I begin speaking before I am completely inside, relieved to take the load off my feet. "What's up?"

"Mister Richards called from the agency." Bob Richards is the government's technical representative on AJC's only affirmative action program contract, which is also our largest. "He won't be able to talk to you again until next week, but wants you to know that they've decided to modify our contact to add six more positions." She can sense that I am trying to do the math in my head. "That will increase the level of effort by about six hundred thousand dollars annually when you include overhead and our fee."

"Can I go out on a limb and assume that my very able office manager has already placed ads?"

"Three out of the six existing employees are acceptable and will transition over to AJC. But for the other three jobs, I put ads in the Post, the Times, the Gazettes, the Blade, the Sentinel, the Afro-American, the Hispanic and the Latin Times…"

"Geez Renee, that's a lot for three new people. Keep your eye on our money."

Oh, Mister C, you know you got a money tree. When we win the ESP contract in a few months, we'll need two hundred more people. Since we need to interview prospects anyway, we should go ahead and start filling up our queue now with candidates as we vet them."

I must admit that she is correct, and is sounding more like Jerry every day. I love her enthusiasm and confidence, but need to temper her expectations. "You mean the contract we don't yet have?"

"We're on a roll, Mister C." She pauses. "But boss. I'm not your *office manager*. I'm the *chief operating officer*." I chuckle at her nerve but note that her voice contains just a slight hint of defiance.

"*The chief of what*—who told you that?"

"It's what it says on my new business cards."

I know she would never print new business cards without asking. Renee came to work for AJC at minimum wage when the company existed almost completely in my mind and on my kitchen table. I have been thrilled to mentor a young woman raised by her aunt in the Trinidad section of Northeast, not far from where my son lives now. I would give anything to inspire her drive in Sonny.

As AJC has grown, I have incrementally increased Renee's salary above a fair market rate for an office manager, and she clearly recognizes the company's potential for further growth. In midstream, she changed her major from cosmetology and graduated from community college with an associate's in management. Over the past year, she has worked part-time on a Bachelor's degree in business administration.

She has devoured material dealing with contracts and project management. She has been exceptional and we depend on her for operations support, particularly resource allocation.

Jefferson Sinclair says she has *a mind like a steel bear trap*. She absorbs everything I tell her and listens intently to Jerry, a minority shareholder in AJC and one of the most gifted project managers I have ever met.

Her effectiveness has helped AJC grow to 200 employees without the unnecessary expense of additional administrative layers. I decide to compromise. "You may list your title as deputy director of operations."

"Okay, I'm all in boss." Though clearly happy, she does not hesitate to follow with the obvious question. "But who is the director of operations?"

"That position shall remain vacant until filled." I do not wait for her response. "Any other calls?"

"Peter Stanton called to confirm your twelve o'clock call. No. That's it. Jerry tagged up. I'll send him a rundown report. There are a few other minor issues. There has been nothing that a good acting director of operations can't handle alone."

I laugh aloud. Maybe rather than emulating Jerry, she is becoming more and more like me every day. "Okay, call me if you need me."

I can forgive Renee for not recognizing the importance of the call from Peter Stanton at UniverSec since I have not revealed to her the significance of our discussions. Peter is interested in acquiring AJC. He also wants to use my company as what some affirmative action detractors might call *a front*.

Using my status as an African American, AJC participates in a special business program. Stanton wants to arrange to have a very large contract awarded to me that we would perform as a team, but Peter would have me violate the rules on staffing under an uncomfortably thin veil of deceit.

I take Pete's calls and keep him engaged as another hedge against insolvency. If I find myself alone at AJC away from Jerry's prying eyes, I might be more inclined to entertain Pete's proposal. Desperate times could call for desperate measures.

I drive north because Jeff wants my opinion of a vacant lot near Logan Circle where he wants to build, with the city's help, a performing arts school for talented DC high school musicians, actors and artists.

Some see it as the flawed dream of an aging powerbroker. Jeff has no one to carry on his name. He is attempting to immortalize it by carving it into brick and mortar. However, he is also my close friend and longtime mentor. Because he has devoted substantial time and energy into helping me to realize my goals, I feel compelled to invest in his.

Driving through the Logan Circle area in Northwest, I see a flurry of residential construction and rehabilitation activity. Workers are restoring rows of brick Victorian homes to their former splendor.

When I locate Jeff's lot near the edge of the U Street corridor, I note that it is larger than I had imagined. It appears to be large enough for a school, but I cannot competently judge without consulting a professional broker. Perhaps Lydia's real estate judgment is better informed than her views on relationships.

My phone rings again, and the photo of a smiling Yvette fills the screen and lifts my spirits. "Hi."

"Hi, I'm fine. Sorry I couldn't take your call earlier this morning before the show. Then I know you got busy. I started to text you afterwards, but my text would have gone on forever."

Though she has spent three years in the city, her voice still carries a Virginia tidewater accent that her years in Pennsylvania could not diminish. However, the affectation is hardly noticeable among the southern drawls that blanket the diction of city residents. An inordinate number of them have roots in North Carolina and other areas throughout the South.

"That's okay, I'm in the car. Hands-free and safe."

"Well, I don't recall your hands ever really being free or safe—certainly not in an automobile. I'm about to go in and eat an early lunch with my daughter. You know how it is when you have children. I just wanted to let you know that I heard the interview. I thought it was excellent, very poised and articulate. Great answers too."

I suddenly realize how much I have been looking forward to her feedback. "I hope I didn't come off too wordy?"

"Absolutely not. I thought you were succinct, responsive and direct. No dead air at all, which I remember was one of your objectives. Right after each question, your answer followed, without sounding at all rehearsed. Great job, August. You're a natural."

Her tone is markedly upbeat, expressing genuine support. Her voice has that enabling quality that instills confidence in one's—in my—ability to overcome challenges. When she speaks to me, her words seem to pump oxygen into the air, and there are times when I simply cannot breathe in enough of it.

Many times, I have come very close to telling her that I love her, but am concerned with the expectations that might create. I know that if I follow Jeff's suggestion and run for office, Yvette would be my greatest asset. However, I do not like his obsession with packaging what Yvette and I share into a political asset.

"You know, he kind of caught me off-guard with that last silly question." Although I do not want to, I sound apologetic. My response to

Reggie Thomas' question could have offended her. For three years, my *Miss Congeniality* has avoided any semblance of confrontation.

Now she surprises me today by saying, "No apology needed for me. I noticed that you were brimming with confidence until then. I thought you might have been thinking about some of your family relationships." *That's twice she's mentioned my family. What's this about?* She says, "Oh, so now we have dead air. You did a fine job, August. That's not what your interview today was about. Just leave it."

I do not know how she knows nor do I know how we have never in three years talked about Jack or Sonny—or Doll. I suggest coming over to her house. "I'd like to come over and talk to you tonight, but I was just over there last week. I don't want to wear out my welcome."

This time, she does not respond in a schoolteacher's motivational tone. Instead, I hear a woman who is comfortable in her own skin and confident about her sexuality. "August, you know good and well that you could never come over often enough. I really don't know if—in your mind and in your world—I'm your woman, your girlfriend or what. But I'd better be the only one you have. Since you know you're the only one I have, you need to get up here and handle your business."

CHAPTER 8

I am near Yvette's house when I receive a disturbing phone call from AJC's preferred mail order pharmacy. "You've got to be shitting me."

"No sir, Mister Caesar." He does not take offense to my profanity, which is good because I think there might be more to come. He continues in his practiced monotone. "Your company's insurance carrier should have provided information prior to the open season. There are changes in prescription drug coverage. You really should contact them."

The voice comes across calm and relaxed no doubt honed by hundreds of similar responses to hundreds of similar complaints. Most of my small company's employees use our health insurance carrier's prescription mail order service to ship ninety-day supplies of medicines directly to their homes.

The arrangement has worked well for us, but an end-of-year change in the list of covered drugs apparently had gone largely unnoticed until male employees began replenishing their ninety-day stashes of erectile drugs. "Yes sir. I understand that the change results in a significant increase in out-of-pocket costs."

During the first few months of this year, we received three dozen employee complaints about our carrier's decision to drop their performance-enhancement drug coverage.

Some of the callers said Internet searches for cheaper prices have yielded online pharmacies that will ship the medication for a small fraction of any local pharmacy's retail price. However, I need to raise my comfort level substantially before leaving our employees with no other option than generic offshore medications.

Ordinarily Renee would extinguish a human resources fire. However, this blaze has burned so brightly that employees have threatened mass defections and resignations.

Thus, I provide assurances that the problem is receiving my personal attention. The notion of employees massing near the exit doors runs contrary to my goal of rapidly increasing the AJC Security Company's valuation to my target asking price.

"Of course, we will at their request reduce the count in their orders if the full price of any prescription is prohibitive." Even though I consider the suggestion absurd, the voice does not sound condescending. Rather, it sounds like a thin solution. I am not looking for a temporary fix.

I end the conversation saying, "No. we'll get back to you."

I conduct a quick audit of my own supplies, counting the one tablet currently in my system and the remaining four that will buy me two additional weeks of erectile certainty. However, my personal prescription orders are not at issue. As a military retiree, I am covered. However, only a few other AJC employees, many of them working their second careers in physical security, have that luxury.

Jerry Lane, my vice president and the oldest AJC employee, has already cast his unsolicited vote to switch carriers, even though he is also retired from the Army. I call Renee to tell her to begin the process of selecting a new carrier. I hope that we can find a temporary fix until the next open season, even if it means direct subsidies of male virility.

It is late when I reach Renee. "Okay Mister C. But what should we do about some of the other concerns? You know, about things like better prenatal care and pediatric services? I mean since you're personally handling this now." I rationalize that I have called her late in the evening after she has put in a long day.

Thus, I temper my response as best I can. "I've heard from at least six females on this same issue. They have family plans that include their husbands as covered individuals. So, if you would please just take care of this as I've requested. Thank you."

The long drive from my suburban office to Yvette's house is an opportunity for reflection. I am lucky to be in this relationship. However, there are limits to the time and energy I can make available for her. I may be overextended, focusing on my company, deciding on my candidacy for office, transitioning my son into adulthood and now ensuring my employees' can sustain erections.

Jeff, the self-appointed architect of the Caesar for City Council movement, often refers to Yvette as my *First Lady*. She could never make love to me before she was in love with me, and I am at a loss to understand what I have done to earn this woman's love.

She has an all-or-nothing approach to love. She and her ex-husband lost their virginity together on the night of her sixteenth birthday, and she still makes love with the wide-eyed enthusiasm of a 16-year old girl. She devours every touch, kiss and embrace with an excitement that suggests that no one has ever touched, kissed or embraced her before.

Her limited exposure in no way diminishes my appetite for her—or my appreciation for experiencing some of the magic that she and David once shared. As a person who cannot even remember the names of half of his past partners, to me, Yvette is essentially a virgin. Making love to her is a special privilege that requires special care. I feel challenged by that responsibility.

Most women have accused me of being commitment-phobic. My single-minded focus on sex has been consistent since I accidentally brushed across little Judy's ass in a crowded fifth-grade coatroom.

The sheer excitement, not to mention little Judy's unexpected silence, dominated my thoughts for the rest of the school year. A half century later, even with diminished erections, I often behave like that same little boy, trying to rub it up against every attractive woman I encounter.

Conversely, despite her lack of exposure, Yvette's maturity is consistent with her years. As a young mother, she did not experience high school dating or the varietal smorgasbord of boys available to undergraduate female students. Yet she understands intimacy better than most. She can quickly assess—but never judge—people with an accuracy that is spot on.

However, she is insecure—especially about my intentions. She has thrown in her lot with a man who has honed passive aggressive uncertainty to an art form. Despite my claims of truth and honesty, in all truth and honesty, I might very well end up as a burned-out old rake destined to die alone as an old nursing home playboy.

Her tastefully updated Monroe Street home rises high above a street transitioning from generations of old Northeast families to a wave of new cosmopolitan urban settlers. I am impressed with the progress her contractor has made. With minimum supervision or oversight from me, he has maintained the house in its elegant past while incorporating modern upgrades.

Waiting at the door, she greets me with a long warm embrace and I hold onto her as long as possible. Then, I turn my attention to visiting her bathroom, admiring the eclectic decorations adorning the interior of her home. It is a seamless blending of African and Native American motifs, including carvings, sculptures and paintings.

The colors if her art mesh tastefully with her furnishings and the whole montage is a perfect backdrop for her smooth Afro-Indian features. As the seconds go by, I am embarrassed about the amount of time I spend in her bathroom trying to squeeze the contents of my bladder through a slightly obstructed pathway.

When I reemerge, Yvette is moving about the house draped in a white robe that accents every contour of her shapely body.

As I gawk, she fills the awkward silence. "So, you were surprised by the political questions in the interview."

"Oh yes, I had not really prepared for that. I think Jeff planted them. *Why?* I don't know. Maybe he wanted to know if I could dance. How do you think that part went over?" I ask.

She responds, "Actually, fine August. He never asked a direct question. He simply set a trap and to see if you would step into it and show your hand. But you answered like you were a concerned well-informed citizen. Look baby, you nailed it. Stop worrying about it."

When she opens her robe in anticipation of an impending hot surge, I can see that she is clad only in a snug sleeveless jersey and panties. I quickly lose my focus. She sits back in her seat to catch the breezes generated by her ceiling fan. I take a seat, waiting for the unwelcomed heat in her body to subside.

"Come on, since the doctor has you on the wagon, let's go upstairs." She takes my hand, gently guiding me out of the chair. I stand up dutifully but then she stops suddenly, turning to face me again.

"August, I had the strangest visitor." As she speaks, she searches my face for clues. "A man knocked on my door and flashed a badge, saying he was an investigator for the government."

She has my attention. "So, what did he want?"

"He said that your clearance was being reviewed and that he had a few questions for me." She sits back down. "He asked how long I've known you. When I told him, he seemed to lose interest, but asked if I had met your family, your sons or any of your old childhood friends. Of course, since I don't even know if you have family, I couldn't say."

Although none of it sounds typical, including the emphasis she puts on the information she claims not to know, I lie. "It all sounds like typical stuff, Yvette."

I am a little more relaxed now. Someone hired the mystery man to dig up something in my background. By now, Jeff has erased the only bogey I can recall. I have been through the government's clearance processes.

I have endured polygraphs and mock interrogations at survival school deep in the forests of the Pacific Northwest. No one has quizzed my friends with this level of intensity—including volunteering to Yvette that I have two sons. I am certain I have never mentioned it.

"August, you aren't in any kind of trouble, are you? I mean about your family or anything in your past?" She has that look again. There is something different in her voice, but I do not detect alarm.

I neither hold nor need a clearance that would send an investigator to Yvette's home. Since the PI knows she would tell me about his visit, he wants to see how I will react. He will be disappointed—unless this goes much further. I expect a little digging once Jeff starts lining up financial support, but hope this political skullduggery does not stir up a hornets' nest.

I must allay any concerns that Yvette's mind may have manufactured. "This is probably about that ESP contract I told you about. We'll need a facility clearance to protect some supersensitive stuff." I would rather lie to than tell her I do not know. "And I don't know why I've never told you about my sons. I have a son I never see in California. His mother and I divorced out there a long time ago. I have another son, my namesake, here in town living with his mother—whom I provide some support but have never been married to. Okay?"

"Thank you for that—and we have to talk a lot more about all that another time—and why it has never before come up in conversation."

I stand up and pull her up from the sofa. "Fair enough. We will, if you'd like. But there's not much more to say. Now what was that about upstairs?"

Without another word, she discards the robe completely and stands, pressing her body against mine before starting up the stairs in front of me, the short jersey top rising over her shapely bottom.

Yvette has over many years, very innocently developed a provocative natural switching motion in her walk. I follow the hypnotic rocking movements as her ample cheeks strain against the fabric of her panties. As we ascend the stairs, I notice for the first time that piano jazz has been playing softly upstairs.

The pill I swallowed this morning begins working before we are halfway upstairs. It occurs to me that there was a time when I would have bent her over at the landing and taken her from behind as an introductory demonstration of prowess. I ignore that dangerous impulse, probably avoiding the embarrassment of explaining to emergency staff how grandma and grandpa fell backwards down the stairs.

In the upstairs hallway, she turns toward her smaller guest bedroom. I resist making a remark about her choice of venue and an equally crude comment about a *service interval*.

I have come to recognize that my urban vernacular has mood-killing power in this house. Once in the smaller bedroom, I embrace her from behind allowing her to feel my fully medicated passion. When I kiss the back of her neck, she whispers my name and turns around to wrap her arms around my neck.

I use my hands to undress myself as she kisses me. After she removes her top, she pulls me down with her onto the daybed. I chance a quip. "You know this my favorite spot in the house." Of course, she does. The bed and the matching oversized ceiling fan are gifts from me. She presses two fingers to my lips to discourage further comments.

I immediately saw the potential in this large daybed, a sturdy wrought iron apparatus matched with a thick, firm mattress on a sturdy coiled box. The arms are perfectly spaced handgrips and footrests. I tested them in the furniture store to the shock of a young salesperson. I wanted to confirm that the arms would enable me to remain semi-suspended and target a single pressure point for extended periods.

However, I sense that tonight Yvette is in the mood for intimacy as opposed to mounting. Confused about her choice of venue, I indulge her pace until I can no longer resist assuming the position.

When I do, she does not protest. Our rhythm ebbs and flows with the tempo of each track of music, but the force of each thrust remains consistent. At one point I think the volume on her stereo has grown inexplicably loud only to discover that we have rocked the wheeled daybed across the floor to the doorway.

I have a passing thought about rocking it back but abandon the idea, noting it would entail doubling the degree of difficulty.

When my arms and legs grow weary from the reps, I resume a much more intimate embrace, commencing a manageable spiral that I hope will inevitably bring us to conclusion.

Predictably, after a few more tracks have played, her eyes pop open as she feels a familiar telltale twitch. When she pulls me closer for a final spiritual bonding, I gladly submit. We mold our bodies into what she believes is an existential, Siamese existence of the *yin and the yang*. I look down and see her staring up at me in anticipation. However, before I surrender, she unexpectedly begins to flutter, expand and contract.

I lose the power of speech and search her eyes for the explanation she does not seem to have. I know she will conclude later that it is a special gift inspired by feelings I could never understand.

A wave sparks and migrates over the crown of my head and down my spine until it trips a switch at the base. My release is from a bygone era of youth and its endless capacity, and requires several spasms to expend. My mouth opens wide and I make an indecipherable sound that exists nowhere else in the natural world.

Her question to me, however, is clear and concise. "August, why can't you just tell me you love me?"

CHAPTER 9

"**L**ook Doll, I'm moving as fast as I can."

"Biscuit, you need to hurry up and get off my porch before AC gets here. I'm going to catch enough of his shit today without hearing him going on about why you shouldn't be here." I shout and watch my father make his way gingerly down the stairs to the sidewalk. He moves slower every year. He is a shadow of the man once known in neighborhood folklore for jumping from a bedroom window, pulling his pants up on the way down—and landing in the shoes he had already tossed out.

I know he has been upstairs long enough to get whatever my grandmother is willing to *loan her son* this month, and August has called to say that he is stopping by my house—*his house* actually—on his way downtown. If he catches Biscuit hanging around here again, my whole day is going down the toilet.

My father shouts back over his shoulder, "Remember, I knew your man long before he was riding around town in business suits. I knew him when he was a wild young dude stealing clothes. I remember when he was into some serious shit. Did he ever tell you about that? Businessman my ass, I know the whole story." Despite his protests, however, I know my father is moving as fast as he can.

While August convincingly plays the part of the corporate executive, I know he hustled right in this neighborhood until all the stores burned down in the 1968 riots. Mentally, he is as hard as these streets.

While the grapevine says that, as a brawler, he came up short, my father seems to ignite a special fire inside him. Arthritis runs in our family like hard heads and soft behinds, and Biscuit's legs have seen better days. Still, he is keeping it moving. I shout out to him, "Well when are you going to tell me the whole story?"

I know he will not. August has confided in me about enlisting in the Army when he was 16 *to avoid trouble*. All that happened when I was just a child, and my father has built a colorful resume of his own.

After he had grown too old to steal, Biscuit Jackson began driving a taxicab decades ago as a cover for his primary work—bagman and tri-state talent scout for a pimp. He never attended high school, never worked for a legitimate employer, never paid taxes, voted or registered anything in his own name.

We have no idea where or how he lives now. Oddly, or maybe as a testament to his craftiness, he has no criminal record, existing only as a shadow. Moreover, a shadow he shall remain until he finally disappears and reappears as a *John Doe* in the city's morgue.

This morning, I watch him, aged far beyond his years, making his way toward a taxicab converted from a stolen sedan. My father has no legally issued taxi license nor driver's license with his real name. However, it appears he still has Esther, or *Cookie*, waiting for him in the passenger seat. She knows better than to show her face here, but I am relieved to know that he still has someone.

"You shouldn't be so hard on him, Ruth. He just started looking for shortcuts after your grandfather died. But he just never figured out how to make that life work for him. Very few people ever do." I turn toward the sound of my grandmother's voice speaking to me from behind the screened storm door.

I can barely see her leaning slightly forward over her walker.

"I'm not hard on him, Momma. I just don't want to have to get into all that with AC today. I know he's going to ask why I quit that stupid job."

"I don't see Sonny Boy's car. Did he know his father was going to come by here today?" While he knows that he should be here to speak with his father, Sonny's car is nowhere in sight. Momma's great grandson is the love of her life. Though he is the mirror image of August, she says that she sees in him the natural gifts of her deceased husband and the wasted raw potential of Biscuit.

"He went to pick up your prescriptions. No, there won't be a problem with parking. He took *his boy* with him so he wouldn't have to get out of the car."

"And you think AC would have been pissed about seeing James here? Wait until he sees his son pull up here with one of Pharaoh's boys in the car." She laughs through the congestion I can hear in her chest, and I make a mental note to ask her doctor about her chest x-ray results and second pneumonia shot. "But forget little *Coolaid*. Does he know that Sonny dropped out of college again?"

"Momma, his friend calls himself *Dee Jay Kool-Aid* and Sonny says he actually makes a living that way. All that thug talk you hear from him is just to claim what they call *street cred*. And yes, *August knows*. Sonny said he told him over the phone last week. He did not drop out of school. He just dropped three of the four classes he was taking."

I feel foolish having said it aloud, and can see my grandmother flash a grin before turning to position her walker for the trip back upstairs, chiming back over her shoulder, "His father needs to leave him alone, Ruth. He tried college but it didn't take. What's wrong with him going to barber's school if that's what he wants. He likes to cut and style hair, and he's good at it. Then AC can put his college money into a barbershop for Sonny. Maybe right there on H Street. What's wrong with that?"

I walk over to speak to her through the screen. "Nothing, Momma." She stops to rest, repeating a refrain I have heard far too many times. "There are three kinds of people in this world. There are difficult people, people who put up with shit from difficult people, and everyone else." It sounds fascinating coming from a person who puts up with Biscuit. "This is what happens when a man has a son too late in life. You end up with an old man and a boy. There's just too much separation between the two of them."

I agree. August may come to support the barbershop idea—but I know that he also will hold out for a business degree. I do not know how to argue with August's logic or his insistence that Sonny's two-year degree should be easy for him to obtain.

However, he cannot dispute the level of commitment Sonny has shown in pursuing the training, state licensing and experience required to become a barber and qualify to be a barbers' manager.

Momma reaches the top of the staircase and disappears into her room. In the silence after my father and grandmother have left, I think about that night I met August so many years ago.

My friend Tonya, then a clerical assistant at Fort Belvoir, asked simply that I accompany her to *a party for soldiers on their way to the Persian Gulf.* We anticipated meeting fresh-faced recruits looking to have a blast before shipping out. However, eyes rolled as we walked into a much older, racially mixed crowd.

Most of the women still wore the conservative business suits they had worn to work that day. Tonya and I arrived in revealing dresses more suited for the kind of *danceathon* we had envisioned.

We stood alone together, painfully out of place, for what seemed like an eternity before the host and his friend graciously rescued us with offers of drinks and hors devours.

The man I heard people refer to as a *sergeant-major* offered to mix *something special* for me. I had never talked to a soldier with so many stripes and ribbons before. "You know, you don't really look like a Ruth. I'll bet you go by something else. Oh, they call you Doll Baby. I can see why they call you that. No, actually, I grew up not very far from here."

He was clearly well socialized and intelligent and extremely comfortable in his own skin. He was polished and, except for dancing like a man who went to Catholic school, seemed cool as well.

Even his no-look swipe across my ass was impressively accidental. Noting my casual indifference, he palmed it. "I love a small woman with a plump round ass." I removed his hand—*after a minute.*

Later in the evening, I encountered this same senior NCO waiting for me outside the upstairs powder room. In the brighter light, I could see that he was substantially older yet either unaware or indifferent to the fact that the object of his lust was a recent high school graduate.

He looked so handsome in his uniform and kissed me so gently and passionately, I allowed him to swing dance me, kind of country-western style, into an adjacent bedroom. He locked the door behind him. I warned, "We're going to get caught."

He laughed, and probably guessed for the first time that I was even younger than he initially thought. "Caught by whom, Doll Baby?" Embarrassed, I stood on my toes and kissed him, resolving not to talk anymore.

I was young but by no means a girl scout, and caught fire when he adeptly slid one large hand under my short dress and inside the seat of my panties. He was not the first one to do that, just the first to do it that smoothly.

He shattered my misperceptions of any social barrier between us, and I thought he would take me right there in a stranger's bedroom while the party continued downstairs.

But instead he led me back downstairs. After a while, and amid burning laser-like eyes and fire breathing whispers, we slipped out of the going-away party. He began priming me as soon as we were in what he called his *pussy car.* I felt comfortable with him from the beginning and snuggled against him with my feet up on the seat.

Driving with his left hand exclusively, he navigated through town with his right hand clamped firmly on my ass. I was impressed, at my young age, with how adeptly he slipped in out of traffic, smoothly escaping stalled lanes and avoiding traffic signals. He accelerated deceptively around traffic without the appearance of speeding, routinely violating traffic rules so fluidly that policemen ignored his transgressions.

"You're an *ass man*, aren't you, Sergeant?" I asked with no response other than his hand becoming even more invasive.

He brought me directly to his house—this house. When I saw him naked for the first time, back then he was like a muscular model. Tonya, who would later forfeit her girlfriend card by gaining first-hand knowledge and incur my lasting disdain for her transgression, told our friends that he was *all-dick*. And she was correct.

He brought me here and made love to me, primarily from behind, in every room of this house. Frequently, he would yell out, *damn this pussy is good*. That Monday, my new acquaintance put on his desert utility uniform and dropped me off at home. He told me he would write, boarded a transport plane and headed to the first Gulf War. Less than ten months after he left, I was screaming my way through the painful birth of his nine-pound son.

To the surprise of no one, August was less than enthusiastic about my pregnancy.

After hearing his accusations, I silenced him with the positive results of a paternity test. When he saw the documentation, I believe he got his first look at my birth date. The sergeant-major quietly accepted his responsibility and began factoring into his financial planning his son and his namesake's 19-year old mother.

I never petitioned the Army to police August's paternity. *I'll always take good care of you both, so please don't make me listen to anyone tell me what I'm supposed to do for my own child. They'll never require me to do more than I'll do voluntarily.*

My decision to trust him proved to be a wise one. August was prompt with his child support, even allowing me to sign a lease on this house at a below-market rent—paid only sporadically.

Our relationship has taken many turns over the years. I have watched him grow older gracefully—but older nonetheless. At times, August is as far away from me as a distant star. At other times, he is right inside my head.

Several single mothers have talked to me about the powerful natural bonds they share with their children's responsible fathers. In fact, the broken promises and unreliability of a suitor pales in contrast to dependable long-term support and visitation—whether voluntary or court-ordered.

I have compared notes with dozens of other single mothers. Some, like myself, share a bond with responsible fathers resembling a kinship. One temporarily cohabitated and talked about being in a traditional nuclear family.

Responsible fathers can sexually arouse some. Occasionally, I act on my feelings, aware that sex with August does not transform our custodial arrangement into a loving relationship.

My problem, according to Momma, is that I never felt worthy of holding August accountable—convinced I have no right to his accountability. When he returned from the Gulf War, I was kicking a crack addiction.

When he came to visit me, the look on his face told me that I would never have him. And, over the past few years, he has focused only on Sonny's personal growth and expanding my catering service—getting us out of his pocket and me out of his life.

I am still outside when August arrives and parks his town car near the house. The black designer series model, its license plates stamped *AJC CEO*, is always freshly detailed and immaculate. It is one of the few remaining in a discontinued line of touring vehicles.

August remains in the car after parking it, engaged in a telephone conversation. I consider ways of letting him know that, if he were to approach me today, he would be in for an uninhibited evening of what he nostalgically calls *project pussy*.

CHAPTER 10

"**O**h Shit."

"What's wrong, Biscuit?"

I peer into my rearview mirror. "That's the same car I saw parked down the street from Doll's house. I made him right away but didn't think he was looking for me." The unmarked blue sedan that has been on the street all morning is now directly behind me—red light flashing from the dashboard.

"This could be a big problem, Cookie, so just keep your mouth shut unless he asks you something directly. Your answer to any question about me is I don't know. Got it?"

"Okay. I know how to act."

"Nobody asked you to act. Just keep your hands where he can see them and shut up." Cookie needs to use the bathroom badly after waiting in the car for me for the past hour. I see that we are in front of one of those new trendy restaurants on H Street. The wait staff may or may not allow her to use it, but I know she will make a convincing case while I deal with this cop.

I am relieved to see him get out of the sedan much too quickly to have called in my license plate. As he walks toward my car, he appears too old to be an active detective. In addition, he has turned off the flashing light and removed it from his dash. Something is not right. "Good morning, detective. What seems to be the problem?"

He does not confirm nor correct my assumption. "I'm sorry to bother you Mister Jackson, but this should only take a couple of minutes." Upon hearing my name spoken by this stranger who has not yet produced a badge, I instinctively turn to look over at Cookie. She raises an eyebrow acknowledging her own surprise but, as instructed, remains silent.

"I would've preferred to speak with you at home, but I can't seem to locate an address for you." I remain silent. "And, of course, there is no need to waste your time or mine asking for your driver's permit or taxi registration."

He is not a cop. "Look. She needs to use the woman's room in that restaurant. I gesture for Cookie to get out, knowing now that someone who has no authority to stop her is detaining me. She climbs out of my cab and walks through the café door, mixing into the breakfast crowd.

"You are James Edward Jackson, aren't you?"

"And you ain't the police. So why don't you just tell me what you want?" He flashes a bronze badge that brings a smile to my face. "Come on man. You a PI in a tailored suit pulling people over with a fake siren. What do you want? You got until she gets back before I pull off and leave you standing here."

"Okay, it's just that you remind me a lot of a guy named Precious Oye Adeyemi." He pronounces the name flawlessly that is still difficult for me to get out of my mouth. "You can relax James. Or do you prefer Biscuit? Look, I'm doing an investigation for the government into the background of August Caesar. He's your grandson Sonny's father, right?"

He has done some homework. I stare at him blankly. He continues, "Well. Anyway, my question is regarding an incident way back in 1968 or 69." He pauses hoping to detect a change in my demeanor, and I may not be able to hide my surprise. "Now, I know two things. One—you were not directly involved. And two—Caesar suddenly joined the Army right afterward."

That is what he wants. He knows something occurred, but has no idea what happened. He has said the right things to get something from me. He has called me by my full given name and told me he knows where my mother, daughter and grandson live.

He is gutsy enough to risk arrest himself for this unlawful traffic stop. Because he has knowledge of my falsified paperwork, he is betting that drawing the attention of the police will be much more damaging for me than any charge he can talk his way out of—or any fine he can add to his expense account.

He is correct. I have the documents required to operate a motor vehicle and this taxi. However, the naturalized citizen they identify returned home to eastern Nigeria 30 years ago and died peacefully in his sleep.

I know that the only way to get him off me is to give him someone else. August brought this heat on me. If he wants to run with the big dogs, this is part of that game. Considering everything I know about him; he should never give me a hard time.

"AC, or August, was just a kid I knew way back in the day. He left town when he was a teenager and stayed away for years before I even knew he was gone. Many years later, he met a young girl here who just happened to be my daughter. They had a kid."

"I need you to dig a little deeper than that Biscuit." I was right. He wants me to give him another name—*someone else to harass. I have just the man he needs.*

"AC's running buddy way back then was an older boy we called *Smack*. Smack is the man you want to talk to. Russell Adkins is his real name. But don't expect to find him in the phone book."

The late sixties were difficult times for me. People write songs about how simple life was, but for me, life was complicated. It was impossible to please my father, so I gave up early on that fool's errand. However, when it came to stealing, I was a natural. I had been a good soldier for a hustler everyone called Pharaoh. No matter how many doors I kicked in or how much merchandize I hauled out, nothing I did seemed to satisfy him. People who worked a lot less got lucrative hustles while I was stuck risking far too much for far too little.

Pharaoh and his brothers fell in love with two delinquent kids who had run away from the foster parents in whose care the city had left them. I was going to pick up an easy $100 each for hauling them back home. Pharaoh threw a wrinkle into that scheme by assigning me as their mentor, of sorts.

Some whispered that Pharaoh was August's biological father. I showed them some things but they blossomed quickly on their own into the sharpest little thugs on H Street. Every night, they walked back and forth from the Coliseum to the Car Barn, over a dozen blocks each way. They wore gabardine slacks and alligator shoes—flashing wads of twenty-dollar bills.

I heard they would be moving on to new things. They would soon be leap-frogging me. Then one day they brought me their plan to rob, on their own, several busy stores in Anacostia.

I could never convince Pharaoh that I tried to talk them out of it. I realized they would simply do it with someone else to act as lookout and drive the getaway car. I agreed to help. The night of the job, things started falling apart—a sure sign to any veteran booster to abort and live to steal another day. However, they were determined.

"Look, the last I heard, Smack hooked up with some young gal who lives in Southwest with her mother—no, this side of the river. I think the city sold them the place years ago. But hey look, if you decide to step to him, don't try this kind of bullshit. Pharaoh was grooming him to be a button. That's all I know. Look man, I ain't gone stop for you again. This conversation never took place."

"What conversation is that, *Mister Adeyemi*?"

When Cookie returns, I go back to tell my daughter what has just happened, hoping that August has not yet arrived. However, as I pull up at the far end of the block, he steps out of his town car wearing a blue suit that rustles in the wind as he walks.

"See Cookie, you can walk a brother out of the hood, but you can't take the hood out of a brother's walk."

"Shit, he won't need to change it for me."

"Shut up, girl." Even from here, I can see him deliberately climb the front staircase with all of Doll's nosey neighbors watching. I can see him cinch his jacket button over a dark wine necktie that stands out in contrast to his white shirt. Doll should have dressed like an executive today, but then whom would she be fooling? However, she would be more confident than she will be in that long, hooded sweatshirt and blue jeans.

AC is not so tall, only a little above average height, though he appears *tallish*. He has managed to maintain his physical appearance well, despite the bit of a paunch we all get near our sixties. I have been close enough to him before to see that his hair is finally graying but not thinning—brushed straight back in waves. I do not know why he will not let Sonny style it for him.

He goes clean-shaven with a complexion some people call *brown skin*—though what constitutes brown skin is in the eye and the skin tone of the beholder. AC's skin looks naturally smooth because he has attended to it carefully for decades.

He is no longer the flashy dresser I once knew but is still a hopeless clothes horse with what I would have to admit is understated elegance.

Cookie interrupts my thoughts. "I bet he one of those men who so strong, people think he arrogant, when he really just confident—ain't he? I bet he ain't got no men for friends. That's why you scared of him ain't it, Biscuit? Don't get mad baby. I know you can whip his ass anytime you want to."

"Cookie, I told you to sit there and shut up." Moreover, I want to whip his ass when I see him stand close enough to kiss my daughter—but then will not. Instead, he stares out at her silently behind a pair of dark sunglasses. It is a mind game—a pimp's move. I know that AC still sees himself as a player. I feel my smile forming. We taught the boy well during his formative years.

I tell Cookie, "If he really wants to be a pimp, he should just get some girls and move downtown. That was my last hustle before I started hacking full time, finding and breaking in girls for pimps—and on my own, diving johns to stickup spots. I ain't proud of it—just the place where life took me. And it ain't too far from where it was taking AC."

Cookie turns to me looking astonished, but I know she is also impressed. "So that's why you talk to me like a ho, Biscuit? You try to be hard, never let on how you feel about me. And you know you never told me how much Miss Rose gave you today. And you ain't told me how she doing."

Normally that would be off limits, none of her business. However, these last several months have been especially lean. She has been carrying me financially most of this year—so I indulge her. "I don't know how much yet. I didn't count it in front of her. I just stuck it in my pocket. But I know I'm going to have to be better at getting Momma to her doctor appointments."

"Oh, that would be so nice."

"She ain't getting no better. She's always going to be fighting heart problems brought on by that sugar she got—plus arthritis, blood pressure and eye pressure." I hear the frustration in my voice, but I do not resent caring for the woman who took care of me, my baby girl, and then the baby boy she had with a stranger. And that first year after Sonny came was a bad one for Doll. AC sent her too much free money and my mother gave her too much free time.

Cookie is back on topic. "All I got is the white man's money this month, baby—bill money. We owe my sister all the food stamps. So, whatever you got in that pocket, we need to stop at the A&P on the way home."

CHAPTER 11

"**S**he's starting to forget things. AC, she forgets where her glasses are, where her medicine is and if she has taken it. Last week, I couldn't find her in the house. When I looked around for her, she was heading toward H Street in her nightgown. AC, she forgot how to go to the bathroom—twice."

Doll looks relieved to have said it all aloud, maybe for the first time. Except for letting out a long low whistle, a few minutes pass before I respond. "Doll, we have to figure something out that is in everyone's best interest—especially hers. I mean, after everything she has done for us."

We are still outside, and suddenly I am annoyed with myself for playing around and not kissing this woman. I need to kiss her partly so those nosey bitches across the street can see her kiss me back, but I need to kiss her because we are family. I know she does not believe that her grandmother's wellbeing is my responsibility.

She gives me a status update anyway. "I have been talking to a consultant who specializes in assisting seniors with their Medicare benefits. No, Medicare pays her. I hope to hear back from her later today. I've been taking her to physical therapy. I've been working out some myself since I'm there. You remember years ago when skinny assed people complained that they could never gain weight? Well nowadays all those skinny people are fitness experts—every narrow assed bitch I know wants to lecture me about how they stayed narrow."

I finally put my arms around her and kiss her on the lips, sucking gently on her lips as much as she will allow. She kisses me back without hesitation. Doll has assured me that she is not in love with me because she refuses to put her sanity in jeopardy that way. "Now you know I genuinely care for August. But that damned AC can be a real son-of-a-bitch."

When we enter the house, I have something else to discuss. "But first, I need to run upstairs to the bathroom and stop in to see Miss Rose. Where's Sonny?"

"He should be back soon. He went to the pharmacy for Momma's pills."

"Okay. But when I come back down, we need to talk about school—and catering." I pause and turn back to Doll before starting up the stairs. "I may also need to talk to you about my prostate."

"Your what?"

Clearly, Miss Rose's health is failing, even more so than the last time I saw her. A mere shadow of that active, vibrant woman I had met long ago, she still manages to flash a smile as I walk over to the side of her bed. She is sitting up, her frail torso braced by firm pillows piled against the high wooden headboard.

Her bedroom furniture is from an early American collection, the queen bed surrounded by sturdy wooden posts supporting a canopy frame. Her cover is a colorful patchwork quilt comforter with matching pillow shams. Above her bed are old framed photographs of John Kennedy and Martin Luther King, Jr. placed between two paintings depicting scenes from the Crucifixion and the Last Supper.

While her bedroom furnishings seem out of place in an otherwise contemporarily furnished home, I understand that the set was the well-deserved reward bedroom for a woman who worked for decades as a colored domestic.

She had been one of the last of the colored women who, with shopping bags in hand, proudly traveled by city bus from their modest residences to clean and cook in affluent homes throughout the city.

After growing up during the Great Depression, she and James Senior learned they could overcome any obstacle through hard work and determination. Her modest earnings had supplemented his salary and the unreported cash that both earned from performing domestic services pushed the Jackson family solidly into the colored middle class. However, her husband's premature death had abruptly pushed them back down.

She reaches out with both bony arms to wrap me in a warm embrace, and I hold on to her for a long time.

I am impressed but in no way surprised with the overall condition of the room, noting that Doll has always maintained it and the rest of the house spotlessly, and a light citrus air freshener accents Miss Rose's space.

The dresser and chest of drawers are polished and uncluttered, and a Formica-topped wheeled bed table holds the only evidence of her infirmary—health care items, prescription bottles, scattered tissues and a pitcher of water. "So, how is the queen this morning?"

Despite her age and health challenges, Miss Rose still smiles with thirty-two original teeth. "AC, did I hear you say something about your prostate?"

Of course, she heard that. "I need to speak with your granddaughter about that first, and I'm sure she's waiting to hear what I have to say about it. But you just rest assured that my doctor detected it early enough to minimize any danger. Now, again, how are you feeling?"

Reluctantly, she allows her own health to be our focus for a few minutes and shares with me conversations she has had with her doctors. She makes a point of reiterating her disdain for nursing homes and reminds me that she never actually took her name off the city's list for a subsidized senior's apartment, and fully expects that she can get a little place for herself if anyone wants an old woman to move out of here.

As always, I smile and reassure her that no one has that in mind. It is a promise I know I can keep. Her place in the home is secure. I purchased the three-bedroom row house—which no longer carries a lien—literally for pennies on the current value of a dollar.

The purchase took place long before off-Capital Hill properties became attractive to developers and investors. Years later, I converted the bottom level, which has a street entrance, into a separate English basement apartment that has become Sonny's private space.

Last year I recorded Sonny's name on the title. His grandmother, whom he refers to as Momma, has no rival for his love. Not even his mother, whom he calls Doll, could ever compete with her for his attention.

None of us could ever repay her for embracing the task of raising Sonny from a baby during a time when I was on the other side of the world and his mother was mentally on the other side of the stratosphere searching for answers in a crack pipe. I am satisfied with the quality of the care and attention Miss Rose receives from her primary physician and the cadre of specialists attending to her various ailments and maladies.

While I maintain an active interest and involvement, her medical attention costs me nothing. Miss Rose has a reliable monthly income in perpetuity and her late husband's low-cost medical plan fills in the gaps of her Medicare and Medicaid policies.

When I hear the young workers complain that over half of social security payments go to people who are not the actual retired workers, I think about Miss Rose and all the undocumented floors she scrubbed on her hands and knees.

I ask her about Sonny. "AC, I'm always concerned about Sonny Boy. I'm as concerned as you are, or more. But no matter what, at the end of the day, I trust Sonny. I've already asked him about that boy, and he says there is nothing illegal going on. The only thing that worries me is that I'm not sure that Sonny would even know the signs of trouble if he saw them."

She clearly has been waiting to tell me this, and I feel reassured that she is concerned about, at least, the potential for trouble. She has something else. "AC, you ain't in any kind of trouble, are you? I ask because a man stopped by here last week saying he *was an investigator.*

He wanted to speak to Ruth, but she had gone to the store. To tell you the truth, I think he knew she was gone. What did he look like? I think he looked like *Grave Digger Jones*. No. He never gave his name and I didn't let him in."

"Did he try to ask you any questions?"

"He said the government had asked him to conduct a thorough background check that included your juvenile records. What kind of bullshit is that? Wanted to know who I was and if I knew you when you were a teenager. No, AC, you know better than that. I told him my name was none of his business and anything he wanted to know about you he should ask you.

"Investigators came around once when you worked for that big company, but no one has ever asked about when you were a minor. Plus, I had my glasses on that day. It was just a PI badge. What fool does he expect to trick?"

What fool indeed? "Good job, Miss Rose. No. I am not in any kind of trouble. Someone has paid him to snoop around looking for dirt where there is none. Jeff ginned up this foolishness by talking about putting me in politics." I need to see Jefferson soon. The investigator must have searched on my name in the city's property database and pulled the deed to this house.

Miss Rose wants to talk about something else. "AC, please recognize the part that Ruth played in rearing that boy. Once she got off that mess she was always there for Sonny."

"I know that. And I'm proud of the way she bounced back and took care of Sonny. I know what she did. Bye. Miss Rose."

"Bye AC and don't be too hard on Sonny either. Barbering is a good business when you're the one renting out the other chairs."

I feel my eyes roll involuntarily back into my skull as I process that increasingly familiar refrain. I do not think I have been hard enough on Sonny. A quick glance at my watch reveals that I have over an hour before I leave to join Jerry downtown. I have already used up an hour that I do not have to spare and still have not seen my son.

Out in the hallway, I hear Doll moving around in her room. When I open the door, she is standing in front of her closet with her back to me as though searching for something else to wear.

She hears my footsteps behind her but does not turn around. "I'll be down in a minute AC. I'd appreciate it if you didn't bust in here uninvited. It's your house, but I still have a lease."

However, her tone is playful and her actions belie her words. Doll has removed her jeans and is wearing only a gray one-piece casual jersey cotton top that is now fitting her like a dress.

She has her hands pushed deep into the side pockets, causing the garment to cling tightly across her hips. Doll looks good with short hair trimmed neatly around the nape of her neck. As she approaches forty, her body retains the same basic form I noticed long ago.

"Where's your son?" I ask the question as I walk up behind her. She leans back against me and raises the elastic bottom hem to rest above her hips. I instinctively drop my trousers, despite not having taken medication. I quickly realize that the flesh will not cooperate—even if my spirit is willing. I back off and try to talk my way out of it.

"Okay but you owe me one, Sarge. I needed a shot of *Vitamin D* today."

"Come on Doll. You know I'm here to talk to Sonny. And I need to tell you both about this prostate business." As I pull my trousers back up, her look of disappointment morphs into sadness, and a shadow comes over her face. I share with her what my doctors have told me about my condition. She does not take the news well despite my assurances.

We also discuss her catering business, which she has not yet seriously launched despite my significant investment in equipment. Jeff has tried to help her get off the ground, hiring *Soul2Go* to cater various events, including all-day board meetings. Renee also has contracted with her for several large AJC employee breakfast and lunch meetings.

These engagements amount to no more than a dozen or so per year, but she must supplement those with referrals and others she finds on her own. Though she does not have a dedicated facility, I am impressed to see that she has matched my investment by reinvesting her earnings in enough additional food preparation and storage equipment to dominate the space on the main floor.

After giving up on seeing Sonny, I leave the house, checking in with Renee for updates and messages. I find out that Jerry called earlier to reschedule our meeting until tomorrow. That is good news. The past week has been entirely too active for me.

However, when my pharmaceutical enhancement is out of balance with my natural aging, my body pays a steep penalty. My lower back, gluts and calve muscles all ache and I crave a long rehabilitative nap. Therefore, instead of going back inside or to the office, I point my car toward the east bank of the Anacostia and the comforts of home.

CHAPTER 12

"**G**ood evening, sir. My name's Russell. Let's see, you're leaving Dulles International Airport and going to downtown DC. So, where'd you fly in from tonight? I figured you must've been on that crowded west coast flight. Are you from LA visiting DC—or getting back into DC from LA?"

He does not utter a sound, as though I have not said anything. Every now and then, I get a fare like this, but not usually a man—or a person of color. On nights like this, I do not know how long I will be able to continue this job as a late-shift airport limo driver. I make good tips but more than anything else, I hate to pick up and drop off strangers late at night. I also hate to put so many miles on my own car.

I have never been much of a coffee drinker, so it's hard to stay awake. Moreover, despite Peaches' easy access to them, I do not take amphetamines. As the hours—and the years—wear on, it becomes harder to stay awake on the same routes I travel three or four nights a week.

This faire is starting to make me feel uneasy. He is wearing an expensive suit and leather soled wingtips. He does not have a single piece of luggage or a briefcase. He has not uttered a word since I picked him up.

He reminds me of someone from the distant past whom I have been desperately trying to remember. My inability to place him nags at me until I can clearly see his face in my rearview mirror.

I do not want to find out the hard way that he has no sense of humor and risk losing a tip, but I cannot help myself. "Hey man, do you remember an old movie with a character called Coffin Ed Johnson? In the movie *Cotton Comes to Harlem*?"

Now he speaks, his voice harsh and loud. "Yeah, you mean the character Raymond Saint Jacques played opposite Godfrey Cambridge's Grave Digger Jones."

"That's exactly right. I don't mean this in a bad way, but you look just like Coffin Ed."

"Yeah, I've heard that once or twice before—that and people who can't remember one detective in the movie from the other. Coffin Ed and I have other things in common—like our preference for carrying a dependable gun. You can pull over to the curb right here. Perfect. Now put the car in park. Don't make me have to say it twice."

I am confused. "What? *You do remember* that you paid inside the airport at the booth, right? Riders don't pay me. Everybody pays in advance at the booth."

He does not respond. Rather, his eyes sweep over the immediate vicinity. He is much too old to be a stickup man, and too smart to rob a driver who does not handle money. Finally, he barks, "You were locked up when that movie came out. So, you must have seen it in your cell block on VHS or Betamax."

I cannot speak.

Then, he digresses. "All you DC boys are just alike. When I was in the Corps, I could smell one a mile away. My friends in the Army used to tell me the same thing. Show me the coolest motherfucker in the platoon and I'll show you the DC boy. Nobody else walks like, talks like or *lies like* a cat from DC. They breeze right through boot camp. The shit starts once you give them *a little freedom*—a little *room to maneuver.*"

When I mumble something about *how personal all this sounds*, he thunders back, "Okay, that's a good idea, Adkins. Piss me off. You remind me of a DC dude they used to call *Smack* who hung out back in the day with a baby hustler everybody called *AC—Augustus Julius Caesar*. Why the fuck would Pharaoh give that name to a baby in the hood?

I have a theory. "Are you sure AC didn't do something to you, personally, man? Maybe y'all had *a little pussy dispute,* or something?"

"Just shut the fuck up, Smack." *Bingo.* "You look just like a damned dope needle. Now, I know something went down that night. He joined the Army. And you went to prison." Now, I feel a slight misty spray on my face.

He talks loud and fast but concisely, popping gum in my ear. AC's name seems to be coming up a lot after so many years. My midnight faire is threatening me with a gun, but is not a cop. He is looking for me—asking about AC, and repeating a debunked old paternity rumor about Pharaoh.

"I need you to fill in the blanks for me, Smack. Now just so I'm clear about everything, you don't report this income on your taxes do you. I know I wouldn't if I didn't have to. I'd just make the boss pay me in cash—which he, of course, prefers—and pocket my tips and any other *miscellaneous income.* You drive your own sweet-assed caddy. He has no liability for an independent driver with a fake business license, no paperwork. He just fills your tank up—right?"

When I do not react, he adds, "Then, just like you, I'd be a brand-new-Cadillac driving *motherfucker.* Now, take it easy Smack. I don't like to see you flinch like that. Don't worry. I'm not a cop. I'm just a private eye trying to add two plus two." I wonder why he would be investigating something that happened in 1968.

"Smack, nothing I remember about those days suggests that a smart little hustler like AC would volunteer for the Army. It was at the height of the war. Sure enough, he suddenly up and joined when DC boys were coming home in body bags. Why would he do that?"

"I don't know."

"*You don't know?* You know you went to the pen. Just tell me why. I know most of it, but all I can do is guess about the rest. My client won't pay me for guesses. Don't worry. AC's juvenile file—expunged. But they charged you as an adult. You paid your debt. There is no reason for this to affect your public housing arrangement—no more than Peaches and her little reefer business. Damn. I can see how she got that nickname. Are you sure you're not *hitting them* both? I said *don't flinch like that*, Smack."

His comments about my living arrangements pluck a tightly wound cord. I have often pointed out the risks of offsetting the cost of their marijuana bricks by selling off lids to their closest friends and relations.

Peaches reminds me that it is an argument I am in no position to win. Similarly, Coffin Ed has left very little room for anything other than compliance. I ask, "Just who are your clients?" I keep my ten-millimeter automatic locked and loaded this late at night, but I have left it in the glove compartment for this seemingly safe Dulles run.

"Come on, Smack. You've looked over at that glove box four times already. Do you really think I'm going to let you get the drop on me with that canon? A ten mil makes a hole like a 45 slug. I know because I've got the same thing pointed right at you. Remember *Coffin Ed*? I promise you won't live to get it open. Keep still and you're in absolutely no danger here whatsoever. Just relax and talk to me for a few minutes, and I promise you I will disappear from your life forever."

"I wish I'd stayed home tonight."

"I would have just come back tomorrow night. I can see your caddy and Peaches' little fat round ass from M Street. Look man, you don't need to know my clients just like you don't need to protect AC. In fact, that's my job. I'm working for people who want to protect him from his political enemies. But they need to know what to look for."

I want to sound tough—to let him know, "I ain't no punk, if you checked me out the way you say you did, you know that. I can smell bullshit a mile away, and I smell some right now in my back seat. If you're on the team, ask AC all these questions."

He starts talking loud with intensity. "The two of you were together, but you went to Lorton Reformatory? Did he get a deal to flip on you? Why didn't they arrest Biscuit? Why did Pharaoh leave you to rot with no bail money?"

I hope he does not really need all the specifics. I speculate about the same things, but the truth is I simply do not know the answers. When I asked Pharaoh, he said the court denied bond. Rather than ask Biscuit a question, I would have probably just shot him on site and gone back to jail.

Coffin Ed is still talking. "Why you, Smack? After all you did for Pharaoh—and took care of his little boy. He could never have survived without you. And the first time the cops put a little pressure on AC, he flipped on you. You did every day of that dime—and spent the rest of your life working shit jobs. You were even living in the DC shelter for a *minute*. He's on the radio talking about his company. He's never even offered you a job at that joint. That's really fucked up—don't you think?"

I tell him, "Look I don't know all the facts. Some of it is a mystery to me. But you have nothing on me. Like you said, I paid my debt. I'm just scared that if you don't get what you want, you'll blow it all up for everybody, just for spite."

He is so close I can feel his breath on the side of my neck. "Ooh, Smack. I wish a motherfucker would. I'd just make a few phone calls and fuck up everybody's summer. Or you can keep flinching and make me squeeze off a hot round into your *apple head*. I'll just lean you over and wrap your cold fingers around your unregistered bop gun. Otherwise, you just talk to me for a while, then go home tonight and crawl into bed next to little fat-assed Shantel."

"What do you need to know, Coffin Ed?"

CHAPTER 13

"**I** know what your problem is, Augustus. You think I'm always going to be here whenever you come by. But one day you're going to stay away too long, come by here and find me gone." Jeff's warning is consistent with his usual dark humor, but carries a disconcerting element of seriousness today.

To visit Jeff at his large brick colonial requires a rare trip west of Rock Creek Park into Spring Valley. When I arrive, as always, his white hair is short and neatly brushed, framing a cleanly shaven bronzed face covered with a layer of a rich *patina*.

Following him back to his study, I pass dozens of photographs of three generations of Sinclair's posing with politicians, ministers and entrepreneurs. For the first time, I notice that he is using a cane. We begin with a chat about the radio interview and my closing comments.

"Reggie clearly had some intel on the fact that people are getting behind your possible candidacy for Jay Spencer's seat. He gave you a surprise ten-minute platform to announce on his show. You were right to hold off on that until you make up your mind and come back to do another interview. You don't want to do anything that will tip your hand just yet."

Jeff has served as my mentor since I was a young sergeant assigned to an Army community outreach project for at-risk city teenagers. With respect to marketing and contract finance, Jeff is one of the smartest people I have ever known. A Harvard trained lawyer, he has been a key player in many of the city's economic development programs, serving every mayor appointed or elected.

We spend an hour discussing strategies to win one of the ESP contracts, which could require AJC to obtain security clearances for several hundred additional guards. "That reminds me, Jeff. Someone has engaged the services of a PI to look into my past."

Jeff winks and flashes a smile. "Don't sweat it. Your little teenaged moment of indiscretion has been erased."

I stare back at him in disbelief. "I thought the juvenile database could still be accessed by certain people within the criminal justice system." Jerry Lane and I had been very concerned about the file. Jeff assures me with absolute certainty. "Not anymore, boy. There is nothing there to access, like it never even existed."

Stunned, I let out a low whistle. "You mean, just like that."

When someone questions his assurances, Jeff can affect an intense, steely glare that looks like a warning label on a bottle of rat poison. "I mean just like that. And now neither you nor I will ever speak of this again, other than for me to ask you if you can think of anyone, *anyone else* still living who knows—other than the other boy."

"Just him, and he doesn't know the whole story. Then there's Doll's father, but he never really knew the facts either. Yes, I know they represent wild cards, but I doubt if Biscuit or Smack would ever tell."

"Code of the streets, huh August? *Biscuit and Smack*—two grown men nicknamed for flaky bread and an addictive opiate." He abruptly returns to business. "So, you got another call from UniverSec yesterday?"

My mind drifts to another possible indiscretion, but the magical disappearance of the file renders that issue moot as well. "Yes, UniverSec finally put the entire deal on the table, in fairly easily decipherable code of course. They want to capitalize more than the law allows on my status as a wounded veteran and a minority contractor."

Jeff pioneered the creation of some local affirmative initiatives in employment, education and housing. I have never heard him discourage anyone else from participating in affirmative contracting. However, he warned me that restrictions placed on minority business owners are inconsistent with natural business instincts.

Since he understands the issues clearly, I decide to state the UniverSec proposition succinctly. "They plan to get a few large deals set-aside and have me front the deals. Even a smaller piece of the pie will net me more than ESP. I could just sit back and watch my valuation soar, and then cash out."

Jeff stares at me blankly as though still waiting to hear the issue that requires resolution, so his response comes as no surprise. "*Cash out or sell out?* Which side of your ass did you suggest that they kiss? Those boys play for keeps."

"Well, I've always been kind of partial to the right side."

"Okay then. I concur with your decision. August, you have never really been through the ringer until some government inspector, who can't stand the thought of affirmative action to begin with, gets a chunk of your ass in his teeth. Don't walk away from that—you need *to run away from it.* Don't even leave open the possibility that you might have an interest."

"Okay, Jeff." I do not tell him that I have participated in several discussions already. After we talk a while longer, Jeff turns to personal issues. "August, would you mind if I ask about your son in California?"

I have not spoken with Jack in several years. After the Navy, he purchased his first fast food franchise in California. Now he owns five, including one right outside the gates of a college campus. "The son who never sees me is the son most like me."

"You think it has something to do with the fact that you both had the same mentor?" Jeff is correct. I fully acknowledge that John Fellows, my former wife's father who served side-by-side with Jeff during the Korean War, devoted an enormous amount of time and energy in me when I was just a smart-mouth teenager fresh out of basic training.

While stationed in California, I managed to impregnate his daughter. We were married before I shipped out, and despite John's disappointment in seeing his daughter's path to college temporarily obstructed, he still embraced me as his son-in-law and helped map out a strategy for my education and career.

Later, my son, Jack, named John Fellows Caesar after his grandfather, followed a similar path—mentored and guided by the elder John. My estranged son and I rarely communicate. His mother and I were divorced when I returned from Vietnam.

I have seen Jack three times in the last twenty years. He now has two children of his own, *my grandchildren*. By now, he also may have grandchildren of his own. "He was never in danger of becoming the kind of thug I was becoming."

Jeff never lets me beat up on myself, since he sees that as his job. "August, your father-in-law and I were guided through life every step of the way. When Korea erupted, John was a career platoon leader in the 24th Infantry. I was a law school graduate annotating my resume with a military reference. My father served in France so I fulfilled my patriotic duty. Hell, the last thing we expected in Pusan was actual combat.

"I was born in this house. I inherited it and a dozen other properties. I've never had to make a mortgage payment in my life. I never had a black neighbor until 1969. My father was a lawyer and my mother a university professor. You can't imagine how little they put up with from me. I caught a cattle-prod up my ass whenever I strayed an inch from the straight and narrow."

"No. I can't imagine."

"We have no children as you know, but Edith has a nephew who sucks up her family's inherited real estate like a catfish." Edith is back and moving about the house. "Despite his considerable efforts, he has been unable to piss away more money than he has fallen ass-backwards into."

I have known Elton Dalton since he was a child, another one of those born late in his parents' lives. Edith Dalton Sinclair's family placed their faith in real estate as a family investment strategy, and managed their properties as a family business.

However, they had no success with procreation. That is, except for the birth of little Elton, who became the sole beneficiary of considerable affection and largess. Elton knows Jeff has implored his Aunt Edith and her family to create a well-defined trust that would severely limit his actions.

As though chiming in on-queue, Edith calls out to us. "Why don't you two come in here and have something to eat?"

She goes upstairs, allowing us to continue in the kitchen. When we return to his study, Jeff gets back down to business. "August, hear me out on something. Once you sell AJC, you can comfortably serve as president of a non-profit and serve on the council—just carefully recuse yourself with certain financial matters with the city."

I know where this going to lead us. Jeff has devoted his time, money and energy into his planned school for gifted students of music, arts and theater. His closest allies reject the idea, pointing out existing public programs. I agree with Jeff that none of them come close to the kind of institution that his father visualized, but I simply have no passion for the project.

In addition to his father's wealth, Jeff inherited his legendary devotion to classical jazz and theater—matched only by the family's devotion to the young people of this city. Having leveraged substantial political influence, I have never understood why Jeff has not yet brought the school project to fruition.

"When I started, I reached out to the very best people I could find. But it's hard to control such opinionated people. Edith and I own the non-profit. I preside as President, Edith as an inactive VP. I've *quietly* transferred ownership of the school site to the non-profit." He pauses as though waiting for the significance of the transfer to sink in.

He looks at me through those steely eyes. "But not even Edith knows about some of the development projects I've shared with you. Edith's family is from the talented tenth school of thought. She doesn't always instinctively *reach down to the downtrodden.* That's why I need someone I can trust to manage these assets of great value and to use them as intended."

He continues before I can respond. "I have a very capable executive director, but he can be replaced with *someone you trust*. Several board members will show you the same loyalty they show me. Now, don't say a damned thing tonight. We can talk about it the next time you come over—*provided you don't stay away too long*. To jumpstart all this, you'll need to be front and center on a major issue or an event—seen by the city and its leadership. It should have no hint of political ambition."

Edith walks into Jeff's study. I rise to embrace her as we engage in small talk. Her eyes are soft but deceptively probing, always subtly sweeping, recording and analyzing. She has been carefully prepared from childhood to take her place confidently among the city's elite.

She has never said anything to me about it, but I have always sensed her disapproval of my friendship with Jeff. I remember that Pharaoh used to warn us about the permanet gulf between generationally affluent black families *and the rest of us*. I, however, have never endorsed the belief, held by many, that they simply will not bridge the chasm. "How is Yvette, August?" She does not wait for my response. "Jefferson, can you give me a minute before I go upstairs.""

Jeff laughs after she has left. "Didn't I tell you she was going to stay on you about Yvette? Boy, you've just begun to feel the tip of that probe. But I stand behind her on that one, since you look a little strange as a sexagenarian with no divorced, deceased, intended or current wife."

Jeff excuses himself, still laughing, and joins Edith in the kitchen. I hear her admonishing him about test results. I hear Jeff respond with finality to another hushed question. *"I'm going to make the best of whatever I have left in the tank."*

When Jeff returns, I want to ask about his health, but decide that he will tell me anything he thinks I need to know. He, on the other hand, continues to plow on into my personal affairs. "So, tell me what's going on with your local family. Tell me about that boy of yours, for whom you shoulder a great responsibility. I won't ask whether you have yet to complete your will and advance directives."

I know this will not be the most enjoyable part of my time with Jeff, but I know he will not allow me to leave without discussing it. Jeff had been my primary sounding board when I came home from the Persian Gulf to find that Doll was in a drug rehabilitation program. Over the years, he has gotten to know both Sonny and Doll. I am certain he will not be satisfied with generalities, insisting on details—*finding out if I know the details.*

"Well, Sonny gave junior college a try for a while, but has now dropped most of his spring session classes." Jeff does not mask his disappointment—with me? "He seemed okay in the fall, but stumbled recently."

"Stumbled?" His eyes narrow. "And what are you doing to *reach out to catch him?"*

I hear myself sounding defensive, knowing the importance Jeff attaches to Sonny's stability. "He has decided that he wants to be a barber. I don't even know where that came from. He likes to cut hair. His mother and grandmother spin the idea as owning a barbershop, which is fine if he is serious, but if he is, then he needs to learn something about finishing what he starts. It's not as if I'm asking him to get an MBA or a law degree. I've adjusted my expectation to an Associate of Business. No part-time job, no work-study—just drive his new car."

"So that's *his new car?"* His question suggests he has seen it, and thought it too lavish.

I am curious. "Where have you seen his car?"

He is reflective for a long moment as though weighing the appropriateness of his next comments. "I saw your son downtown last week with *your baby-mama."* I laugh aloud at Jeff's purposeful mispronunciation. "I saw them while waiting for Edith to come out of Macy's. Doll's pants looked like someone had spray-painted them on her. I could see clear up *the crack of her big ass."* I smile at hearing how matter-of-factly he speaks with Edith somewhere in the house.

He continues. "Now I was just a casual observer, mind you, but young leisurely Sonny, *August Junior,* appeared to be sitting in the driver's seat waiting for his woman just like I was waiting for my woman. And when

Doll rushed out the store, ass bouncing every which way, she seemed apologetic." Jeff looks at me quietly. I do not speak.

"I don't have to tell you how confusing a situation like that can become. No boy, nothing incestuous. I'm talking about the misperception a young adult son can develop. How many times during your community work did you encounter young men who unwittingly become husband figures for their single mothers—even though they have done nothing to earn such a lofty designation?"

I feel that it is my turn to instruct. "Yes, I do understand. But some of that's impossible to avoid. To survive, a single woman pieces together the best support network she can. If she has an adult son, he naturally assumes responsibility in the home for stuff like transportation, facility maintenance *and security*. In some instances, he may become a partial breadwinner as well. But once done, that arrangement is impossible to undo—even if a responsible suitor tries later to enter the mother's life."

"So, you are of the mind that it's okay?"

"I am of the mind that it is inevitable. Jeff, unless the estranged father is going to step in early and assume those responsibilities himself, frankly, he doesn't have a damn thing to do with it. A new man simply has to *make a choice*."

He closes the folder filled with notes I brought for him. "And you have not and do not plan to step in. And this is your position. Okay." Then he looks down again and adds, "Of course now if you're over there *banging that girl*—that could be another kind of problem."

CHAPTER 14

"**G**ood morning, Lydia. How's Marsha? I haven't seen her around for a while."

"Good morning, Miss Tate." *That's right, you nosey bitch. Keep walking that little rat dog before I let Canuck give her what she wants—and what you desperately need.* I don't need any *block captain* bullshit today.

Today is my sixtieth birthday, but I have not had a steady girlfriend for a year now and thus no Marsha to make plans for me today. My morning has begun like any other. I have finished my pre-dawn stretches and have taken Canuck out for a one-mile jog.

I am ready for work and about to pull out of my driveway when—against my better judgment—I decide to invite August to join me for lunch. Two weeks have passed since he insulted me by canceling a date via text message. Over four weeks have passed since I last saw him.

A little male company might be nice today. August requires no maintenance, and fits well into my schedule. After all, I dread the thought of reopening auditions to fill my need for occasional male companionship. My last experience with new candidates was, at best, disappointing.

There was pretty boy Ray. I was not concerned that Ray was much younger. Women like a little candy every now and then. However, Ray never learned that ringing the bell was an intended outcome—not a pleasant surprise. A tad older candidate, Len could quote statistics from ten college conferences, but could not recall which of his women preferred to parry and who liked to thrust.

Matt was age-appropriate, smarter and more engaging, but when his wife's surprise audit uncovered a deficit in his bottle of erectile medication, she sent him texts with maps and driving directions to our so-called weekend *hideaway*.

However, she accused me of being *the little ho* her cousin saw with Matt in Aruba. It was not I. But I thanked her for the heads up as well as her high threshold for bullshit—and wished all three the very best.

I have a reason to call August today. My son, Aaron, asked me to obtain a status report on the issue that brought us together—my son's security clearance. Joshua, my former spouse, has been absent—physically and financially—for most of Aaron's life.

However, Joshua's recently documented involvement in a domestic terrorist group could jeopardize the security clearance that Aaron's job requires. Proactively, we sought a security consultant with defense experience.

When a client recommended AJC, Aaron scheduled a 9 AM meeting with August but met with Jerry Lane. As I waited in the lobby, August reported for work at 11 AM stating that Jerry *always takes the lead on these cases*.

He invited me to join him for coffee in a small shop next door, palmed my ass as he held open the door and commented on my firmness like a judge at the county fair. He then told me he had fallen in love with me on first sight. I marveled at how convincing he could make that bullshit sound.

Today August agrees to have lunch with me in the park. I tell him, "I've got some great leftover pasta salad in the icebox and I haven't pulled out of my driveway yet. Do you want me to go back in and get it?"

He agrees without hesitation. It occurs to me that I have never seen his wallet. "That sounds good to me. Is it homemade?" August's careful money management would be an attractive trait if I saw him as a marriage prospect. Of course, I do not. "Do you have to get back to the gig after lunch?"

He knows that women like his deep voice. I allow the advanced audio system in my sports car to reproduce his rich bass through the speakers. It fills my car's cabin with a presence that stimulates more interest than I want my voice to convey. "Yes, I'm afraid so. I have two potential buyers coming in back-to-back this afternoon." I do not expect to hear disappointment, and I don't.

"That's cool. But don't forget to throw an extra pair of panties into your purse." My mouth opens but I have lost the ability to form words. Before I can achieve coherence, he continues. "We can probably find a quiet spot near the water."

I shift uneasily back in the driver's seat, fighting an instinct to rescind the invitation and end the call. Of course, that would not faze him either. "Sure, August, that sounds fine. But just so I'm clear, you want me to bring what?"

He responds as though confused by my confusion. "You should bring an extra pair of panties—unless you already have a back-up pair in the car."

"No. I don't." I am annoyed to hear a stutter in my response, and try to settle down. "So, tell me, AC, why would I carry around an extra pair of panties?"

He answers matter-of-factly, as though explaining the importance of maintaining proper tire pressure. "You always get so juicy. You should never go anywhere—certainly not with me—without slipping an extra pair into your purse."

For emphasis, August affects an urban accent to contrast his otherwise flawless diction. It is a *duality in his personality*. He seems to be in a balancing act, straddling the world of his birth and the world of his rebirth. I have dated other guys from east of the river. I remember when we used to invite a few to spice up our high school parties. I want to rebuke him but hear a playful quality in my voice that belies my protest.

"Don't you think that's a little presumptuous? I mean, even for you?" I listen for jest, but hear none and his voice remains steady and adamant.

"What else are you carrying in that expensive leather bag today that would be more useful?"

"I don't know, maybe some cash I can use for a cab if my date turns out to be a jerk?" I consider hanging up but he relates his intentions with such graphic specificity that I feel moist midway through his monologue. When he wraps up, I finally speak in a voice I barely recognize. "And what makes you think that I would let you do all that? August? August, are you still there?"

I remain in my driveway a long time, thinking about four weeks ago and the long drive back to my house after we played a few sets of early spring tennis. I rode all the way home cuddled against him in a middle seat like a schoolgirl. While we both acknowledged our juvenile behavior, I enjoyed every kiss at every stop light.

Upon arriving home, I teased playfully that I was tired and just wanted to call it a night. Instead of pushing me into the house and taking me like the thug I wanted him to be, he said he understood and abruptly drove away, leaving me standing there with my intact panties soaking wet. Thirty minutes later, he expertly broke through my back door wearing a nylon stocking over his head and face. I could not get enough.

I go back into the house annoyed by how easily I allow this man to manipulate me. For some reason, I could not tell him that I have been maintaining extra panties for thirty years. Walking back into my bedroom, I take a fresh pair of panties out of my top drawer and change out of the wet ones that are no longer suitable for work. I grab the bag of inexpensive extras I have been intending to divide between my desk drawer and glove box.

Instead of putting my slacks back on, I pull from the back of the closet a wool flannel skirt. My reflection in the mirror has gray strands of hair that I refuse to color. She reminds me that I am much too old for this kind of behavior. I avert my eyes from Canuck's stare and my judgmental reflection as I tuck a pair of crotchless panties into my purse.

About an hour into my workday, I call August to cancel our noon rendez-vous in the park, but he has forwarded his mobile phone number to his secretary. In her annoying voice, his *Girl Friday* asks if I wish to reschedule. "Tell your boss that I can't meet him until after work, and I will catch him then if I can." I hang up abruptly, certain that she will convey to him the disinterest I try to express, and know that she will also put her spin on it.

Checking recorded voice messages later, I listen to August's request that I meet him at a café on U Street at five. I decide to send him a text: *Call me when you upgrade our dates to weekend getaways.*

To my surprise, the day turns out to be busier than I had expected— even busier than my lie to August described. Yvette Saxton surprises me by emailing a meeting request. I schedule her for the lunch hour made available by my canceled lunch plans with her boyfriend. I wonder if she got uptown early and stopped off at the bookstore before seeing that quack psychiatrist.

At exactly noon, Yvette arrives dressed in a form fitting knit dress that highlights her taught figure. I speculate that losing that protruding bottom would probably bring tears to August's eyes. I still think we could be mis-taken for sisters, but she is slightly more generously proportioned.

"It's good seeing you again too, Lydia. Oh thanks. No this is just an old dress I like to wear this time of year. But now I must say that's an interesting outfit you're wearing."

"It's just a joke I'm playing on an old friend." I have forgotten that I am wearing what could be a modified parochial school uniform. However, I am more interested in the opportunity now at hand. I wonder what will happen if I turn up the heat a little more.

When I consider it, I can almost picture her jumping up and running from the building. However, when she sits down on my office sofa, I cannot resist sitting next to her. I am pleasantly surprised to see that she shows no discomfort, even as I openly appraise her.

I hope my tone suggests my lack of interest in conducting business. "I was wondering if I would see you again, Yvette. No, I knew you were seri-ous. Many people take my card, promise they will get back to me and never do. No, I don't let it bother me—it's just business." I laugh and touch her hand for an extended moment. She does not pull it away. "Men do that too," I add. "Don't you hate it when a man just wants to find out if he can—and once he knows he can, he never does?"

She smiles knowingly but does not respond. Then she turns to look directly into my eyes. I see that I could lose my way easily in hers. I begin our meeting, struggling to avoid going too far in a direction that might derail the progress we have made. I tell her about several options she could pursue for her gallery, and by the end of the noon hour and the last of the pasta salad, we agree on next steps.

With the serious business concluded, I cannot resist getting back on message. I redirect by asking if she ever saw the other person at the bookstore again. She laughs, "Oh no, I left before he could find me. Besides, as you know, I'm in a committed relationship. Then she asks, "So how are you doing in the guy department?"

This is my opportunity to convey to her an important piece of information. Looking directly into her eyes as I speak, I respond, "Yvette, for the past three years, I've only had *occasional sex* with one man—with the same man. Oh, that has been more than enough. Besides, there is nothing more important to me than consistency, safety and peace of mind."

I want to lay everything out on the table, and feel frustrated that I cannot. "I called him recently after a long hiatus. *What did he say?* He said I should carry around an extra pair of panties in my purse." Yvette's eyes widen. "That's right—at my age. What do you think about that?"

She does not speak right away, but her facial expression indicates she wants to know how I reacted. I reach into my purse and take out the crotchless panties. I almost panic when she shows a little discomfort. Before I can change the subject again, she responds, keeping me on message. "Do you mind if I ask your age, Lydia? Oh, happy birthday. Do you ever think about whether you'll have anyone when you're older?"

I lie. "Not for a second."

"Really?" She does not believe me but does not belabor the point. Instead she refocuses on me. "And so, you still get really wet. Is that a problem—I mean, for him?"

I am so thrilled to hear the question that I require every ounce of restraint I can muster to maintain a calm demeanor and a level tone. "He's a very touchy-feely kind of lover—one of those intuitive men. He's also a borderline pervert who likes to leave them on me. Even if we just make out in the car, he knows wetness, and I mean soaking wetness, will be a problem for me if I have somewhere else to go. Funny thing is, I've been packing extras all my life. Yes. I get very, very wet."

"So, is that because of him or just a natural inclination?" Her voice suddenly sounds cracked and strained. She pulls a hanky from her purse and clears her throat. She closes it quickly but not until I see a trace of black lace inside. She wants me to know.

"Both. But this is probably the main reason." I reach over and pull her arm toward me. I try to convey August's girth, but my thumb and index finger are not long enough to encircle her wrist.

Nevertheless, she gets my message, giggles and takes my hand in a way that men simply do not understand. It is something my previous girlfriend understood, but she did not understand how to share it with just one person. A feel a chill up my arm and I think she detects it. "Yeah Lydia, I know exactly what you mean."

Emboldened, I move closer, my voice just above a whisper. "Now I do like it when he drills me with it. He likes to hear me holler. He knows better, but won't accept the fact that pounding—or even thrusting hard—has no role in sensual touching. Only women truly understand the interplay between emotional and physical contact."

Yvette says nothing, so I go on. "A man has a genetic disposition to deliver the meat, and trust me, I syphon everything he has to squeeze. But only women know the power of subtlety."

Yvette leans back against the sofa, breathing through her mouth as though the air in the room has a distinct new flavor. I lean back with her but merely hold her hand. Instead of kissing her I decide to let the moment pass—for now.

Just then, Sonya's voice explodes over the intercom like a police officer with a bullhorn. "Lydia, I'm sorry to interrupt your meeting." She speaks softly and apologetically into her speaker, but in this moment, her voice seems to blare. "The Payne's have called three times to ask if I can come over this evening to discuss the listing. But I just don't know the Hill that well."

As I gather myself, I hear Yvette mumble under her breath, "Yes, the pains indeed."

I flash a smile at the thought we share. My niece is riding the subway today. "Sonya, tell them we're both coming by. They are on the way to your house." Yvette straightens up in a way that tells me to get back to business. "So, Yvette, can you tell me anything more about that Logan Circle project?"

She clears her throat again. "I still don't really know much about it. As I said, a very influential older couple has raised money for it. Do you know of the Sinclair's? Of course, everyone does. Their nonprofit is Renaissance Partners. What's my price range? You know, it hasn't occurred to me but they've never said."

Sonya and I have already familiarized ourselves with the only remaining space in that area where anyone could build a non-residential project of any significance—and then someone with solid connections.

Before we wrap up, Yvette promises to give me her opinion of some art I purchased for my home. When we stand and embrace, our girl's kiss catches and lingers on the corners of our lips. I wonder if the ever-observant Sonya will detect the way her chest rises and falls as she attempts to steady her breathing on her way out of the office.

I go back inside, switch off my call forwarding and ask Sonya to come into my office. Sonya is the first person I have managed in 10 years, after mentoring dozens of sales agents and associate brokers during my career.

Just as I was about to close my office, my sister persuaded me to transition my business to my niece. "Sonya, have you been out to lunch? Then what did you eat? I know having a baby will do that to the Davenport girls. But you can't take the weight off by not eating."

Knowing her baby is now three years old, Sonya waves off my comments. "Also, that developer called about the Logan Circle property." Sonya allows the words to trail off, hoping I will talk about my inside track.

I decide to fill her in—somewhat. "Considering the location, I'd expect a lot of opposition from the neighbors to anything but maybe the luxury condominiums my favorite developer wants to build. If I could sell Sinclair on another location, maybe he'd sell to my client. With the condo listings, I could leave you on a path to success—and the means to hire a personal trainer."

August's secretary calls to cancel the appointment we no longer have. Just as I am about to suggest that she delete my number from her files Renee continues, "But he wants to get your professional opinion on the feasibility of building a school near Logan Circle." I inhale. She adds, "Please hold for the address of the vacant lot." I do not need it. I have the whole story, and Yvette, August and Davenport Schwartz Realty are all right in the middle of it.

Later that evening, I drive Sonya to help her close the listing with the Payne's at the far-east end of Capitol Hill. After getting the required signatures from our new clients, I drop Sonya off at her home in last gentrified residential pocket this side of the Anacostia. As a forecasted storm begins to develop, we both note that my small favor has saved her husband the trouble of taking their toddler, my grandniece, out in the rain.

When we arrive, her husband is standing in the doorway waiting for his wife with an umbrella. We exchange waves as the youngster peaks out to watch her father come out to the car and shepherd her mother, nice, and dry, to their front door.

I am about to head west toward home when I receive a call from August asking for my initial assessment of the Logan Circle location for a new school. I have not driven past it because I am already familiar with it, having daydreamed for over a year about obtaining it for my clients.

He sounds anxious, although I cannot be certain about his enthusiasm for anything. When I mention that I am only a few blocks away from the Souza Bridge, he immediately invites to his house to discuss it during happy hour.

Since the noon hour, Yvette has been on my mind and my nerves are still tingling. I want to refuse his suggestive invitation and the wrestling match that may ensue, and hurry back across town.

I remember how the rain always extends the Washington rush hour, and picture traffic uptown creeping slowly through the park. I head east, and cross over the bridge into Anacostia, the area my stuffy girlfriends call *East-of-the-River*. I hit a lull in the traffic and quickly breeze through several lights.

In no time, I am near the city's southern border with suburban Maryland in an affluent pocket of Anacostia that some Washingtonians still call the Silver Coast. I find a parking space and dash through the rain—with no umbrella escort—up the long flight of concrete steps to his colonial. His door is open, but no one emerges. Rather I see a shadowy figure lurking in the dark foyer.

I become very aware that I am wearing an outfit that resembles an adolescent school uniform—down to the tops of the white socks visible just above my boots. August surely has already spotted and reacted to the outfit he can clearly see.

I step inside, and he is all over me, kicking the big wooden door closed so hard it rattles its frame.

When I protest and demand my happy-hour birthday drink, he places something in my hand that I try unsuccessfully to encircle with my thumb and index finger. He lifts me up on a foyer table, hikes up my plaid skirt and alters the slit in my crotchless panties.

He has lost much of the density I remember from three years ago, but seems sufficiently medicated. When lightning flashes through the foyer window, I look out through my legs from an inverted squat. A wild-eyed man glares down at me, grabs both my ankles and lunges through the gate.

After bonding with Yvette, this is not what I crave. My scream triggers a primal response and he bucks like a wild beast spooked by the storm. Anxious to wrap this up, I tighten my gluts and push my feet into his shoulders repeatedly until he yells something in Ebonics and slumps to the floor. I can feel his hot, labored breathing on our essence as it overflows and soaks through the seat of my panties. I left my purse with my fresh panties in the trunk.

My legs dangle over his shoulders. He looks victorious, and though I was somewhat locally orgasmic, his ambush has been ill conceived. He is still breathing heavily. I wonder about the long-term effects of erectile dysfunction drugs on men. I hear myself saying, "How about the miracles of modern medicine, huh August?"

Speaking haltingly, he responds, "You know, we're both too damn old for this. But answer me this. Suppose they came up with a pill that made vaginas tighter or caused them to snap? Do you think men would ridicule any woman who took them? We'd keep a stash around the house for you."

I counter, "And if they had made birth control pills for men, would you take them? I'd have six children by now. I ain't old yet, AC. Sixty is the new 50." Then against my better judgment I ask, "Is this—how you do it to Yvette?"

"First of all, *sixty is sixty—period.* I don't know who started that. Second, I know what you want to do to Yvette. Go ahead and try. That would really be something, wouldn't it?"

"What are you talking about, Augustus?"

"I'm saying that I know what you want to do, and I support it whole-heartedly. Oh, come on, girl. You know you do. Lydia Annette Davenport. Oh, yes you do."

CHAPTER 15

"**Y**ou see, Kelly, I've suspected all along that you were still into men. I've never accused you of anything before, but now I see this text message from a scumbag like August Caesar. I know him. I don't care what he tells you. He wants to fuck you."

Of course, JoAnne is correct—considering August has tried it already. If I called him right now, he would drive over here and *at least try* to fuck us both.

My fiancé has been livid all morning. My close friends have warned me that indulging her insecurities will stretch the limits of my patience. Their warnings stem largely from their spot-on perceptions of her as a spoiled brat—her sheltered upbringing by committed parents with professional pedigrees.

My father left me with his two sisters while he was away at sea. Neither he nor my well-meaning aunts had a clue about college. While I can never thank them enough for raising me, I handled the educational and professional aspects of the journey out of my neighborhood solo.

Jo thinks there is a *difference* in our sexuality. I lost my virginity to a boy long before I understood that I was not attracted to boys. I told her about the years I languished in confusion through failed relationships in high school and college. However, I had not anticipated how a woman who has never shared her body with a man would receive that information.

She is unlike most of my previous girlfriends who at some point experimented with male partners. My *gold star femme* has been confident and self-assured since puberty. She has had a supportive father who loved her unconditionally. I have known few lesbians or bisexual women, of a certain age, who can make that claim.

Our current problem arose after she insisted that we share our passwords and allow mutual access to e-mail, text messages and phone records. While it was difficult for me to fathom such a compromise of privacy, in time I grudgingly agreed. I had nothing to hide. However, I was unprepared for the regularity or the scope of her sleuthing, which try as I might, I simply cannot abide.

While I regret that August's text message to me was so brazenly inappropriate, it was also funny. I also regret confronting the reality that the woman to whom I have pledged myself does not trust me. "Yes, I hear you very clearly, Jo. I have told you the truth about our two meetings, but you refuse to accept the truth. Now I hope we can work through this, because your refusal to believe me actually presents a bigger problem."

Jerry Lane's husband, Jordan, introduced me to August. Jordan could not say enough about his friendship with August who served as best man and the only straight person in their wedding party. Later August became godfather to their daughter—artificially inseminated by pairing Jerry's frozen sperm with the egg of Jordan's twin sister.

According to Jordan, it is not a question of August's acceptance of our sexuality. Rather, he has never implied that there is anything to accept. Jerry, who in no way suffers fools easily, has postponed a third and final retirement because of his confidence that his minority share of AJC will secure the future for his family. For me, their endorsements trump any comments about August's rakish propensities.

Jerry had asked me to give August my perspective on a proposed regulatory change that affected AJC. As a government-contracting officer, I am always willing to help small business owners who lack the resources to hire in-house or obtain procurement expertise.

We met one morning for coffee, and our conversation remained professional—at first. In my work, the few small contractors have the time required to understand the buying process.

I think August misinterpreted my admiration for the time he must have invested in learning the regulations. He morphed seamlessly from serious entrepreneur to inspired pimp, shifting his focus from the contents of my head to the bulges in my sweater and jeans.

Outside the café, he backed me against a big ghost of a town car with a fistful of my hair in one hand and half of my ass securely palmed in the other. As he conducted a vacuum-sealed mouth probe, I wondered how he assumed it would appeal to me.

When I told him that I was a lesbian, he backed off immediately and apologized for his mistake—but not his transgression. However, with that *bit of business* out of the way, his professional attitude and subsequent respect toward me never faltered.

My sexual preference notwithstanding, I could not imagine that August could have the time, energy or the libido to accommodate a substantially younger woman who runs five miles every morning—*probably before he is out of bed.*

August is like my father's friends, *old school brothers* who have been chasing women for so long that they cannot ignore a prospect. They are all military veterans who adhere to a strict *no-pussy-left-behind* code of ethics. In addition, if they mistake a woman's interest, they rationalize that the woman *sent them mixed signals.*

I will confess that, during August's third visit to the men's room in the café that morning, I had entertained the thought of him as a platonic friend—a possible wig who could spread around a little testosterone at my family gatherings.

My aunts would swoon over a handsome cookie-cutter version of Pop, and Pop would hit it off famously with another career military man. August could help me deal with the people who set me up with every Clydesdale who can hold down a job.

I still laugh aloud when I think about the year I agreed to serve as my friend's Thanksgiving beard. In return, he was supposed to serve as my Christmas holiday wig.

My performance at his family reunion was flawless. However, he disappeared from my aunt's New Year's party and entered Cousin Henry's bedroom just before midnight. Someone discovered them and reported opening the door and seeing Fran with Henry's ankles in his hands.

Though Francis has remained my close friend in the aftermath, no one has seen nor heard from Henry since.

Last week, August invited me to another meeting. I hesitated to accept, suspecting he might be just giving *it another shot*. However, he asked if I would be interested in serving as executive director of Renaissance Partners, a community services organization started by Jefferson Sinclair.

I have always admired Sinclair's approach to community empowerment through economic development, and August said he was going to resuscitate some of the projects that languished as Sinclair aged. I was thrilled. I have been searching for something to give me a respite from the tedium of analyzing proposals, executing awards and administering grants.

Though I am concerned about his reckless behavior becoming his downfall, I agreed to consider taking the job. August and I are very much alike, having escaped some of the same traps and made similar journeys. Like me, he is comfortable with all people.

I believe our backgrounds give us an edge, the ability to tap into reserves of inner strength when external sources dry up. Most significantly, rather than shedding the traits that tie us to friendships with people east of the river, we embrace them and incorporate them into our professional personas.

I have come to see in August the person I want people to see in me: A woman who never seeks validation. A woman who can spot a fire before it starts to flame, smell shit before it stinks, and walk through sand without leaving tracks. I have quickly developed a keen interest in the opportunity he has offered to me, convinced that our professional relationship would be phenomenal.

However, first, I must deal with August's reckless humor on my phone and its impact on this spoiled brat I have come to adore. As I look at Jo, I see her lips moving but I have not heard a word she has said for some time now. "Kelisha? Kelly, are you even listening to me?"

I hazard a guess. "Yes, yes. I understand how you feel about August, but we may just have to figure out how to deal with this. Look Jo, you're a cop. Like you, I work with men—young, strong virile men, who make suggestive comments all the time. I know how to handle that. We both do. I don't know why August sets you off the way he does."

Now she knows I have been ignoring her. "You haven't been listening to a word I've said. Kelly, August is the man who's been dating my mother for two years without a commitment."

The notion of him dating a missionary like Yvette derails me for a second, but I recover. "*Without a commitment*—they're in their sixties, Jo. December marriages can be very complicated—especially regarding assets. What kind of commitment is she looking for?" *Why does everything have to be about commitment with this woman?*

"Well, she claims she doesn't need one."

"Then what's your problem? Is that it? You're the only one here *with a problem*." I know I am losing patience, but something is clearly missing. I simply do not understand the root cause of her angst over August—or her involvement in her mother's very personal affairs.

Jo is livid. Her voice cracks when she asks rhetorically, "Then why is she in therapy? I know my mother. This old fake assed pimp has her all confused. She's never been with anyone like him before. Now she's found out he has grown children and a couple of baby mammas." I wince whenever the urban term used endearingly by some is so pejoratively used by others— *others like Jo and her family.*

"Found out? I knew about the boys and one of the mothers after two conversations."

My revelation—such as it is—catches Jo by surprise, as though I have been withholding secrets from her. She asks, "How did you find all that out? And what made him tell you?"

I can hear the sarcasm in my words even as I pronounce them, but can think of no other way to end this absurd conversation. "I don't know. Maybe when I asked him, *So August, how many children do you have?* How could Yvette spend all that time with him and never ask that question?"

Jo comes back immediately with a question that makes perfect sense in her world and absolutely no sense at all in mine. "How could he be with her for two years and never volunteer that information?"

I am condescending. "That's just DC, Jo. People here don't volunteer information like that. You meet a couple here and the woman introduces her escort as *her friend, Fred*. You then have everything they intend to tell you about Fred and frankly all you need to know. After that, to ask any more questions becomes intrusive."

"That's why I say guys from DC ain't shit."

"Now wait a minute Jo, all my friends and the men in my extended family are from DC. My father is from DC."

"Really Kelly—we're going there?" *Suddenly I want to slap her little ass.* I give her a moment to better compose herself, to realize how thin the ice is beneath her feet—*beneath our feet.* She recovers, "Okay, okay. I didn't mean that. I'm just upset. Why? Because he's a hustler, that's why."

"So am I. I think that's the piece you may be missing."

"Kelly, please. You don't know what I know. No, I can't tell you. But trust me. Look, I just need to know something so I'll know if we can get past this." It sounds like my princess wants to draw a line. It is the wrong move.

She may as well say goodbye to me now—regardless of whether I decide to work for August. But what does she know? If it is enough to make her this hysterical, she will have to tell me at some point.

I decide that Jo deserves a fair warning. "I know what you're going to ask me, Jo. I urge you not to draw a line in the sand. Please don't test my resolve. If August's campaign starts poling well early, I'm going to have to decide quickly—just to beat the rush. Executive Director of Renaissance Partners is some really serious shit."

"And you don't think your career in grants management had just a little to do with his offer to run Sinclair's non-profit?" She has asked a novice's question unworthy of a reply.

I respond anyway, happy to point out her pretentious gullibility. "Now, you're being silly Jo—or maybe *just plain stupid*. Sure, it does. Or maybe you think they'd bet a rich man's money on a lesbian they don't know because they like the way her ass looks in jeans."

"Not funny Kelly. Not funny at all. We'll see where this so-called campaign goes. Promise me you won't quit your day job. I can't tell you. Just promise me."

CHAPTER 16

Jefferson W. Sinclair III is Dead at 88

"Edith, I was just over here talking to him not long ago. I just don't know what to say." I cannot see the headline inside the folded newspaper spotted with August's tears. However, the words are etched in my mind forever.

I called the paper's editor to tell him that Jefferson would be pleased that his bio is on the front page rather than back with the obituaries. I am pleased that the well-researched write-up references Jefferson's rarely noted but praiseworthy civil rights record.

August, however, appears devastated by the loss of his longtime mentor and friend. He sits dejected in Jefferson's study, unsure about what to say to me. He must know that I have been preparing myself for Jefferson's departure.

However, he also knows I learned late last night that I would never again see my husband working at his favorite desk. August is here to implement one of my husband's advance directives. He thinks he should also comfort me. Nevertheless, he appears to require more attention than I do.

I would like to comfort him but I am neither emotionally nor physically equipped today. In fact, I need a nap. I only hope that he can summon the strength and composure to perform the tasks required by Jefferson's directive.

I assume that there are strategic reasons my husband has entrusted August with his final arrangements. As always, the wishes of the deceased trump all opinions to the contrary. I am trying to show patience for this man who appears ill suited for this role.

My husband enjoyed many associates over the course of his long and active life. In recent years, he became so reclusive that some people expressed concern about his absences.

Except for those who served on the board of his non-profit, only a few have spoken to him at length during the last decade. Jefferson had no siblings. He has never gotten along with my family. Yet his fondness for August has never wavered. I was pleased that Jefferson derived such joy from the son I could not give him.

At first, I suspected August might have ulterior motives for cultivating such a close relationship with a man over twenty-five years his senior. I was concerned that August might be interested in the considerable resources my husband inherited and acquired—and continued to hold separately.

Then I wondered how he could know. Jefferson and I never flaunted wealth. Like everyone else except members of my immediate family. There is a good chance that August has no idea of our net worth.

In fact, as soon as he arrived this morning, he offered to make up any shortfall in funds required to pay for Jefferson's final expenses. While it would have been a clever ruse for a young man trying to deceive me, I concluded that his offer was heartfelt—further evidence of his genuine love for my husband.

Nevertheless, I have never understood why Jefferson picked August to fill the shoes of Jay Spencer on the city council. The person who inherits that seat could become council chairman. However, without Jefferson here to back him, August will never prevail.

After all, what would be his campaign slogan? *Sixty is the New Fifty?* Right now, I need him to show me the Old Sixty, the good old *reliable sixty*. Most of all, I need him to understand that death can bring out the best and the very worst in people.

I begin with a pep talk. "Yes dear, your friend has returned home. Yes, he would have greatly appreciated this kind of news coverage while still alive.

But right now, he needs you—*I need you*—to reach deep down inside and find the strength to ensure that his wake and funeral services are all done in a manner befitting the man we knew."

He nods in agreement and gathers himself. Then he decides that this is the time for me to get to know him better. He tells me the story I already know, one that I may die if I have to hear one more time.

"Edith, I don't know if Jeff ever told you this, but I ran away from my first foster home when I was eight and my last when I was twelve." There is a mixture of sadness and pride in his voice. "The odds against me ever befriending a man like Jeff were enormous.

Jeff taught me how to use my past as a trampoline rather than a crutch. The notion that I can distance myself emotionally is simply a dog that will not hunt. But you can count on me to do this the way Jeff deserves—*the way you deserve, Edith.*"

They are compelling words and I feel relieved to hear him speaking coherently. Jefferson always treated August more like a younger contemporary than a generation removed. I search for the words that may help him. "I'm an old woman, August. Old age gives you an advantage at times like these. Unless you're just silly, the longer you get to cheat death, the more familiar with death you become."

It appears I have his attention, so I go on. "My pastor delivered a sermon once about what he called *death's shadow*. I remember he said that younger people couldn't understand the nuances of living every day in death's shadow, of understanding that any night could be your last—*any nap your last*. The longer you live in death's shadow you come to be at peace with your own mortality."

I quickly add, "But that means nothing when dealing with the death of your longtime partner or friend. I say you can never be fully prepared at any age for that. When it arrives, only grief and its cleansing properties will sustain your sanity. I'm not asking you to distance yourself from your grief. Jefferson knew you would be feeling it. He wants you to—what's that you say when you don't think I hear you guys talking? Oh yes—*cowboy the fuck up*. And don't tell anyone you heard me say that."

I will with considerable effort, emerge from this grieving process intact. I just hope this young man can be the rock that Jefferson has assigned him to be. I try to jump-start him.

"Now, I'm available, emotionally and financially, to assist you in any way. The people coming over from my church will also be at your disposal." August nods his understanding, but does not comment. "You can get the ball rolling by calling the funeral home. Do not delegate that task. They will assign a coordinator to assist and guide you, and they will link up with the hospital morgue. Just be there. If you stay in the driver's seat they won't try to steer."

August takes out his stylus and begins to write on the screen of his phone. I am astonished as the device converts his cursive chicken scratch, complete with indentations and bullets, into readable text right before my eyes.

"Then, contact the cemetery. Don't delegate that task either. They know the Sinclair family plot. However, before doing anything, especially contacting our church's office, read what Jefferson has prepared for you so that you can familiarize yourself with his wishes. This study will be off limits to anyone but you. As you know, that door leads to a small bedroom and bath. I'll make some fresh coffee and leave the pot warming on the kitchen counter. Help yourself to anything else you see."

I watch as August opens the folder that Jefferson gave me over a month ago. It contains several documents, including notes describing a few provisions of his last will and testament. I resist the urge to watch his face as he reads the notes. I will withhold the will from him for as long as I can legally, just to see if he inquires.

I am most confident that Yvette will help him through this, though both will have to learn to work together. Never a matchmaker by trade, I introduced them three years ago for no other reason than because they were both in my house at the same time.

I would have never recommended to Yvette that she become involved with August. Left alone in the kitchen just long enough to pour a cup of coffee, the gregarious Caesar established a beachhead.

Yvette is on the way here now to move in with me until two weeks after the funeral. She will also supervise the people my church sends over to screen my phone calls and serve as hosts until after the funeral services. I hope they can keep their hands off one another in my home. I have overheard enough to know that August and my husband shared the same nasty preferences.

Reminded of my own challenges that will ensue when my house is full of people with good intentions and limited common sense, I walk away to take a nap and leave August to his tasks.

Just before I go upstairs, I hear August dialing the ancient rotary device Jefferson insisted on keeping for his desk phone. August is forcefully expressing his expectations for results and accountability. It is a good sign.

I gave him a spare set of keys and left another complete set on the kitchen counter with my notes for Yvette. Relatives, friends and neighbors will descend on my home tonight. Right now, I just want to rest and dream about my old friend with whom I shared so much.

I dutifully supported but did not share my husband's wish to establish a private school. To my dismay, my husband backed up his commitment with a contribution to Renaissance Partners of valuable real estate that has been in his family for two generations.

Many detractors thought his school plan ill conceived. Most are surprised he had that kind of wealth. My nephew Elton will be at the forefront of the opposition. I know I must tell August soon, but wonder how long I can keep Elton from finding out about Jefferson's decision to make August the trustee, essentially a beneficiary of a portion of his estate.

CHAPTER 17

"**A**ugust. Who is Ruth Jackson?" When I hesitate before responding to her straightforward question, I know Yvette interprets it as guilt. "I see. Why don't I tell you what I know, and you decide, how much more you want to add? First, her name is in my folder as a preferred caterer. I called her to see if she could get something over here tonight."

After a day of mourning my old friend, this may be just the kind of theater I need. I try for deadpan but can barely suppress a smile. Only Jeff would find humor in arranging, in death, such a predictable confrontation.

It is perhaps his *final prank and testament.* It has never occurred to me to tell Yvette about Doll's catering business. "She's the woman everyone calls Doll, my son's mother. I just told you about her last week when you asked. She caters events—some for Jeff." I do not tell her that Edith and Renee also have hired Doll for numerous meetings. "So, could she accommodate you?"

"Oh yes. She's prepared to start tonight, and she can take care of our needs over the next few days." I nod, pleased to hear that Doll is taking her business seriously.

"Well then, that's good, right?"

Yvette appraises me for a few seconds. "You're just a smooth operator, aren't you August? You know, this is not the time. You have more important things to do than tap dancing. And it may be my fault that I've not compelled you to share more, but you should offer to tell me things I should know."

"Tell you what things, Yvette? What Sonny's mother does for a living?" I try not to sound dismissive.

"I mean things like how Doll knows the Sinclair's. How she seems to *know me*. Why your *son's mother* is so concerned that she has not heard *from you* since it is so unlike you not to return her calls."

I laugh because Yvette looks at me as though I am a student caught outside the classroom without a hall pass. I laugh because she sounds like a girl who just found her best friend's love note in her boyfriend's book bag. It makes her attempt to portray the adult in the conversation less than convincing.

I try to maintain a straight face. "Yvette, you must have *said something*. She's just trying to pull your chain with a little drama. And she does not know you." We go back and forth for nearly a half hour before she settles down again.

I remind her that I have barely mingled with Edith's guests and that Yvette's overreaction to Doll's ribbing is keeping her from providing the assistance she has pledged to Edith.

I try to wrap up. "We have a lot of time to spend together over the next several days and we can discuss this as much as you wish. Right now, I need to get out there with the guests. And so, do you."

While I am gathering instructions and other documents into my briefcase, Yvette responds to a knock on the door. "Just come on in." A Missionary opens the pocket doors as I continue to go through my papers. I hear her announce, "Lydia Davenport says she's in the neighborhood and wants to know if it's okay to drop by to talk to you.

I wince at Lydia's timing and make the mistake of answering without bothering to look up. "Okay Joyce. Could you offer her some refreshments and tell her I'll be out in a few minutes?" Hearing no response, I look up to see clueless expressions on the faces of both women. Yvette's expression is sheer consternation.

"I think she was *talking to me*, August."

"Oh. Okay."

"*Oh Okay*, what, August? Joyce, give us a few minutes before you bring Lydia back."

I start lying. "I didn't know you and Lydia were already acquainted. So, I have no reason to think she would be here to see anyone but me—since I hired her to be my real estate broker."

Of course, ironically, we are both lying. Knowing Lydia as I do, by now my name has come up in conversations between them. I simply continue packing my briefcase, certain that by now, Yvette has established the link between the three of us.

I understand how having that out in the open would probably alarm Yvette. *However, why play this game? Does she have some emotional need to convey—and convey to whom?* "Okay, I see you didn't know. Sorry I never mentioned it before." Is this supposed to be *gotcha moment?*"

"August, I called Lydia earlier to cancel an appointment scheduled for tomorrow. She's also the real estate broker helping me find a location for my art gallery. I told her I was here helping Edith, and she said she might drop by to pay her respects."

I look over at her showing no emotion. "Okay, so she could be here to see either of us—so what?"

"So, why would she be here to see you today? Are you that urgently in the market to buy some real estate?"

"Lydia sent a text the afternoon she heard the news that Jeff had suffered a massive stroke. I told her today that I would be spending a lot of time at the Sinclair residence." I try not to sound defensive. "She knows about Jeff and the school. I've been getting some real estate advice from her to help me prep for my meeting with the board."

She turns on a dime. "What meeting with which board? I don't know what you're talking about." I do not understand why this is making her so emotional.

I decide to go on the offensive. "So, what if you don't? Why should you? I haven't discussed this with anyone. Before he died, Jeff asked that I serve as President of the board of directors for Renaissance Partners. He was gone before I could give him a response. Then I found out today that he had already willed half of the non-profit's stock to me—whether I take the gig or not. I guess it's to push me further toward accepting his propositions."

Yvette looks as though she suddenly has a lot to process. "Edith told me that Jefferson transferred title to their Logan Circle properties to the non-profit." She begins to whisper. "August, do you know how much that real estate is worth?"

"I do now that Lydia has told me." Since we are both lying about our relationships with Lydia, I want to state that mine has been strictly professional. I also want to downplay the notion that the stock holds great value for me personally. "But I do not *have* anything, Yvette. Renaissance Partners owns the properties, plain and simple."

Yvette remains silent, as though trying to reconcile what she has learned with whatever she thought she knew before. I finish gathering my things and put on my jacket. "So, Yvette, are you two going to meet back here? If so, I can clear out and let you have the room."

I continue to provide information. Her lack of knowledge may be at the root of her anger. "Yvette, Lydia helped me prepare talking points on changing the proposed location of the school. If they agree to sell the property, I have no problem with her turning a tidy commission for her work since, if she doesn't, some other broker certainly will. The school should be in the community it serves, and we should sell the Logan property to help fund it. We may even get some land from the city. Jeff died before I could tell him, and now I can't do a thing without Edith and the board."

She studies me as though noticing for the first time some birthmark on my forehead. "August, do you really have the time to get all this done?"

"I have no interest in owning AJC a minute longer than absolutely necessary. My plan has always been to sell it as soon as the valuation hits a certain number. Can I smoothly transition out of one and into the other—not without help from very capable people I can trust. I really need to know if you're one of those people. Edith is going to ask you to help me."

"And how do you know—would you feel about that?" Strangely, she asks the fumbled, revealing question like a psychiatrist.

"I doubt if she cares how I feel about it, but I like the idea. That's also one of the things I hoped you and I could talk about." *I had also hoped to speak with her about the sleeping arrangements at the Sinclair mansion, particularly regarding coed visitation.*

She stands quietly as though trying to gather the nerve to ask me something. "Okay, but just one more thing, August. Are you the one Lydia told me about? Are you the man who makes her pack extra panties in her purse?"

"Why would you ask me a thing like that?" I sink down into the chair. "I don't know who he is, but I do like his style."

As soon as the door abruptly slides open, I know that Joyce has not briefed Lydia in advance on the room's mood and occupants. However, I also know that Lydia has come here to have a little fun—but not at the risk of a losing a large broker's commission. Lydia walks in and stops in front of Yvette, already aware of the game she needs to play. "Hi. When I spoke to you over the phone, it occurred to me that you two must know one another."

She expresses her condolences, kissing Yvette softly on the cheek. However, her innocent gesture, customary between two female friends in an hour of grief, causes Yvette to stiffen and lean away. Lydia turns to me. "August, I am so sorry to hear about your friend." She walks toward the desk but I remain seated, struggling to maintain my composure.

Yvette turns to leave the room, making eye contact only with Lydia. "I guess the two of you have a lot to discuss."

I stop her. "Yvette. I believe this is your meeting, is it not?" I get up to leave the two women alone, certain they now have far more to discuss than I do.

"But Yvette says, "No, you go first. I'll talk to you later, Lydia, if you have any free time." I wink at Joyce to acknowledge her mischievousness as she closes the doors behind them.

Lydia spins back around to me. "Oh man, that was bat-shit crazy." However, her expression of concern morphs into open laughter. "I am so sorry. Do you forgive me, Bat? I couldn't help myself." She leans over and kisses me fully on the lips, and sits down in front of the desk. "Oh man, you and Yvette."

"No, you mean you and Yvette."

"And you—and who else, huh August?"

I do not respond. A voice comes over the house phone's intercom system. "August, I hope everything is going alright in there, dear." Edith's voice is strong but holds some concern. "The ladies have done a wonderful job out here, but we would like to see you come out for a bit longer and say hello to some of the people. My pastor has arrived, and I'd like you to get a chance to talk about the list of speakers."

"Yes. It just occurred to me that I haven't come up for air."

"But as important as that may be, it isn't principally why I buzzed you. John Fellows called to offer his condolences and asked if I had your phone number." She pauses to allow space for my reaction before continuing. "He's traveling from California to attend the funeral—accompanied by his grandson."

I am still silent. I have not seen John since he attended a Korean veterans meeting held in Baltimore over two decades ago. I have not seen my son Jack since he was in the city briefly years ago. It has not even occurred to me to call them.

She gives up on soliciting a reaction from me. "I believe he said that his grandson read about Jefferson on the Internet. I'll see you when you come out dear."

I immediately begin composing a telegram to send to John and Jack, but Lydia interrupts my thoughts, and returns me to the confusion at hand. "Come on. Say something, man. You look like a kid caught with his hand in the cookie jar."

I look up at her. "I don't know. Maybe you can clear something up for me, Lydia." Her eyes answer my question even before I ask it. "Are we both in the same cookie jar?"

"If we're all in the same jar, August, there's no room for anyone else. Hell, who're we trying to kid? There're no cookies for anyone else."

CHAPTER 18

"**W**hat's going on Nay?"

As I sit nude on the side of my bed rummaging through my briefcase, I know Bernard requires an explanation for the abrupt change in my behavior. Just a few minutes ago. I had been expressing joy, loudly, as he repeatedly impaled me to the beat of love songs from the seventies.

However, the sound of the boss's ringtone made me pull out midway into a deep satisfying squat. Unaccustomed to me dismounting from my favorite position, Bernard should be suspicious.

"You getting dressed right now and going where?"

I apologize, "Baby, I've got to drive up to Spring Valley. Yes, tonight. I need to take something to my boss so he can sign it."

"Nay, you mean way uptown in Spring Valley—*white Spring Valley*? American University Spring Valley?" I understand why Bernard looks confused. Perhaps if it were midday, he might believe that I need to drop everything right now, and travel west of the park to get my boss's signature on a letter.

Just a few minutes ago, I was hovering over him with a tight grip on the top rung of my brass headboard. His large hands tightly squeezed my ass with each dip. Despite feeling the burn from my hamstrings to my calves, I soldiered on, driven by the sheer depths to which the orca plunged inside of me.

Yet in an instant, I was scrambling across the bed for my smartphone. "Not a problem Mister C. I was just getting in some lower bodywork. How many reps? Oh, I lost count."

Bernard had responded to my wink with a slight smile, but he cannot be pleased. He waited patiently for five weeks before I was comfortable enough to get naked with him. It occurs to me that I may be asking too much. He will never understand how a phone call could so quickly supersede the ecstasy I had been expressing.

Perhaps no one would understand who did not work for demanding people like August Caesar and Jerry Lane. Rather than explain it to a person who works a standard shift, and seeing no reduction in Shamu's enthusiasm, I decide to set my alarm and get a little more before I leave.

As I reposition myself to straddle him, I apologize again, "I'm sorry, Baby, I meant to turn the phone off, but once I heard my boss's ring tone, I couldn't ignore the call."

He places his index finger against my lips and asks, "How much time is there left on the clock? Oh, fifteen minutes will work."

After a few more sets of deep squats, we are about midway through our departure window and I am on the verge of insanity. In one motion, I find myself rotated onto my back. I lock my hands under his shoulders. He demonstrates the extreme depths to which the orca can dive, at times using it like a crowbar. He disregards several requests for intermissions, clearly accustomed to hearing them and understanding that, while loud, they lack genuine resolve.

Bernard could be the beast I have been waiting for. After he agrees to drive me to the Sinclair residence, I am almost ready to announce that the job is his—if he does not say anything stupid.

After a quick stop by the office, he pulls his surprisingly comfortable extended-cab pickup out onto the street and begins the long drive that will take us from Southeast to our far northwest destination—and he remains deliciously silent until we are off the Whitehurst Freeway.

"So, what's your boss doing in Spring Valley?" Four years ago, I would have felt the same way about traveling west of the park at night. But I have not given a second's thought to going out to one of the city's wealthy residential communities. There are adults who have spent their lives in the city without going west of the park to do anything other than stroll through Georgetown, visit the zoo or shop within walking distance of a subway station. The location of the city university in Vann Ness is an aberration, an up yours from a prior mayoral administration.

"Have you ever heard of Jefferson Sinclair? That's right. My boss was close to Mister Sinclair. He's at her home right now preparing for his public viewing and funeral services. I need to get his signature on the letter I just picked up from the office. No. I am not a secretary, though I have been one and proud of it. I'm now our company's deputy director of operations."

We ride in silence as Bernard, who normally uses speed limits only as points of reference, carefully comes to completely stops and slows down for Washington's notoriously long yellows. We arrive at the huge colonial and see a police cruiser, a dozen luxury cars and several chauffeurs standing around conversing.

Bernard lets out a low whistle. "Oh, so this is why you talk the way you do?" He does not say the words with malice but they prick me much more than they should. "No. I speak this way because when money talks, this is the way it sounds." I regret saying it immediately.

I must avoid using shutdown comments that sound like put-downs against backdrops of relative opulence. "Look man, I just got lucky and hooked up with some hard-driving hustlers who are teaching me how to ride the money train because they need somebody to keep it running on schedule. I'm going to drive until the wheels fall off."

"Cool down Nay-nay. I love the way you talk. I'm sorry if that sounded like a crack. I know you think I just stock shelves, sell gas and change tires. I also manage the place. Ramesh is teaching me the franchising aspects of inventory, retail fuel and auto repair. I've got money saved and have been keeping my credit score hovering around 800. I just need to better understand the finance end—business plans and loan packages."

It occurs to me that this is the most interesting conversation I have had with any man in years, and I cannot wait to hear more. I ball up my fist and punch him in the chest—hard. "That's the kind of shit you should have told me right out the gate, punk." I punch him again—harder—and open the door. He simply laughs and replies, "Just hurry up before a brother gets arrested sitting out in front of this place. What the hell is this anyway, a museum?"

I walk up to the house and manage to get inside without drawing attention to myself. Several people are leaving just as I reach the doorway so I walk in unannounced through the foyer, and hear conversations from about a couple dozen people remaining in the home.

Getting a glimpse into the drawing room, I can see Mrs. Sinclair's well-dressed visitors mingling. Assuming the hostesses are near the food, I follow the aromatic trail back to the kitchen. I am surprised to find Ruth and two other women wearing aprons, busy with food preparation. I am just about to call over to her when I notice three older women in what appear to be church ushers' uniforms.

"Yvette, I know it's none of my business, but you need to get back in there and break that up. Don't worry girl, I got your back." I have seen her but not actually met Yvette before.

She is strikingly pretty and looks much younger than her age. However, I have spoken to her over the phone many times, often when she was not at her best. Her calls are now fewer and farther between. This evening she is clearly on the back end of a long day.

She tries to calm her friend. "We need to remember why we're here. Only a little ho like Lydia could walk in here uninvited and hang out in the study with August behind closed doors." So, *Miss Thing* is back there somewhere with Mister C. I never thought older people carried on like this.

I am certain that if I stay long enough, I will learn everything. However, there is a bona fide stud behind the wheel of a truck—talking like he can also *walk the walk*. I need to find August Caesar and remember to knock before I go in. Just then, Ruth literally floats across the large kitchen to embrace me, speaking so others can easily hear.

"Oh, how have you been doing Renee? I haven't seen you in so long. Thanks so much for arranging that spring break trip for August Junior." *August Junior? Spring-break?* Sonny has been on break since the day he enrolled. There is clearly a hell of a backstory unfolding behind the scenes at the Sinclair mansion. I only hope that they have not allowed it to spill over into the guests. "Uh, I'm fine, Ruth. I see you're on the clock tonight."

"Well, I was told that Jefferson wanted me to do it and you know I want to be supportive." Ruth turns to the three women. "Yvette, this is August's right hand, Renee Webster. Renee, this is Edith's dear friend Yvette."

Yvette does not come over to shake my hand. She simply shrugs and shakes her head in disbelief. With her eyes in danger of rolling back into her skull, she manages to force a smile.

"Renee and I have spoken on occasion. Renee, these are two dear friends of mine and members of my church's Missionary Society. By the way, *Doll*, when do *you girls* expect to finish in the kitchen? You know, Mrs. Sinclair expects it to be spotless when you're done." *Oh boy*.

I am on my way out of the kitchen area before Ruth can respond. I decide to find the study on my own rather than walk through the house with a dramatic tour de force. As I pass through the large drawing room, I hope the last of her guests can see that Mrs. Sinclair's strength is waning even as she soldiers on. A hostess hurries to get ahead of me and leads me to a set of sliding wooden doors. She simply gestures to the doors and walks away with a cracked smile.

As soon as I knock, the doors open and a well-dressed woman about Yvette's age, and almost as pretty, walks out of the study. "Hello. Are you Renee? I'm Lydia Davenport. I'm so pleased finally to put a face with the voice—and to meet the real brains behind AJC. Go on in. I think August just received a phone call."

She is very gracious in contrast to the way she normally treats me over the phone. She looks amused about the confusion her presence here has probably caused. The boss looks remarkably relaxed for a man with three women jousting in the same house.

With the letter signed, I leave the house and see in the shadows Lydia and Yvette standing very close together in the private driveway. They are engaged in deep, hushed conversation. Though they are beyond the security light's coverage, even in the shadows I can see that there is no animosity between them.

My curiosity peaks on several levels, but I have issues of my own. I have taken much longer than anticipated to get the letter signed and get out of the house. I have not known Bernard long enough to tell if he is angry about the delay.

"I'm sorry, man. I hope I didn't keep you waiting too long, but I couldn't avoid it. The lionesses are in-charge of the zoo tonight. I really appreciate you being so patient and understanding."

When I lean over to give him a peck on the cheek, he does not so much kiss me as make out with me. I do not break away until he is ready to let go, and by the time he does, I am refocused on what I hope is our mutual plan for the remainder of the night.

"Bernard, would you mind if I asked you to turn to the jazz on WDMV and just cruise back across town in silence? I have a lot to process."

"See that's what I mean. I love it when you say shit like that. *I have a lot to process.*" He drives home in complete silence. Instead of WDMV, he takes the liberty of popping in a private play list he has stored on a drive.

It features tracks with Thelonious Monk and McCoy Tyner, but also includes several other past and present jazz pianists. He makes almost every light, turning down Rock Creek Parkway to catch the crosstown expressway.

Still silent, he follows me into my house, walks uninvited upstairs to my bedroom, removes every stitch of his clothing and stretches across my bed on his stomach. After locking up, I join him. I remove my clothing, unable to take my eyes off his two pouting muscular mounds flexed like sculptured marble with dimples carved deep into their sides.

When I finally lay down beside him, he remains face down, allowing me to massage the smooth marble until I motion for him to roll over. When he does, the orca is so packed, it twitches at my touch.

CHAPTER 19

So, you're August Caesar's son?

Since it is biologically correct, I have been answering in the affirmative to that question, acknowledging the blood relationship more in one day than all the previous days of my life combined.

While dozens of people have come over to introduce themselves to me and my grandfather today, this woman is the youngest of several particularly attractive women who have very deliberately crossed the wide banquet hall to ask me something about August. I sense that the fact that little or nothing to contribute may be more enlightening for them than any peculiar insight I might have shared.

People have been really looking forward to meeting me, studying my manner with an almost disconcerting intensity. If they found anything that might remind them of my father, it would be news to me. *Oh, I see you have your father's eyes.*

In anticipation of just this sort of popularity, my grandfather has made me promise to wear my most cordial social mask. It has held up well against the strain of so many references to a *sperm donor* who has meant so little to me.

I am here only to support Pop, to take care of him in his twilight years the way he took care of me in my early years. I am in the throes of acquiring my fifth fast food location, and already feel that I am risking losing the deal, attending a charade on the other coast.

Pop had been determined, more determined than he has been about anything in a long time, to attend this funeral of his friend. Together they survived the 24th Infantry Regiment's controversial defense of Korea's Pusan Peninsula, and going north after Inchon. Pop remains active in his veterans' group attending reunions and funerals, but not one that required a transcontinental trip since the 1982 Baltimore reunion.

His photographs taken with Jefferson Sinclair are among his most prized possessions. As the unit removes Mr. Sinclair's distinguished name from the roll that grows shorter each year, my grandfather wanted to be here and I could not in good conscience allow him to make this trip alone. *So, you're August's father-in-law. Did your daughter make the trip also?*

In a hastily sent telegram to Pop, August had expressed his condolences belatedly and invited us to stay at his home during the visit. It was difficult to resist the opportunity to observe the way he lives since I will admit to a passing curiosity. I declined because I sense that Pop has a hidden agenda.

As he travels deeper into his winter of life, I know that part of him still holds out for the possibility that August and I will find a way to reconcile. I can almost guarantee him that we will not.

I never truly understood my deep resentment for August's absence until I had children of my own. In a way I do not understand, I almost envy the support and love they receive from my wife and me.

My mother married August so young that she was able to outgrow him the way people grow out of acne. I on the other hand, never grew out of a need for a father even though there was never an hour in his day that Pop did not make available to me. However, I must refuse any request he makes for me to bond with August, and I appreciate that he has thus far spared us both that agony.

All day I have shown civility to people who must if they are rational human beings, detect my complete lack of interest in their relationships with August. I rise again to greet another female visitor to our table.

I am prepared to answer a few general questions but I am determined to ignore any that I deem too personal. I see that my grandfather has finally decided that standing up to meet them all may require more stamina than he is willing to tap into.

Yes, I'm Jack Caesar and this is my grandfather, John Fellows. No, he is my mother's father. Yes, most people say that I favor him. Yes, but I was in the Navy. No, other than my own military postings outside of San Diego, I have lived in California my whole life.

While I confess that conversations with August's friends and associates have been modestly illuminating, I am concerned that the persistent interaction is beginning to take a toll on my grandfather. We only arrived in the city last night and Pop does not sleep well in unfamiliar surroundings—particularly not in a fancy hotel like the one August arranged for us just outside Georgetown.

The woman standing in front of us is stunningly attractive—much too young to have a romantic interest in August. Curiously, she lingers longer at our table on a fact-finding mission so obvious that it even brings a smile to Pop's face. *No. Yesterday was the first time I have seen my father in many years. My mother lived in California as well. No, I have no other siblings from my father except for a half-brother here in the city. I have not yet met him.*

Pop and I have already decided that it would be silly to try to hide our estrangement and that specific questions about my mother will be off-limits. I try to deflect any further questions from our table visitor with one of my own. "Actually, I was wondering how you know my father." I feel very odd referring to him that way.

"Oh, I'm sorry for being so rude. I've been so busy talking about August I've not actually introduced myself. I'm JoAnne. Detective Sergeant JoAnne Saxton. What do you want to know about my weapon? No, I carry a nine but prefer a 10—you're right, it makes a big hole, like a 45. My mother is very close to August. Is your father sitting with you?" She looks around feigning surprise that he is not sitting with us, apparently hoping to instill concern in me. So maybe she is not *exactly a friend.*

"He's spent as much time with us as he can. He appears to be in high demand today, and his place is really near his old friend's widow and dignitaries. He has had to orchestrate this entire weekend." *Why am I taking up for him?*

The brief moments he has managed to spend with us today have been more than I can remember ever being with him. I am impressed with the job he has done coordinating a huge service that rivaled any I have ever seen—with its long list of eulogists, soloists and testimonials. The procession stretched for a mile with a large contingent of police escorts on motorcycles, sedans and utility vehicles.

Much has revolved around August. Representatives and senators, mayors and council members all seemingly interested in meeting this man who has been front and center during the entire event.

While there is no designated master of ceremonies, he has emerged to speak, instruct, or to vector. Primarily, he has maintained order and flow. He is clearly the person in charge. Everyone involved has deferred to him to make decisions on the fly or to provide clarifications to vagaries I would swear he has purposely left vague.

Several television camera crews cover the entire event. All have taken time to interview August. Mr. Sinclair's widow constantly redirects people to him. Through it all, August is everywhere at once. He had a minister recognize Pop specifically and seated him at the gravesite ceremony with Mr. Sinclair's widow and her family.

I know he will never forget these kind gestures and will cherish his memories of this trip. For those reasons as well as the genuine affection Pop and August have for one another, I must grudgingly admit to being glad we came.

Turning to Pop, JoAnne offers her condolences. "I was very sorry to hear about Mister Sinclair. It sounds like the two of you enjoyed a very special friendship." When she turns on the charm, her voice drips pure honey and sweet tea.

"Yes ma'am. I enjoyed a very special relationship with Jeff in Korea, and we both remained close through correspondence, phone calls and our active participation in our unit's veteran association."

I listen with interest as Pop encourages an expansion of the conversation, wondering what there is about this woman that has his interest and which bit of information he is trying to obtain by volunteering more of his own. "I also had a very close relationship with August before and after his service in Vietnam. I like to think that I was the link that first strengthened the bond between August and Jeff."

However, JoAnne shows little emotion, in sharp contrast to Pop's very emotional revelation. "That's a coincidence. The Sinclair's were the link between August and my mother, such as it is. I don't know anything about that, but I can tell you what I do know." She is growing increasingly heated, even hostile. JoAnne appears about to comment further, perhaps with specificity, when a voice from behind her interrupts.

"What is it that you know, JoAnne?"

As she turns, my gaze follows hers to the woman who was the first to greet us upon our arrival and seated us strategically at the repast. I have seen her huddling with August throughout the weekend and now seeing that she is an older, more gracious—perhaps even more attractive—version of JoAnne, even Pop quickly connects the dots.

I wonder if Pop has noticed that, as Yvette has made the rounds through the hall, she has frequently found her way over to our table. This has been true particularly during our visits from other females. Pop gingerly invests the energy required to stand, even though he and Yvette have already met.

Yvette holds out her hand, allowing Pop to hold it in both of his as he thanks her for taking such good care of us. She graciously accepts his thanks but remains focused on her daughter's earlier comment. "What is it that you know, JoAnne?"

The younger woman instinctively backs off from her earlier posture and decides to hold back the comments we so much wanted her to share. "Oh, I was just telling Mister Fellows that I do not know much about August's time in Vietnam. Well. Anyway, it was very nice meeting you both."

Pop and I assure her that it was our pleasure and I, along with several men at adjacent tables, are powerless to resist gazing at the way her derriere swings as she moves back across the hall.

I must turn my interest back to Yvette who I now know has a full court press on our table. Recognizing that the trail has now gone cold with her daughter, Pop abruptly shifts his focus to her. "So, JoAnne tells us that you and August are very close. The two of you look so much alike. You're her mother, aren't you?"

The laser glare she shot toward her daughter disappears, replaced by a warm and gracious manner. "Yes. Her father and I have been divorced for over seven years. August and I have enjoyed a very close relationship for about three years. We're both going to be on the board of the community service organization founded by Jefferson Sinclair. Edith and I became fast friends after I arrived in the city and joined her church. She's president of the church's missionary society on which I also serve. In fact, she introduced me to August. I've been staying with her since Jefferson's passing and assisting August with the funeral services."

She provides the information chronologically and concisely as though we have a right to a briefing. I decide to join in and satisfy my own curiosity. "Then the two of you must make a very effective team because this weekend has gone amazingly well. My father appears to be right at the center of everything without officially being designated anywhere on the program."

She smiles and nods her head slowly. "I see. Like father like son."

"How is that?"

"It's just an observation based on an observation." She continues to show the knowing smile and her response produces a big grin on Pop's face. "Well, I need to get back to my chores. If there's anything you need anytime during your stay—if you can't reach August, please don't hesitate to ask me. In fact, there'll be people at the Sinclair mansion again tonight and you are most welcome to join us—you and young Mister Caesar."

I like her very much despite the liberties she takes with our *family* association. The men in my vicinity watch her as she replicates her daughter's exit, stride for rocking stride. I think that my father must be a very lucky man, and I wonder if he knows.

CHAPTER 20

"**M**ister Caesar, it looks like you're going to be okay. The bullet entered and exited cleanly, barely penetrating your lower right side. From the looks of this wound and the loss of blood, it must have been at least a 45-caliber round."

I am not sure I overhear the medevac technician correctly over the noise of the helicopter's engine and blades. However, my memory of the thundering report and the force of the projectile suggest his estimate of the caliber is probably accurate.

The shooter fired at point-blank range and missed badly, after reconsidering. When I saw that big barrel, I thought I was a dead man. The muzzle flash from the blast illuminated a whole section of the parking lot like a flashbulb, revealing a clear photo quality image of my shocked assailant, weapon in hand.

The unmistakable crack of the discharge was sickening, as was the molten hot lead that tore through just a pinch of my lower right side but still hurled me into a car parked behind me.

My knees buckled, and just before losing consciousness, I heard tires spin on the gravel pavement, lurch forward and speed down the road. The two EMS technicians who arrived on the scene looked young enough to be my grandsons, but I prayed a prayer of thanks that someone promptly vectored them and their lifesaving equipment to my location. "Hey, give me his name again. *August Caesar?* Stay with us, Mister Caesar, we're doing everything we can."

I wanted to pull off the oxygen mask and tell him to save his energy for the effort it will take to stabilize me. I wanted to tell him that I am far from ready to go anywhere. In fact, with my second retirement long done, I am starting the third more relaxed phase of my life.

Bullets have struck me twice before on both ends of my military career. The first time was as a kid on a faraway airfield surrounded by rain-soaked jungle, and then twenty years later standing too close to the edge of a facility surrounded by desert sand.

However, never so up close and personal as tonight when I could see the cold hatred in the shooter's eyes. I have seen eyes like that before, but at this point in my life, I never imagined seeing them on the face of someone aiming a firearm at me.

I had stopped on the way home from work to pick up an order of Chinese takeout. I had been walking through the restaurant parking lot toward my car when I passed by a parked vehicle. A quick visual sweep of the lot had not revealed any danger lurking about. The evening had been warm enough that the open driver's side window did not raise a concern.

As I walked by, someone stuck out the barrel of a rather large handgun, but it was too late to avoid the inevitable. After I passed out, a stranger revived me. I am not certain whether I owe my recovery to successful cardio-pulmonary resuscitation or the garlic stench he blew into my lungs. I was, however, very grateful that he took the initiative.

After a few minutes had passed, someone shouted, "Where the hell is that ambulance?" Almost on cue, I heard a distant siren growing louder until I saw the emergency lights strobe and flicker across the night sky.

"*He's been shot.*" An attendant leaped out of the truck and began to administer care, followed by the driver. "*I don't know. I didn't see it.*" I know that, if I were them, I would be wondering why anyone would shoot me, and I hoped they assumed that the motive was robbery. "*It looks like he's lost a lot of blood.*"

The attendants moved quickly and efficiently, cleaning out the wound and controlling the bleeding. They lifted me and placed me on a platform, which they loaded into the vehicle. *"That was the medevac team. They're almost here."*

That was when I knew it was serious. The notion of a helicopter evacuation had not even entered my mind. I had needed only one during my four tours in Vietnam and one during my two tours in Iraq but had never thought I would need another one stateside.

The police cleared a spot on the road for the aircraft to safely land. I was impressed with the professionalism with which the ground team briefed the medevac crew on my status, and felt like I had been in very good hands. I thanked them both.

"We're going to take care of you from here, Mister Caesar." From the point of exchange through the flight to the hospital, the quality of their training and the level of their expertise had been evident, and there had not been a moment in which I did not feel safe. Curiously, I regretted most not being able to look out from the helicopter over the sloping suburban landscape.

"Okay Mister Caesar, you're doing good sir. We're almost over the hospital roof now. We're going to land on the helipad."

After being rushed to surgery and attended to by a steady procession of medical personnel engaged in a flurry of activity, I wake up in the recovery area of an intensive care ward. I estimate that it is shortly before daybreak when I am left alone in a room to rest, connected to several tubes and cords but confident that all is well and that I will be fine.

I close my eyes to enjoy a much-needed nap. However, my first non-medical visitor arrives—a man who identifies himself as a police detective. I manage to mumble a request before he can say a word. "I would prefer not to have any visitors other than immediate family."

"Yes," the law officer replies. "That would be standard procedure in a shooting. We have already issued those instructions, and a uniformed officer will be right outside your door for a while or until we can get this thing sorted out."

He walks over to the side of the bed, and looks down at me as if assessing both the physical damage and my state of mind. After asking a series of questions related to my identity, residence and employment, he moves on to the events that transpired that day and my "reasons for being at the "scene of the crime".

I tell him that the scene of the crime is my favorite local Chinese take-out restaurant and my reason for being there was to pick up the food I had called in. I lied that I did not see the shooter who could have easily killed me. "Mister Caesar, do you have any idea who would do this or why?"

I shake my head and shrug without answering him. "Did the shooter look like a woman? I ask not to be sexist but because men don't usually miss at that range. However, anyone could reconsider at the last second and allow the gun barrel to drift. Or, depending on strength or experience, a big caliber weapon could recoil and get away from the shooter."

"The shot came from nowhere. The impact from the slug must have thrown me around some. I simply did not see who fired the gun."

"Then you never looked into the car to see who was holding the gun—even when it flashed? I know a lot of victims close their eyes or look away, but the doc tells me this ain't your first rodeo."

"I understand that you've got a job to do, detective, and I hope you catch whoever did this to me. However, if we're finished here, I would really like to just lay back and get some sleep now."

He does not believe me and probably has investigated enough shootings to know that I am not telling him the truth. I do not care. I know exactly who pulled the trigger and I think I know why. However, the shooter can do nothing for me behind bars.

"Okay then, I'll leave you to it. But I hope you don't mind if I stop by tomorrow to see if there are any details that occur to you later." He walks over to a cabinet with a note board attached.

"I'll just pin my contact information up here for your reference. I'll add just one more thing, Mister Caesar. It's never a good idea to pursue or confront a shooter without the police. People have been determined to try, but it never works out quite the way they think it will. Some end up doing some jail time themselves. Others end up dead."

I close my eyes and try to concentrate on a happy thought to take into my slumber. I try to focus on the good times, but instead I dream that Sonny is just a toddler and I have lost him in a city that I do not recognize.

I look for him in a place with which I am not familiar. I can hear his voice. However, by the time I get to him, he calls out to me from somewhere else. I cannot possibly find him and I am powerless to stop searching for him.

CHAPTER 21

sleep through the remainder of the night and drift in and out of consciousness as doctors, nurses and technicians attend to me for most of the second day. On the third day I awaken, feeling remarkably improved and strong but still slightly groggy from pain relievers. My first visitor of the day, other than hospital staff, arrives just after breakfast.

"Oh, August, I couldn't believe it when they told me. Who in the world would do this to you?" She is wearing the same type of white uniform she has been wearing at Edith's house during her stay there. She walks over to the side of the bed and kisses me lightly on the lips. There is tenderness in her manner and touch that I find comforting—as though she has a special gift for this. Even at this hour, I cannot resist. "I told the police I thought you did it."

"Don't play around like that August. It's not funny. All the news stations ran your story that night and throughout the next day. I half expected to find them here. No, they're already affiliating you with Renaissance Partners as Jefferson's successor. No. They have not yet mentioned that you are also president of AJC—just that you're taking over Renaissance."

"Then that's a good thing. That's a very good thing." AJC does not need the publicity while we compete for an important contract. "So, then you're dressed for the cameras?" I wonder if she knows how good she looks in that uniform. "I have been trying to figure out for a week if you altered that thing to fit you. Or did you just grow into it?"

"Stop, August. I'm dressed for my usual rounds. Three of the people on my list are in this hospital today. No, this is not the same dress. The other one is in the cleaners. You wrinkled that one beyond the capacity of normal ironing to correct. But you need to focus on getting well." She moves in close and whispers. "You were all over me. Did you really expect me to do that in Edith's house on that beautiful sofa?"

I share a secret. "Jefferson would have wanted me to put it to good use. You see, he told me back in the day, Edith was bent over that couch so much you can still see her knee prints in the cushions." I suddenly realize that my side hurts when I laugh.

"You need to quit. I could have gone the rest of my life without knowing that." She quickly changes the subject, becoming very serious. "I want you to stay at my house when you leave rehab. I can make you very comfortable in the downstairs den where you'll have access to everything you need. Besides, it seems that we have a lot to discuss and plan."

She lowers her voice. "Edith—who I'll never again be able to look in the eye after today—got around to telling me about Jefferson's wishes for Renaissance. Yes, you were right, generally, about her hopes for me. She wants me to help you, to serve as a paid board member. I will assume any title you will agree to bestow, but I will not replace her as vice chair. She'll retain that position but won't be active, just wants to preserve her vote."

I anticipated that move. I am impressed with Edith's strategic thinking. She knows that Yvette's presence on the board will always guarantee her two votes—plus the other two members she has in her pocket already. She will also have a dynamo in Yvette to get things done. Yvette's compensation may be a more difficult issue if I can successfully lure my new executive director.

Yvette interrupts my thinking. "I don't want to interrupt your rest and recovery with shop talk, but I do have just two questions I need you to answer honestly before I can give my answer to Edith. One: Do you think there will be a problem with the two of us working together? Two: Do you envision a role for Lydia beyond site acquisition?"

I say no to both. "Now why are you looking so puzzled? Are you still concerned about changing the location?"

She moves a chair close to the side of the bed and sits down closer still, crossing her legs as if to sharpen her focus. I begin slowly. "No one except Jefferson has ever wanted to establish the school near Logan Circle—not one soul. Most don't want it at all. He had a romantic notion about establishing something in the U Street Corridor. However, the kids he wanted to reach, although there are some in Northwest, are primarily from three of the city's wards, two of them east of the river. That's where we need to concentrate our efforts."

I reach for my water bottle and she springs up to help. I manage on my own. "Renaissance owns the real estate outright. Lydia can get a small fortune for the property from a consortium of developers—without even breaking a sweat. I'm thinking about a strategy that leverages all that cash and taps into the school system's assets. We have a board that'll be energized by the change in location."

"August. What are you going to do about Elton Dalton? Whenever Edith doesn't consult with him, I think she feels like she's going against her family. He could make trouble for you."

I wave off the thought, "Elton won't be a problem."

"How can you be sure of that? Maybe you don't know how he stirs up trouble when he can't have things his way. You're so gung-ho about this project." When I shrug, lay back and close my eyes, she stops probing and looks for ways to help. "Then we need to develop an airtight proposal with everything laid out so that we can run it past Edith. We could do that together but you didn't say whether you'd take me up on my offer. Okay. Well, just let me know after you've thought it through. I promise to stay out of your hair."

My eyes are open again. I am not yet ready to tell her about Kelly. "Yvette, I need to ask that you keep this to yourself until I have had a chance to completely flesh out all the details. She nods her head but frowns. "It won't be for long."

"August, you know I don't feel comfortable keeping this from her. After all, I'm in it because she asked me." She agrees to wait, though still somewhat reluctantly, and stands up to kiss me goodbye, saying she will stop by again in the afternoon. I know she will keep my confidence—for a while, anyway. However, she is clearly very uncomfortable keeping my confidence at Edith's expense.

I fall off to sleep again and do not awaken until well into the afternoon. I awaken to the sound of two voices that are familiar yet register as distant echoes from the past. "I thought you were going to sleep all day. A person who did not know better would think that you had never been grazed before."

John's smile is warm and takes me back to an earlier chapter of my life that I thought was so very complicated but now know was so simplistic. It was a time in my life when my future hinged on decisions I struggled with. But now know it was a time when the decisions were quite clear.

I had the good fortune to rely on his seasoned judgment and the objectivity he demonstrated even when my bad decisions involved his own daughter. "Wake up boy. We only have one more day before we get out of here and head back home. I can't believe they sent a chopper for you with that little scratch."

"I thought you guys would be back in the Bay Area by now. Why are you still here?"

"Well, I heard that one of those women finally put a bullet in you, so we thought we'd stick around to see if she got a chance to finish you off." I can see that Jack not only looks like his grandfather; he also inherited his black sense of humor. John lets out a roar that is probably audible throughout the ward.

I am fully awake and upbeat. "Come on, Jack. It's not a bad wound, but the stiches hurt when I laugh—or cough. But what I want to know is if you are telling me that you two sentimentalists had to make sure I was okay before you left?"

"Well, that's the way I was raised, August." Sarcasm drips from Jack's words.

"Jack—stop."

"That's okay, John. He's just speaking his mind. I would rather use this opportunity to find out how he feels." We may never have another chance to air our feelings.

John's thinking is from a bygone era adhering to a lost code of behavior. "Not when a man is down, Jack. You kick a man's ass when you can stand toe to toe. When he's on his back, you save all that for another day."

"And if you don't have another day, if you are all out of days? What then?" Jack asks the question and turns to walk out of the room, but John reaches for him and pulls him back.

"You can make another day today—but not necessarily anytime you want." The force in John's tone disarms my estranged son. In that same tone, he continues. "August, we were trying, well, I was trying to wait for the right moment to tell you something, but everything has been so hectic and now this."

I feel the bottom drop out of my stomach. Though I have spent very little time with Jack, our exchanges have always been cordial before now. Since their arrival in the city, his attitude has been unusually quiet and combative. Now, I suspect that I already know what John is going to tell me.

"My daughter was diagnosed with breast cancer over five years ago. Now don't look at me that way. You were once married to her, but there was no reason to drag you into that. Her parents, a *loving husband*, her children and grandchildren surrounded her. There was no role for you, no reason to invent one, August."

The similarities between John and Jeff ware astounding, particularly with respect to their direct confrontational styles. During the silence, John quietly leaves the room, and I understand that he is providing this space to allow me to speak with my son honestly without abridging my comments for his grandfather's sake. I wait a moment for it all to sink in before speaking.

"Jack. Please look me in the eye when I'm talking to you. You can get my meaning from listening to my words, but you get the truth by looking into my soul. I'm sure your grandfather has told you that one. I remember how many times he said it to me." He sits down in the chair next to my bed and looks directly at me, reminding me that his eyes are identical to Sonny's eyes, identical to mine.

I go on—long. "I was doing my first tour in Vietnam when you were born. I was one of those guys who enjoyed being there because it gave me time to think about how putting myself in harm's way had somehow been a better alternative to being here—or at that time to being in California. Your mother was just a kid and I mean a very young seventeen. However, her wisdom increased very quickly and she seemed to have aged substantially each of the four times I came home on leave from the war.

"By the time I ran out of war to hide in, she had become wise beyond her years. She was a Berkley graduate with a rabid antiwar posture. She could not understand how I could spend four tours of duty as an occupying enemy of the only truly legitimate Vietnamese government. At any rate, she had become wise enough to know that hastily marrying a young street hustler had not been her best judgment.

Though I returned to the States as a changed man, she understood that the man I had become and the woman she had become were strangers with disparate minds."

He does not want to let me off easily. "And, so what about the son you had together? Did that account for something?"

I do not want to get off the hook. "You were everything, Jack. I fell in love with you the first time I saw your picture, and melted the first time I held you in my arms. You are past old enough now to know how a court would have ruled on custody in that case.

I managed to get myself stationed at Fort Ord for a few years to spend as much time with you as she would allow. She wanted me gone. Before I left the area, I gave her the divorce she demanded and moved on. But during the time I stayed at the Presidio, your grandfather helped me chart a course that changed my life forever."

Jack looks at me with tears welling in his eyes. "I don't know what I would have done without him either. But you don't know how much I resented you."

"Yeah, I'm afraid I do know. On Father's Day, on your birthday, on those days when your classmates' fathers participated in school activities, when their fathers rooted for them at pickup games—even when they stunk. When you just needed to come home to see a father who was willing—no, compelled—to put your needs above his own. Yes. I know exactly how much you resented me."

"Yes. Pop has shared all that about your past with me."

"I'm not making excuses, Jack, but my mother's long gone. I never knew her. My father was a drug addict with problems and demons of his own that were beyond my comprehension. My foster parents were insane. They were all dead before I returned from the Army. I have never hidden behind my father's absence as an excuse for the way I have behaved with you—just as you clearly did not allow my absence to affect the way you raised your sons. So, one of your sons is a law student and the other is an aspiring surgeon?" I am changing the subject because I think we are exhausting each other, and I am certain that Jack will let me transition us somewhere else.

"They are your grandsons, August. They know that you exist and they know where you are. They know you never stopped sending child support, even after Mom remarried. If you want them to know who you are, I can't lie to you, that would require you to dialogue with each of them—but I suspect that you would never tell them this story about mom again, would you? I didn't think you would. You also have a new great-granddaughter. Her name is April. Yes, after Mom."

"Jack, I am so very sorry—even after the fact—to hear about your mother. I don't want you to misconstrue anything I've said today as a criticism of her. I would've been damned lucky to have her in my corner."

"I was blessed to have her in mine. You know, August, I think I joined the Navy to sort out some things myself. Nothing aids introspection like pulling mid-shifts across an ocean or two. You and I are not reconciled by a long shot, but this has been very therapeutic."

After a while, John returns and asks nothing about what has transpired. Instead, we talk about flying to California for an extended visit, which I immediately commit to do while John retains his mobility and wit. We also talk extensively about Jack's fast food franchises and his sons' accomplishments. We talk about Jefferson Sinclair and what he meant to all of us.

CHAPTER 22

"**M**ister Caesar, it is important that you understand that while there are several methods of treating prostate cancer, the best method for each individual hinges on a number of factors, not the least of which are age, lifestyle and physiology.

"I am making my recommendation only after considering all of those factors. And knowing that this is your third opinion, I also have taken the extra step of collaborating with colleagues. I strongly recommend radical prostatectomy as soon as possible to remove the entire cancerous prostate and a minimal amount of the surrounding tissue."

I have been turning the doctor's words over in my mind for the past three hours. I awakened this morning to his dire concurrence with previous findings and recommendations.

After hearing the same speech from three of the most respected specialists in the area, I am convinced that, no matter how many more doctors I might consult, their conclusions will be the same. I will have to select the best surgeon to perform the surgery and perhaps move to a hospital out-of-state before going home. I find the notion depressing and am having some difficulty processing it.

Two visitors interrupt my thoughts.

"Hey, AC."

Their timing could not be worse. "Hey Dad, how are you feeling?" Sonny walks through the door behind his mother. To look at him is to go back in time and look in a mirror. Jeff used to say that I *spit him out*. I know that I should not, but cannot help making a comparison between my two sons: the very stylish and distracted Sonny and the very conservative and focused Jack.

My eyes instinctively sweep over him from head to toe, noticing first a diamond stud in his ear. His stylishly patterned baseball cap is still, inexplicably, on his head. He is wearing a plain white long-sleeve tee shirt that is simplistic in its design but constructed of a rich silk blend. I cannot see below the shirt but, thankfully, he has properly cinched his pants at the waist. I am disappointed to see the outer edges of a tattoo peeking out of the band collar of his shirt.

"Where the hell have you been? No, I'm not asking you why you haven't been here. I'm asking where you've been for the past few weeks. I waited for you for hours in Northeast the day we had agreed to talk about school."

"Oh. I meant to call you about that. We had a problem at the pharmacy that day with Momma's prescription. It took them hours to fix it over the phone with her doctor. They said it had something to do with drug interactions." He looks away as he speaks, aware of the flimsiness of his excuse.

"Then why didn't you respond to my messages?"

"I had a friend with me. I didn't want to get into all that with you while he could hear us." I want to stop my interrogation. However, I find that I cannot. I am aware that the young man in question is a member of Pharaoh's family. Sonny's friendship with him reminds me of the negative influence his great grandfather exerted on my own misspent youth. "Who, Coolaid?"

Seeing Sonny always reminds me that I have not spent nearly enough time helping him develop into the young man I had so hoped he would become. My health issues remind me that the time remaining for unfinished business is finite.

Soon, I will have an invasive surgery followed by a long rehabilitation period. I do not know where or how to begin a conversation with him, so I continue to criticize him. "You've had weeks to get back to me. Tell me why that dude is always with you, Sonny? Has he enrolled in college? Are the two of you studying together?"

Doll lets out a deep sigh. "Damn, AC, can we not get into this now? I mean, is this the best time and place for this?" I do not take my eyes off Sonny. Though he has been trying to maintain his composure, he reacts as though he intends to chide me for my negative reference to his friend. Instead, perhaps sensing my resolve, he merely looks away, electing not to respond. Doll is still talking, attempting to intervene. "We came here to see how you were. Now look at your blood pressure and pulse readings. Can we just relax for a minute and have a family visit?"

I glare up at her, ready to accuse her of coming between my son and me. "*This is how a family visit goes,* Doll. I appreciate both of you being here but there is no cause for concern about my health. It was really just a scratch."

They both shake their heads in disagreement. "Just a scratch? AC they flew you to this hospital by helicopter. We were here the night it happened but when we got here, you were out like a light. We didn't bother waking you up, but I saw all the shit they had hooked up to you that night and there was a lot more going on than just a scratch. I think you lost a lot of blood for an old man."

She smiles the way one looks at an old geezer in a wheel chair who stubbornly insists he has not lost a step. I am surprised they visited me that night. I remember telling the police that only immediate family members were welcome. I guess police officers in the DMV interpret immediate family structure liberally. "I didn't know you had been here," I admit.

"Sonny asked me to follow him out to get your car off that lot rather than leaving it out there after the store closed. It's parked in your garage now. Sonny goes by every evening, picks up your mail and hangs out around the house for a while."

I had not even thought about my car. I assumed Renee would take care of it. "Thanks, Sonny. I appreciate all that."

"Yeah, Dad, after going a few rounds with the cops, I took your keys. Nobody touched the car before I got there. By the way, it rides on a sheet of glass. It took me a minute to remember your home security code, but it came to me. But Dad, Doll is right. You didn't look so good that night, and not all that much better the next day."

I have never gotten used to hearing Sonny refer to his mother by her first name. I think about Jeff's observation of their behavior downtown. Doll, with her affinity for dressing in current urban styles, could pass for Sonny's older sister—or *girlfriend.*

She adds, "And I've been calling you, AC, but you have your cell phone number forwarded to your assistant. If you think I am going to talk to you through that little girl, then you don't know me at all. But that don't matter—for now. What was important is that, even though you didn't know we were here, we knew you were here."

I apologize, "Look, Sonny. I'm sorry that I jumped all over you like that. But I've been concerned about you. Your mother's right. We don't need to get into right now. But the issue isn't going away. And neither is my need to hear the explanation for your absence from Mister Sinclair's funeral."

Again, I compare Sonny's inexcusable absence with the maturity and flawless manners exhibited by Jack during the funeral and the repast. Jack doted on John the entire time and several people complimented me on my son's impressive bearing and manner—compliments of a type I have never received about Sonny.

Notwithstanding their age difference—he is older than both Sonny and Doll—Jack's maturity is still an unpleasant reminder of just how ineffective I have been in socializing my younger son.

Once on that train of thought, I contrast Doll's irascible nature with Yvette's graceful poise. However, I am considerably more comfortable with Doll's street sense and raw wit. Over time, we have come to enjoy levels of comfort and familiarity that I find soothing and relaxing. *Maybe we really are family.*

"AC, I think you've been in that bed too long and starting to get a little cabin fever. You've been a little cranky, but now that we've all calmed down some, let's get back to our original question. How are you feeling today?"

"Well, I can tell that they've been gradually reducing the amount of pain killer. But I like that. I am starting to feel a little something in my right side but I don't believe it'll be anything that I can't tolerate. I should start standing and walking tomorrow. I've probably never mentioned it but I was shot twice while serving overseas—once in Vietnam and once in Iraq. Both times with AK-47s."

Sonny's eyes widen. He has been unimpressed with almost every other aspect of my life, but riveted by this revelation. "No, you never told me that."

Before I can elaborate, Sonny's phone rings and he leaves the room to answer it. Doll moves in closer fast, glaring and lowering her voice to admonish me just above a whisper.

"August Caesar, what's the matter with you—acting all high and mighty with Sonny? What person hides in the dark to shoot an old-assed man? You walk right into it with a bag of Chinese food in one hand and your limp dick in the other hand. You need to dial that bullshit back a notch. Tell the truth, AC. Which one of them crazy bitches shot you?"

"I don't know. Which one did you piss off the most that night at the Sinclair residence?"

"I don't know what you're talking about. I was asked to provide catering services and I did." She clearly has been anticipating that I would ask her that question, and has her position all mapped out.

However, I still want to hear it. "Yeah, but I believe you also provided something else. *Like what?* Like fireworks, from what I hear."

She is undeterred. "If they couldn't handle it, they shouldn't have started it. I didn't like the way Yvette was trying to *carry me* in front of her church crew. She was bossing me around and treating me like the hired help. Then throwing her relationship with you—*whatever that is*—in my face. I came clean with her about who I was when we first talked over the phone so there would be no unnecessary bullshit. I just stood my ground."

I understand but have a point to make. "*Standing your ground?* Doll, when you provide services as a contractor, you are the hired help. Just like when I put people on a contract, we're the hired help. The only things you're supposed to focus on are customer service, your bottom line and repeat business. You were there as *Soul-to-Go*, not Sonny's mother."

"*Sonny's mother?*" She says the words as though she could taste them—*seasoned with too much red pepper*. She leans in even more. "Is that why my bedroom window has a crack in it? Is it because you like to come over sometimes and *fuck Sonny's mother?* No wonder those bitches don't know where they stand."

I lay silently, so she continues. "And who was my customer, AC? Yvette?

Hell no. *My client* was and is Mrs. Sinclair, who expressed nothing but appreciation for me responding on a moment's notice to her need for catering. She and her guests raved about the quality of my food. I stayed up all night—two nights in a row. I wish I could've done that official repast—that's where the money is."

Her voice rises. "I thought you'd be proud of me, *Sarge*. She paid me in full plus a healthy bonus. I picked up five new gigs. I knew what I was there to do. But that night, your *little sexually fluid friend* was making trouble. Then, you had another one twisting her ass through the house in an usher's uniform. The angrier she got the harder she twisted it. AC, you fucked them both in that old woman's house, didn't you? Remember, I know you."

I do not try to convince her that I struck out—or maybe I do not want her to know. I also resist the urge to joke about back rent. "You know you didn't have to insult her."

"They tried to carry me first. And oh yeah, you need to know they got together before the night was over. *On whom? On your monkey ass—that's whom.* It was right after Renee limped in and limped out." She laughs heartily. "Who the hell was in that truck with her, *Mister Ed?*" Girlfriend was looking and walking *brand new.*"

I laugh with her despite the pain. "And you say *I got jokes?* Hey look baby, before I pass out again, I need to talk to you and Sonny about something else."

"*Baby?* Oh, now I'm *your baby?* This is some new shit? Oh man, AC. Is it time for that surgery already?"

Before I can respond, Sonny's face appears over her shoulder.

"Is it time for what surgery?"

CHAPTER 23

"Jordan, do you mind if August and I talk for a while?"

"Uh oh, time for shop talk. Not at all Jerry, we'll just be down in the cafeteria. Buzz us when you two are finished, baby, and we'll meet you in the garage."

Jordan leans over the bed and kisses August softly once on the cheek and again on his forehead, brushing his hair back gently with his hand. "Tell Uncle August goodnight, Taylor. Now, you need to be focusing on getting well and getting out of here, Aug. Work will always be there."

August appears upbeat. He tells my husband, "Thanks, Jordan. I'll remember that when Jerry starts to grill me after you've left."

Jordon flashes a smile that makes me melt and walks out of the hospital room. "Goodbye, Uncle August. I hope you get better soon." Taylor climbs up on the chair next to his bed and kisses August on the cheek. My husband and daughter leave the two of us alone. I feel proud of my ten-year-old's maturity and the ease with which she maintains her composure at her uncle's bedside.

August knows that raising her has not been without its challenges. She has had to understand why her fathers are as old as her friends' grandparents. She has had to contend with people who will never choose to understand why she has two fathers.

Jordan has been insistent that we not compromise an inch on openness and honesty lest we lose Taylor's respect. We do not want her to lose the self-esteem she needs to deal unequivocally with any attempts to marginalize her family.

While I am from another time and space that sometimes still makes it difficult for me to relax in some settings, Jordan's authenticity is remarkable. I credit him with helping her to persevere.

Much has changed since my days when no one ever asked and no one ever told. My resolve is an acquired trait that pales next to Jordan's tenaciousness, which pales next to our daughter's fearlessness—often in the face of rabid stupidity.

I believe that she already sees August, for whom her love and affection are appropriately unconditional, as her family's unconditionally reliable and predictable friend. At minimum, he is simply the best friend I have ever had. I have never known my husband to research doctors as thoroughly as he did to find August the best prostate surgeon.

Every year, hundreds of former government and corporate retirees commence second or third careers with small government contractors. Most of these graybeards work either as employees or as consultants. The IRS taxes them as businesses.

A smaller number peel off subcontract work from former employers, and use it to jumpstart new ventures. I am among those who take equity positions in promising contractors like AJC in exchange for providing expertise, access to financing and new sources of revenue.

I met August just briefly in Vietnam when I was a rifle company commander in the 101st Airborne Division. We reconnected during our second careers with a large defense contractor. As a contractor, August seemed like a good fit for me. His casual style belied his dogged determination to succeed. Most alluring was his plan for a mandatory five-year exit and cashout. I have kept my end of the bargain and August has kept his. He has given AJC a solid five years, doing business within a changed environment, more competitors and less flexibility.

I get to the point since I do not know when August might fall asleep. I have a lot to say. "August, I really need to ask you about this nonprofit. When I hear news accounts of the shooting, the reporters focus only on you becoming Sinclair's successor in his community ventures—nothing about AJC."

When August says nothing, I continue. "They talk about your new relationship with Renaissance Partners and rumors about your political plans. I don't hear a word about AJC—not necessarily a bad thing. I hate to bring this up now, but I just couldn't stop wondering if there's something I'm missing—something you think I should know."

"Jerry, I've been expecting you." August states it as if he welcomes the opportunity to allay any concerns—the same openness and honesty that has been his trademark. He sits up a little more in bed, waving me off when I try to help. "I planned to sit down with you, but then all this happened. First, I'm still committed to everything we planned—maximize the money we can get for AJC and get out. Guard contracts are going to dry up further after ESP. If we lose, we'll only get a few crumbs."

He pauses a moment for my concurrence, which I indicate with a nod. However, I remain silent watching his face intently for clues as to any information withheld. "But if we win, AJC sells for our target number and you get the agreed upon share plus your bonus—what's the matter Jerry?"

"Nothing August, I'm just listening." I remember his promise of a substantial bonus if we hit the tipping point within five years. However, he made the promise in a bar at happy hour. I thought by now he would have conveniently forgotten his pledge. "I apologize if I sound suspicious, but I'm just afraid that getting into all that political stuff might shine a light on us that we don't need."

"I agree. That's why I'd never done that damned radio show before now. But there may be a problem." He lowers his voice to a whisper—never a good sign. "There has been a PI snooping around my friends looking for information about something from a long time ago."

I understand the problem immediately. "Oh shit, August. Not that. It could fuck up everything for all of us." I am beside myself as I think about gambling as we have with our futures. I do not understand why August would not table any political announcement until after the sale. "Why would you even start talking about this new stuff now?"

"I didn't, Jerry. Jefferson Sinclair did. That's why he arranged the radio interview and set up a campaign committee. He called in a favor to delete my juvie file from the police department's database."

I am unimpressed. "That's a slippery slope, August. You never know when that kind of thing will turn up in the hands of a determined government investigator. I feel exposed right now. In big city politics, you don't even know whose following who." I try changing the subject—preferring not to discuss this delicate matter in a semi-public place. "So, do you think you can run a nonprofit and AJC—even for a brief time?"

"Let's just say that it's much more attractive now than before. There have been recent developments." I do not want to know what that means. "But since when have I run AJC, Jerry? I never really wanted to and never have. I've given my all in the areas of relationship management and business development. But you run the company day-to-day, and groomed Renee as a heck of an effective office manager."

"*Office manager?*" I try to suppress a smile. "I don't think you've been paying close attention to her, boss." I would never have thought that the person I had to teach proper phone etiquette five years ago would today be doing the work of a chief operating officer. "August, I don't spend any more time at AJC than you do. I study the detailed status reports, solve problems and review all incoming and outgoing communications."

August's look of surprise says it all. I am surprised that this has been a revelation for him. In fact, he is incredulous. "Christ, Jerry so she has been signing everything—running everything? What about our new human resources manager and our new bookkeeper-CFO-type?"

I chuckle. "You mean the people she recently recruited, interviewed and hired. They eagerly support Miss Webster in any capacity she requires of them. Remember that she wrote their job descriptions. They report to the COO. But as you know, there is no COO nor is there a director of operations."

"So, people don't see her as just a secretary?"

"August, no one sees her as a secretary—except you apparently. She's been smart enough to keep taking your calls. That keeps her in the loop. Who do think customers speak with when no one can find you—when *you can't find you*? She hired an assistant to handle basic admin tasks. To be clear, she asks me for help with anything she doesn't know how to do, but she never asks the same question twice. August, who did you think was handling consultants, prime and subcontract administration, all aspects of HR, in-house IT support, billing, payroll, payments processing and corporate purchasing."

"I thought you were."

Now I am shaking with laughter. "She outsources some stuff. But it's basically just her." As I speak the words, I realize the list of duties is extensive, even for a business with only 200 employees. Renee has quietly absorbed an enormous amount of responsibility—and an enormous amount of experience. "She's really quite remarkable."

"You mean you don't think we should fix this?

"Fix what August? It's not broken. But we need to break her off a piece of the sale—if there is one."

CHAPTER 24

t is late when I leave my real estate office and return to the hospital. I had come to visit him earlier, but August was in deep conversation with a visitor. Long after all his friends and associates have departed and the dinner hour is well behind him, I make my way clandestinely back up to his floor. Amazed at how easy it is to get by everyone late in the evening, I see only a few disinterested nurses and attendants down the long hallway.

When I peek in on him, August is awake, appearing to surf on a notebook computer. When I see him reach for his eye drops, I move ninja-like past his cloudy cataracts to a counter against the wall. I must be presenting a shadowy figure, perhaps he thinks I am a nurse. He asks, looking at me as he would a haze, "Did you forget something?"

Without a word, I walk into the bathroom. A moment later, I am running water. He looks vulnerable and confused—frightened perhaps. I return with a small pail filled with soapy water in one hand and a washcloth in the other. When his vision clears, he realizes that he has an unauthorized, late-night troublemaker. Still without a word, I set the pail down on his empty food tray table, pull back his covers and lift his hospital gown.

When he speaks, the joy in his voice is unmistakable—disconcertingly so. This is not the indifferent wannabe pimp I know and love. "Lydia, how did you sneak in here at this time of night?" With the warm soapy washcloth, I wash him thoroughly in soothing strokes. "What do you think you're doing?"

I don't like this man. I want to ask him what he has done with the block boy formerly known as AC. "Shut up, punk. What do you think I'm doing?" Despite my doubts about my ability to arouse an erection—particularly in his insecure, non-medicated state, I think it feels good. I watch him lay back and allow me to pursue my objective. I wash him thoroughly, doubtful that he has sufficiently bathed here. After several minutes of caressing, August's mind apparently taps into an erotic place.

When I achieve acceptable swelling and elongation, I lower my head and open my mouth wide enough to accommodate his increasing rigidity. The growth startles me since I expected far less, and I apply my patented combination of suction and manipulation. I take satisfaction inducing involuntary moans from a man who has experienced this sort of thing in every corner of the globe. "Oh shit, oh shit, girl."

He is almost shouting. I reach up and slap him across the mouth with my free hand, and raise my head to speak. When I do, he reaches desperately for my hair, attempting to reposition my mouth. "No, please don't stop now."

"Then just be quiet and stop acting like a little bitch before you get me busted." However, he cannot be quiet. So, I continue, praying that the whole ward will not remember me as that old woman they caught blowing the old gunshot victim scheduled to get a laser beam up his ass. I look over to see his curled fingers tightly gripping the bed's side rails.

I know he is bracing for the euphoric charge that I want to ignite inside his big head. Just before the surge commences, I gently squeeze his sack with the palm of my free hand and even manage to work a finger up his crack. With no resistance, it parts, welcoming me inside to that strange dark foreboding place. As he releases the first of his discharge, the horse jumps around in my mouth like an unattended fire hose. I hear his head repeatedly slamming against the mattress.

To his credit, he tries to suppress the noise; however, he makes an unmistakable growling sound through his clenched teeth that is easily discernable by any passersby. Since I have no idea what to expect when next we meet, I unabashedly continue sucking until he is flaccid.

When I look up, his heels are digging into the mattress, straining his gluts and calves with his torso lifted slightly off the bed. Out of breath myself, I ask between gasps, "Damn, how long have you been saving all that?"

For a long time, he does not respond to what is, after all, a rhetorical question. Though he rests his body back on the bed, he remains essentially in his pre-ejaculatory posture. After I have rinsed, spit and peeled open a fresh bubble gum wrapper, I hear him speaking through labored breaths.

He sounds spiritual, emotional. "You knew you were coming up here to get the last of the summer wine before I go up to New York for surgery."

"AC, we just get better with time." I do not know what to make of him. "What's the matter with you? You never get depressed."

"I've never had a major surgery before. I see life in a new way. I've been laying here thinking about business, about family, about my time growing up."

I discourage him from going any further, "Geez, don't make me have to sneak up here, get you off *and* be nice to you too. Let that old shit go, man. You had to dig yourself out of a deep-assed hole. I know pampered people who couldn't even eat success off a silver spoon. Don't trip because they're taking away a little piece of your hardware. You punks kill me with that."

He is determined to show me this version of himself, still speaking with agonizing sensitivity. "There are things you don't know. I've worked hard for some things. I've also cut some corners. Sometimes I've walked straight and narrow. Then other times I wander so far away I can no longer find the line."

"Don't beat yourself up over that. You have a lot of company in that space."

"I want to tell you something."

Nothing good ever follows those words. "You ain't on your deathbed, August and I'm no priest—no need for a confession."

He is direct. "I fucked up, Lydia. I told a lie to participate in an affirmative action program. No, don't be silly. I didn't lie about my race. I lied about my past. As a youngster I committed a felony. It was a stupid thing for me to do—dumber than the offense."

I am engaged now. "You lied on a government form?" He nods. It is a stupid thing to do. I think about the thousands of homeowners who feel secure despite smoking guns on government forms in their files. "Is this little indiscretion going to ruin your life?"

He becomes thoughtful and does not answer right away. "I don't think so. That's the crazy thing about it. I only have one prime contract. You can bet they're going to take that away. Hell, *take it*. The problem is that we won't be eligible for the deal I had been hoping we'd get, so I can't get the money I wanted. I'll have to conduct a going out of business sale, a fire sale, because I just don't want to do this anymore.

"Okay, then don't do it anymore. Yes, it is that simple." I want to know—since we are sharing. "Hey, I've envisioned you hustling goods and stealing cars and such. Tell me AC, what exactly did you do? I know a little bit about peer pressure. What was it?"

"But you don't know anything about this kind of peer pressure. It was not *dare or double dare*. It was *do it or don't come home*. The thing is, I should never have been there. People who really knew me also knew I didn't belong in that liquor store. The judge even could see it and allowed me to join the Army. That night in the store, I was shaking so bad. I think I was more concerned about people finding out that I shit my pants than I was about the possibility that we might get caught."

"So, it was you and Crack. I'm sorry, *Smack*." I want to laugh but know that would be inappropriate. He has told his story with the solemnity of a murderer confessing on death row. However, the only thing this misfit is guilty of is a lot of petty theft, and making a colossal fool of himself—that and a bit of reckless endangerment, mainly as a danger to himself. However, lying on that government form could be an even bigger problem than he thinks.

He has a question for me. "What's the story with you and Yvette?"

It is an effective mood killer. "Just because you feel haunted by all your ghosts—and there are a lot of them, AC—you want to talk about mine. First, that may no longer be any of your business. However, I will say that I'm still taking her slowly—and I mean very slowly. But the trilateral arrangement I wanted may be out of the question. She's—we're—just very uncomfortable about not knowing where your dick has been. You got the hookup tonight because you're up here feeling sorry for yourself, and I can be a pushover for a sad story."

I climb into bed butt first and scoot back until there is room to curl up in front of him for a spooning. However, he wants to kiss me for a while, and I turn around to oblige him—knowing the freak loves the aftertaste in my mouth. Once again, he tries to lapse into that melancholy mood. "You know, that may be the last of the summer wine."

"Shut up and take your old crazy ass to sleep."

CHAPTER 25

My son James is in rare form today. "I can't say that I believe AC was able to get out the way at the last second—or if somebody just got cold feet at the last second. They didn't just miss the mark at that distance." James has been fueling speculation ever since finding out that a shooter had merely grazed August's side from just a few feet away with a large handgun.

He starts up again. "And even in the dark, the kind of big flash a ten or a forty-five makes—he had to see who did it. I'll bet it was one of those women."

Back from taking me to my scheduled doctor's appointment, my son sits next to me on the living room sofa. We have been watching Tonya and my granddaughter work on the other side of the counter that separates what remains of the living room from Ruth's home-based business.

I am proud to see Ruth preparing lunch for sixty people at a nearby conference. Two other women working on-site for Soul-2-Go have already served the conferees breakfast. Soon, they should be setting up for the morning break.

My son's theory about the brightness of the flash makes sense to me. I am inclined to agree that August must have seen his attacker. James is too scared to take me to see him, since August still blames him for something he did 40 years ago. From what I hear, August has been too calm about the recent attempt on his life—too calm even for a cool customer like him.

I would have expected August to be raising all hell. I would have guessed that he would be either leading the effort to arrest the shooter or working to convict him. I also would not be surprised to hear that that the shooter has washed up under the Sousa Bridge at the colored folks' marina. Instead, I hear that August is staying close to home quietly proceeding with his recovery.

I know that Sonny, who has done a yeoman's job of aiding his father's recovery, has expressed frustration over August's refusal to discuss the incident or the case. I have received two visits from the detective investigating the case. AC has not told the police any more than we know.

I try to silence my son. "Hush your mouth, James. What do you know about guns?" Ruth and Tonya chuckle as I express doubt about my boy's involvement with firearms—even in the face of the overwhelming evidence on his long resume. Aware of James' experience in such matters, Tonya and Ruth readily defer to his authority.

"Tell her, Biscuit. You used to run with the big dogs." Ruth laughs good-naturedly at both of us, but she is also concerned about me. This has not been my best month. A few times, I could not get myself up in time to get to the toilet.

Although I have been sleepwalking all my life, Ruth is now exaggerating how far I walk away from the front porch. I admit my glasses and things sometimes show up in the icebox. They have barred me from using the microwave. However, Ruth somehow has convinced August that she needs James around more often to help take care of me. My son has suddenly become my doting taxi driver and daily companion.

At first, we were all concerned that August might find out that James occasionally sleeps over in the bedroom that was Sonny's before my great grandson took over what we now *call the English basement.* James' commitment of time and attention also has freed Sonny to log additional hours at a nearby barbershop. Traveling to New York with his father and back and forth to Hillcrest has given Sonny an excuse to stop pretending to attend college.

After becoming increasingly more tolerant of the barbershop idea, August has helped his son develop a business plan and his first loan package. In addition, one of his college-educated women found a cheap commercial space. In no time, Sonny will complete all the requirements for his master barber and barber manager licenses. August will co-sign a loan on equipment and a building on H Street, which has once again become the hottest strip in Northeast—after burning down in 1968.

At just 25 years old, Sonny will start out with barber stations on the main floor, a nail salon on the lower level and stations upstairs for independent women's hair stylists. At his father's insistence, he will also have a part-time bookkeeper. August's time in the hospital and his recovery has given them the chance to find each other, spending more time together than at any other time in Sonny's life.

However, AC will never fully trust James. My son has done something unforgivable, but neither will tell me exactly what. It is as though AC would rather forget—but never forgive—the whole thing. However, James's support for me so far appears to be trumping August's need to even the score.

Intrigued by James' shooting theory, Tonya offers her own. "Doll, I think AC knows who did it but has something to gain by sitting on it. No. Maybe not blackmail. But I don't think he would hush up about it unless there was something to lose by giving up the shooter."

Knowing her theory makes perfect sense, Tonya looks around the room at each of us—shrugging in response to our silence. I think she may be on to something, but I know Ruth is not comfortable with her talking about August under any circumstances. For years, Ruth could not even look at Tonya after she found out about her getting together with him 20 years ago. Ruth claims to be over it, but Tonya should know better than to mention his name in her presence.

As James gets up to help Tonya carry the boxes to Ruth's new company van parked in the rear of the house, he leans in with a whisper. "So, Doll, you must be making pretty good money with this catering thing."

My son's comment, while harmless on its face, triggers the defenses his daughter employs whenever he refers to money. While she welcomes this new generosity with his time, Ruth suspects it will eventually come at a price. However, she should not call it extortion. Rather, she should understand that his request for payment would be the product of a mind that perceives her ability to pay him as her *obligation to pay him.* "I'm doing okay, Biscuit. After getting a few breaks and a lot of new leads I seem to be working my business all day every day now."

As James walks out with an armload, his daughter turns to look at me. However, I merely wave my hand again. "James didn't mean anything Ruth. He's just glad to see you doing so well." I know Ruth has no faith in her father and no illusions about his motivations. Only he can change that. Only she can choose to accept him. I am just so happy to be alert today that neither can steal my joy.

"I know, Momma. He's just Biscuit being Biscuit."

I want to change the subject. "So, what about you and this new person I hear you talking to on your cell phone deep into the night? I keep listening for a new voice in the house."

"I swear, old woman. You always hear the things you're not supposed to hear." I have not heard anything—just enough low talking to know I could set a trap. Now I have confirmation of my suspicions. Her silence tells me the subject is not open for discussion, but the she decides to give me a little information.

I am so thrilled to see Ruth smiling that I do not care what follows. She says, "I just met him. Roland works at the auto dealership where I bought the van. Momma, I told you we just met. He knows what he wants and what he needs. I don't know where this going but we won't be affected by *Occasional Dad.*"

I am not comfortable with that reference and feel the need to remind her of a few facts. "I know you don't think you owe him anything, but he helped you pull all this together. I ain't saying you haven't worked hard Ruth. I guess I'm just asking if you think anyone else would've done it for you."

"Momma I know this wouldn't be a business without him. And there ain't many men who would make this effort—even if they could. But this shit is a lot of work. It's 24-seven. And Momma, the shit is lonely. You can find good people, but when the shit hits the fan, there's nobody but you. AC says, in business, the only hand you can count on is the one at the end of your sleeve. Have you seen AC here lately?"

"Not since the day you knocked out that back window." I double over and snicker, but at least I do not start wheezing again.

Ruth laughs with me. "So, everybody's got jokes today. You know what I'm saying. I appreciate AC, okay? But he just helped me pave a road out of his pocket and out of his life so he can make his next move. Then he can walk around with that phony bitch with a clear conscience."

"And who is that?" My granddaughter has made a reference I do not understand. It makes me feel left out of the loop.

"Don't even worry about it, Momma. He'll fuck it up. AC ain't never going to treat her the way she thinks she deserves. But she has it in the looks department—like a queen, like a southern belle."

I hate when Ruth talks as if she may not be as good as some other woman, so I do my duty. "She ain't got nothing over my grandbaby."

"Thanks, Momma. But she does."

This is a moment for a strong dose of tough love. "And you see yourself as what, Ruth—an ex-crack head who comes from a drug addicted prostitute and a small-time gangster who gave you to his floor-scrubbing momma?"

"You know that's not what I mean. But you're lucid today, ain't you?" We both laugh through tears and she walks over to kiss me on the forehead, putting her arms around me and holding me tight. "August's got his own problems. If he was smart, he'd let us take care of him. He's a fish out of water in politics, and he'll always do shit to remind people of that."

"So? Do you think people will hold that against him?"

"Momma, I know they will—like that PI asking questions—pulling Biscuit over with crazy Cookie in the car. They'll say once a slick hustler, always a slick hustler. Tonya, with her little whoring ass, was right on the money."

When I stop laughing, I bring up something that has been on my mind. "You know, even after going to the best doctor, he may not be able to do stuff anymore. Some men go down after that surgery—they lose their mojo or something. Others try to play it off like nothing's changed. But everybody knows they cut out the little pump that makes the fizz."

"They cut out what that makes the what, Momma?"

"Child, I know what I'm talking about. Brother Caldwell had it."

"How do you know what Brother Caldwell had?"

"I know about everything Joe Caldwell had. A man gets that surgery about right at the time he's trying to deal with slowing down. It was a lot rougher in Joe's day, but AC won't be able to make the fizz. Joe used to say you get a rush but without the flush."

"Momma!"

"Oh, hush girl. And listen to me because I know what I'm talking about. AC don't love nobody else like he loves you. We're the only family he ever had—even if he has another boy out west. I love him. You know you love him too. You're just too scared to claim him. Now get that window fixed before something flies in here."

"Funny, funny, Momma. You know just like AC knows. All he got to do is decide that he wants to be with me, and he'll be set for life. I swear, all things considered, I'd do anything for that man. But he needs to make up his mind.

CHAPTER 26

"**S**o then, you're telling me that they're putting me out of business."
I have been giving my very expensive attorney a hard time, but I am no longer upset about what I have allowed to occur. I accept responsibility for a colossal lapse in judgment that will result in life altering repercussions. After all, it is my fault.

Jerry and I discussed it at length five years ago and took a chance. I distinctly remember saying something absurd like: *Pick up the dice and roll them.* So, instead of disclosing the juvenile arrest at the time I submitted my application, we simply gambled on the government not finding it—and deciding whether omitting my old juvenile offense indicated a character flaw. And they did not find it until someone decided to point it out for them.

"Why no, Mister Caesar, they're not putting you out of business at all. They went easy on you if anything." His determination not to give in on this point is both interesting and annoying. I have paid for the privilege to vent, right or wrong, and I have paid him to listen.

"I can only repeat what I have already told you, Mister Caesar. Again, all this stems from a misrepresentation made by you on your original application. You indicated on a federal form that you had never been arrested—even though you had been. The government received and acted on information to the contrary that, as you have indicated to me in confidence, you are not able to refute."

He pauses again before continuing, ostensibly to allow time for me to remember some critical piece of game changing information. If I had some,

I would share it. I do not really know why I bothered to hire him and his expensive law firm. "As a result, the government finds that your omission speaks to the issue of character, an important element on which your eligibility hinges."

In other words, they now have reason to doubt my character—*not because of the old arrest, but because of the omission.*

"Therefore, your program eligibility is being terminated. In addition, you are now ineligible for any more program deals. Your existing federal customer will terminate your contract. And, of course, you will not be awarded any that may be pending."

"And how is that not putting me out of business?" The meeting has been a colossal waste of time on a morning I would prefer to be anywhere else. The city's schizophrenic weather is experiencing a positive mood swing, wedging a gorgeous sunny day into a week of otherwise depressing skies.

So, wasting it on an unproductive downtown meeting seems an unpardonable sin. The swank offices are impressive, with a large conference room overlooking a bustling downtown intersection. The busy cosmopolitan scene below is in direct contrast to the laid-back parking lot visible from AJC's bland but comfortable accommodations in a suburban strip mall.

I think about how I minimized my own overhead costs years ago by negotiating a modest lease when another failing contractor slipped out in the wee hours of the night. Now AJC could be making the same kind of midnight departure.

As they have been lately, my thoughts drift to Renee. She will have to find a way to recover quickly. Both Jerry and I know that the government's case is valid and we have no one to blame other than ourselves. But she has been all in, unwittingly hitching her wagon to a falling star.

My lawyer attempts to spin the outcome differently. "One positive coming out of this is that they're not coming after you criminally or for unjust enrichment—nor freezing your accounts. You can sell off company assets. You can withdraw any earnings that you have retained at any time. I would strongly recommend that you consult with one of our tax attorneys before deciding how to do that."

We do agree on that point, but I do not need a high-powered attorney to tell me that. I look over at Jerry who keeps his head down and does not look back at me. Our careful frugality has left us with substantial retained earnings. Though it is but a small fraction of what we had hoped to take away, I have offered Jerry the same percentage—though not the amount—we agreed to on the now defunct sale of AJC.

So much has changed in a very short time. Jeff died without fear. He died arranging to manipulate the occasion of his own funeral to achieve one of his last political goals. I almost died, saved only by a last second of hesitation from a man ill-suited for the mission he had assigned himself. However, he succeeded in reminding me how fleeting and tenuous life can be.

Jeff's last words to me were about family. Jack's grandfather is fading before our eyes but he traveled across the country to arrange a talk. I see the gap between my two sons and regret not doing more to close it. Two men with no sons of their own were committed to helping me. So, rather than dwell on the loss of money, which now is water over the dam, I have spent the last week moving on and addressing a few things I can change.

CHAPTER 27

"**R**enee, maybe you should just call me *August.*"

Mr. C has made a remarkable recovery in just a few short months. He is walking independently up and down the stairs with impressive dexterity. He has shorn from himself all vestiges of the medical apparatuses that, during his earlier stages of recovery, had become vital to his daily routine. He now prefers standing as though it is a strategic posture rather than the best way to relax.

August, as I should call him now, has been standing in front of the window watching Sonny climb into that lavish candy-apple-red sports car. Sonny seems older now. He is spending more time with his father than he has since I have known him. Since August returned home, Sonny has dropped by daily to get him out of bed, bathed and dressed.

August has always engaged gardeners and house cleaners to take care of home maintenance. Sonny has filled in all the critical gaps, delivering, warming and sharing meals prepared by his mother and taking care of the required spot cleaning and laundering. Most impressively, Sonny cleaned and changed his father's dressings and bags daily and carefully maintained his supply of prescription drugs and medical supplies. August's double surgeries appear to have been the catalysts they needed to bring them closer together.

Over the years, August has talked about how he gutted and redesigned his home, making optimum use of internal space and natural light. Prints and paintings cover the walls. What should be a two-story dining room serves as an office and the home's nerve center.

He has appointed the adjacent living room as one would a posh lounge, an extension of his office. Its plush leather sofa and chairs nestle around a huge circular coffee table that has as its centerpiece a spectacular detailed globe made from precious stones. African stone carvings and buffalo soldiers, stare back at me from tables, curios and the wide mantle of a huge brown-stone fireplace.

"Okay. Then *August* it is, but calling you that may take some getting used to." Then August looks at me very strangely, and my mind races to anticipate what may be coming next.

"Renee, how would you feel about coming with me to work at Renaissance Partners?" The words do not sink in at first and I almost miss their significance. The news report was are correct, confirmed by his offering me a job at his new organization.

"Thank you, August." The sound of speaking his first name has a strange resonance, but suddenly seems appropriate. "I appreciate you thinking about me and I'll get back to you as soon as I can."

He continues going through the motions. "I can offer you one year's gross severance pay from AJC, and a competitive salary. We also want to give you a hundred basis points of the final AJC sales total, whether you stay or go. I'm making the offer right next to the kitchen where we sat at the beginning of this journey—although I would prefer that we were meeting here under better circumstances."

I almost laugh at what the salary might be, and calling my equity share *100 basis points* instead of the one percent that they equal. I need to use this opportunity to obtain answers. "So, what about the company? Did we win the ESP competition?"

"Well. We'll never know."

"What does that mean?" My stomach tightens and suddenly I feel warm and clammy.

"Well, Renee, this is very difficult for me to talk about, but there were some discrepancies found in our paperwork. No, our *original paperwork*. I would prefer not to elaborate any more. I'll say that it was entirely my fault and I apologize for any inconvenience that it causes anyone—especially Jerry and you."

I stand frozen—immobilized by his partial revelation. My mind races as I try to imagine what he could have done that was so wrong. I cannot imagine him gambling with our livelihoods at stake. I try to measure my words carefully. "I still don't understand what you're saying."

He speaks plainly. "Our biggest contract will be terminated and we are ineligible to receive the ESP contract—even if we won. Renee, AJC is going out of business."

"As of when?" I feel tears pooling in my eyes.

"As soon as I can close a deal, but, for all practical purposes, it's already official."

I hear a phone ringing. As he answers it, he steps out on his porch to speak privately, I send a text to notify Bernard, the man who has emerged as my life partner, confidant and fiancée.

When Bernard asked for help with his business plan and franchisee documents, both Jerry and Mr. C were generous with their time and recommendations. While I was not surprised that they gave the matter their serious and thorough review, I was not aware of the level of knowledge Jerry possessed about franchising. I also was pleasantly surprised by their comments about Bernard's financial records, his pristine credit report, substantial savings and a balanced, if minimal, investment portfolio.

Jerry backed up his endorsement by pledging a low interest loan. Bernard accepted his offer once he realized Jordan's expertise and family connections, as well as the efforts they would undertake to protect their investment.

I must admit that I expected August and Jerry to eventually sell AJC. I had overheard them discussing it using easily decipherable code words.

Also, their huddled whispering and secrecy seemed a bit much. However, I had not anticipated this.

Because they kept me in the dark, I have continued in secrecy to develop my skeletal business plan for a company called *RENCO*, which is currently just a paper shell. I am grateful for everything these two men have taught me. I have learned that, the need for sound paperwork notwithstanding, no one is truly in business until they have revenue.

Therefore, when I get a call from Bob Richards while August is still outside, I decide to walk out in the front yard and take it in private. Our government program manager is returning my call about an upcoming business opportunity for AJC. As we talk, I can still see August through the window. He is also smiling, perhaps about his underpaid office manager who will clean up his shit.

Bob asks, "So, is anyone else in the office today Renee?" Normally I am not inclined to engage in Bob's banter when he blasts August's mobile management style. I decide on a different posture today since I want to find out how much he knows—and how much good will I have established with him.

"Well, you know how it is Bob. The clean-up woman has to do what she has to do." He laughs heartily, happy that he has finally gotten me to play along. "Bob, what have you been told to do about AJC?"

He answers immediately, "I've been told to shut it down any business we have with the company—start terminating everything and shifting the work to another firm. I was hoping you could shed some light." He does not know the specifics, but is beside himself over not having them.

"Renee, your customer service is superb. It's too bad you don't own the company. I'd work with you in a heartbeat."

I do not miss a beat. "Bob, you know, I was wondering if I might be able to stop by your office one day this week to discuss something with you." I need to milk AJC's contacts for everything I can get.

I know that Bob hears something different in my voice. He is intrigued. "Well you can't be coming over again to talk about AJC. Oh Really?

RENCO? I like the sound of it. We can't do anything right away, but I'm all ears. How about tomorrow morning?" I disconnect, pleased that my quest has begun in earnest with excellent timing. August always says, *relationships and timing*, My phone rings again.

"Hello, Miss Webster? Peter Stanton. I see I have you again, as per usual. Look, I don't have time to wait for a return call today. I sense that something is going over there. Can you please tell me if you are personally working on anything that impacts my company or your relationship with my company?"

"That's difficult for me to say over the phone, sir. But I can fill you in. I'll be downtown tomorrow. What does your schedule look like for lunch?"

I hear the door swing open and look up to see Jerry smiling. "So, are you out here taking care of business?"

"I'm just a working girl, Jerry. You know all that stuff is way over my head."

CHAPTER 28

When the phone rings, I step away from my meeting with Yvette and Renaissance's new Executive Director. I have been waiting for this call from Elton. However, I cannot believe what I hear my nephew saying. "Now Elton, your aunt's hearing is not as good as it used to be, so could you say that one more time? It sounded like you said you agree with August."

"That's right, Aunt Edith. Whatever he wants to do is fine with me. His proposal makes a lot of sense." I need a short nap after spending the morning in strategy sessions. I sense *relief* in Elton's voice. It is as though he is relieved to shift responsibility to August. That is completely out of character for a young man with his control issues and insecurities.

Because we are dealing with an issue fundamental to the direction of Jefferson's nonprofit, I must be sure I understand my nephew correctly. "We're all aware that Jefferson gave August authority to implement his vision. However, August's new plan changes Jefferson's vision significantly. Therefore, I thought it only fair to allow you to weigh in on it. Then, of course, there are the other less savory recent developments—revelations about his past."

Elton responds immediately with no change in tenor. "I understand and I appreciate being consulted, but I stand by my earlier response. August should have the freedom to implement Uncle Jeff's vision. In fact, I agree that he should move the school." I wait for him to seize upon August's indiscretions. He does not. "As far as that stuff goes, everyone plays fast and loose with the rules from time to time. They just caught him, that's all. I'm not so sure anyone will care. It doesn't come close to disqualifying him to head Renaissance."

When I say nothing, he continues. "August has an exceptional grasp of what Uncle Jeff was trying to do. That's why he chose him to head his community development projects—the things that were important to him. Think about it, Aunt Edith. I believe the school—and the election—were just window dressing, sweeteners for August. And I think August knows it. We're blessed to have him." He pauses to allow space for my response, but I have none. I am speechless.

I can only listen in silence as he continues to amaze me. "Now Aunt Edith, I know you've already put a lot of time into this and you want to implement your own agenda. You need to step back from this thing and stop working so much. Promise me no more hands on. Let Yvette and that new exec do the work. If they can't, August will have to find someone else. Don't worry about me. He'll think he has me under control—that'll be to my advantage. We need only protect your half of the non-profit."

For the first time, he sounds like my father, and leaves me room for little more than compliance. "Okay dear. Please ask your mother to call me when she gets a chance. Bye now."

I cannot tell whether my nephew has fallen on his head or finally opened his eyes. When he first learned that Jefferson had chosen August to head Renaissance Partners, Elton had been livid to the point that I was concerned about his state of mind. He had gone to my siblings desperately asking them to appeal on his behalf. My only defense at that time had been that I was fulfilling Jefferson's expressed wishes.

I had assumed that once Elton learned of August plans to revise Jefferson's wishes by selling the property and establishing the school east of the river, Elton would realize that August would end up with a considerable war chest. I was certain my nephew stubbornly would take the position that the changes invalidated August's willed mandate. I had expected him to charge over here primed for a fight.

When I search the corners of my mind for an explanation, I find one in a dark place I never use to process Elton's actions. Suddenly a chill runs down my spine as I contemplate the only logical explanation for his behavioral shift. At first, I am shocked that Elton could summon the nerve. But I feel a strange, perhaps twisted, sense of pride. I realize my spoiled nephew may have what it takes to protect the family legacy. My adrenaline rush is reminiscent of the way I felt when my baby sister and I would hide outside my father's study. We would listen wide-eyed to his conversations with men and women who loved nothing better than a good fight.

I take a moment to regroup, to collect my thoughts before returning to Jefferson's study where two women anxiously await my return. With some effort, I replace the beaming expression that surely is in on my face with one of nonchalance. I announce the news to them as soon as I walk through the doorway. "Elton concurs with August's proposal. He looks forward to the project."

"You have to be shitting me." Yvette's sounds more like the irrepressible August than the smart and focused woman I have come to know and admire. I like it. She apologizes unnecessarily. "Please excuse my language ladies, but Edith, you have to admit that it's quite a shocker."

I concur but merely shrug. I have spent hours listening to two intelligent women develop rebuttals for Elton's anticipated objections to August's proposal—and perhaps even August's continued involvement. Now I know we do not need them. At first, I had planned to listen to arguments from both sides, only to support Elton in the end. Then, I read the comprehensive arguments August and Kelly had drafted with the help of their real ostensible estate broker.

Their proposal includes a risk management plan that anticipates every possible setback and correction plans that I cannot logically refute. They have budget projections based on thorough research and reasonable valuations. He has not attempted to obscure the relevance of the sale—nor hide the proceeds from the windfall.

I have come to understand Jefferson's faith in him. I am beginning to wonder if my husband orchestrated August's exposure for the city's leaders—or for me.

August was astute enough to refuse Yvette's invitation to develop his game plan while recovering at her home. I have asked enough of the right questions to know he has not been to see her since his procedure. Predictably, he sought buy-in from his supporters on the board, and gave a copy of the draft to Yvette—to proofread.

He knew she would share the advance copy with me, and intentionally omitted substantial text. It was his notice to her—and to me—that planting her close to him will never necessarily work to my advantage. However, despite his obvious suitability for this endeavor, August is not suitable for an at-large council seat during a time when the council desperately needs to be in steady hands.

Kelisha speaks up. "In anticipation of the board's official confirmation, August directed me to start drafting an implementation plan with action items and timetables." I am impressed with her. When August hired such a young beauty, I was skeptical about her qualifications. However, Kelisha has quickly digested a trove of information and already speaks with confidence and familiarity.

Kelisha also shows diplomacy in handling Yvette, who occasionally appears to be difficult for the sake of being difficult—no doubt distrustful of any woman who has gained August's unconditional trust. Kelisha also handles me well. She has no requirement to travel across town to brief me in my home, but the deference demonstrated by her presence here today further bolsters the endorsement I have already given.

She has the proper temperament to coordinate the cast of characters that Jefferson appointed to his board. August clearly hired her for those capabilities as well as to help him compete for public grant funds. And that lends credence to Elton's theories—regardless of his motivations.

In time Yvette will accept as I have that, surprising as it may be, August has used only the promise of professional development to lure this remarkable young woman from the stability of a federal job into the uncertainty of a non-profit, city politics and priorities. If I am wrong, I will have a savage and intolerable catfight on my hands—albeit an entertaining one—that I am much too old to referee but still too young at heart to resist.

Over the past 30 years, August has slept with at least a half-dozen women he met in my home. His dalliances have placed me in uncomfortable positions with people I counted as friends, women who perceived his relationship with Jefferson as an endorsement of character. They had not been old enough to know that same promiscuous fire had once burned in my husband's loins. If the two of them had been together back then, I might have shot August myself.

Yvette speaks up in predictable fashion. "Kelisha, don't you think the board essentially has spoken—that you have the green light to proceed? Whom else would you be concerned about—once you have concurrences from August, Edith, Elton, Reverend Tolliver and me?" I have worked with Yvette on several major projects and her commitment to excellence is unquestioned. Even though her people skills require work, I am confident in her honesty and her ability to protect my family's interests.

Kelisha's tone remains the same. "Yes Yvette, from the perspective of a board member, you're correct that we can confidently make those assumptions—if only just among us girls. But the executive director has official responsibilities to the entire board—that is if we are going to run a legitimate and unimpeachable organization." I see that Kelisha's patience with her could wane and I stop Yvette before she can escalate an irrelevant exchange into a pointless skirmish.

When I stand up again, they instinctively stand with me and the three of us walk toward the front door. "Kelisha, thank you so much for coming over on such short notice. I look forward to having you with us. When will you give us your full-time attention?"

"You have it now, Mrs. Sinclair. As I have told August, I canceled my wedding plans, but still plan to take a celebratory hike through part of the Pacific Northwest. But other than being absent for that month, I am all yours."

Her words are music to my ears. I will not be involved with Renaissance Partners for one day beyond the vote to abandon the Sinclair Academy project. However, I will need to know what else August is planning.

Yvette wants to remain on the topic of wedding cancellations, an issue clearly troubling to Kelisha—a young woman she has not met prior to today. "Oh, my daughter is going through a similar circumstance. I think she's been devastated by it. She looked so beautiful in her dress."

Kelisha ignores Yvette. "You know, I'm much more comfortable with people calling me Kelly. Would that be okay?"

"Yes, that's fine with me dear. I like the sound of it," I say in response to her request. As we watch Kelly walk out and start her car, Yvette turns back to me with an expression of strange bewilderment. I can only shrug, uninterested in contemplating the reason for her angst.

I start up the stairs for my nap. "Please lock the door when you leave, Yvette. No, I hoped you would hold on to those keys for a few more months. Come and go whenever you please, dear."

CHAPTER 29

open the door to see an unexpected visitor. "Hello Yvette. I don't believe we have an appointment today."

"We don't, and I apologize for not calling but I was afraid you wouldn't see me." Yvette is aware that I discourage patients from dropping in without an appointment. Since I have an unusually heavy caseload, my first instinct is to lie-to tell her I have a patient running late. However, I also feel compelled to see her again. She is one of the most stunningly attractive and poised clients I have ever had. Despite having seen her identification cards, I still cannot believe she is a day over forty-five.

"Come on in. I honestly thought you had given up on therapy—perhaps given up on me." There is a part of me that wishes she would, before I say or do something unethical.

"Well, maybe I don't really know why I'm here. I just felt a need to come in." As always, I invite her to choose from one of the two facing leather chairs. I know that she finds it to be an annoying and disingenuous gesture since any rational person can determine which chair I prefer.

Most patients make the obvious selection, but some have had to find out how I would react to them selecting the therapist's chair. Today, for the first time, I watch her walk over and sit in my chair. I try to avoid looking between her legs. "It's been months, Yvette. Why do you think you wanted to come in today?"

In a prepared opening statement, she says, "I was unsure about continuing the therapy because I sense we'll always be merely on the periphery of conclusions." She goes on to tell me that she wants me to be more forthcoming with my analyses and that she prefers to hear my thoughts in real time. "I see no reason to wait ten weeks to hear what you're thinking," she says.

This is no emergency. This is her power move to compensate for her powerlessness to control other aspects of her life. I do not want this session to spiral into unproductive streams of consciousness. I begin by saying, "I think you know that we've already gone much further than just the periphery. While I'd hesitate to call them breakthroughs, I believe you've come a long way since our first session. As far as real-time analyses, we'll see about that."

Since I am determined to help her organize the thoughts she wishes to convey today, I do not allow space for another reply. Instead, I continue. "Right now, I'm very interested in hearing about what's transpired over the last few months. How you've dealt with it and whether you've changed anything—specifically in your relationships. What I think you may need help with is employing a clear thought process as you deal with the issues before you."

She begins by telling me that there is no longer a question of August's polygamous nature or his suitability as a mate. "I actually have become well acquainted with his other woman, Lydia, whom I had already seen several times in the bookstore downstairs before our sessions." That gets my attention.

She tells me about August's sons, Jack and Sonny, and about Doll. "I just don't see a role for me. Doll and her grandmother live with Sonny in a house they rent from August. If August were to run, his voting base is more likely to see them as a family. They would see me as who, *the one he be with up in Michigan Park?*"

I try not to laugh or point out that Sonny is beyond the age of legally required child support. I never understood her desire to marry August. Few of my patients get married after sixty—unless they have never walked down the aisle. Remarriage is rarely in their best interests unless it provides one party with needed greater security.

Yvette talks about the shooting incident and August's prostate cancer surgery. She discusses Jefferson Sinclair's death, her growing relationship with his widow and her new working relationship with August at Renaissance Partners.

She expresses confidence that they can work together despite their prior involvement. Despite her certainty that August has had a relationship with Lydia, Yvette expresses no animosity toward her. When my pencil ceases to race across my pad, I sit quietly for a long moment, staring at her and wondering why she has not called on me sooner.

"Yvette, a whole lot has happened since the last time we talked. Frankly, I wonder where to begin and how much time we should devote today to each of these developments. How've you processed it all? Who shot August? *He told you he thought you shot him.* Really? Okay, so what happened after the surgery?"

"He turned down my offer to stay at my house during his recovery period—electing instead to recover at his home over in Southeast. I found it hard to believe that he was recovering alone. *Why?* Because I read up on the recovery process—in anticipation of taking care of him at my house. It's challenging, to say the least.

"He says that his son spent hours with him every day and drove him to his appointments. August and his son have never had that kind of relationship—for Sonny to drive across town to adjust and clean bags daily. Sonny changing dressings? Cleaning him up daily following that surgery? No, I don't believe it—not from what I understand about the kid August can't find for weeks at a time."

I am stuck on what she thinks may be a minor point. "So, in three years, you'd never been to his house? Oh, once to pick up a proposal recently. And you just met his son? Oh, you've still never formally met him. Who do you think helped him in his recovery process?"

"Doll Baby helped him, I guess." Now she sounds emotional, in a way that only scorn can manifest. Seeing my expression after her last remark, she quickly clarifies, "And before you ask, I have no definitive proof of that—and I don't care."

"I see." She struggles to talk about it without crying, as though she detests crying in front of me. Many of my patients pay me to have someone with whom they can cry.

"Well, even if I see no future with him, I don't care to be lied to. I can't believe I put his address in my navigation device and drove by his house to see who was there. No, I didn't see anyone." She pauses to collect herself. "I never saw Doll, but I drove by the Northeast house a few times and never saw her there."

Her confession highlights a point on which some colleagues and I disagree. While they would emphasize the importance of trust, I do not discourage satisfying a healthy dose of skepticism with a little old-fashioned tree boxing. Nothing sooths quite like visual confirmation, even though the casual observer would never guess that Yvette, a strikingly beautiful woman at any age, would ever play that game.

"So then, you say that you are now all done with August?" I hope she does not detect my enthusiasm.

Her sudden smile tells me she does. She appears to relax and compose herself, now confident in her ability to assert control in a familiar scenario. "I guess so. That reminds me. Even JoAnne appears to have lost interest in detesting August. At first, she was pre-occupied with wedding plans. Now that her marriage is off the table, she has just lost interest in everything—except making lieutenant."

She waits for me to say something but I need a minute. She continues, "Anyway, it turns out that my daughter's groom was a bride. Can you believe that. I never knew. I could've been helping her deal with her sexuality all those years. But she hid it from me and confided in David—*David.*"

My pencil is racing again. Before I can look up, she is back of the subject of August. "I spoke to Sonny when he answered August's house phone.

Again, I'm not proud of it, but I asked him if his mother was there. He hung up. August called me minutes later. Oh, he said that Sonny was the only person who'd come over."

Yvette's tone has become collegial, as though we are just two friends having a chat. Recognizing that her daughter's sexuality is a topic for another day—perhaps its very own day—I ask, "Speaking of which, how about the plans for your gallery? Oh, so nothing's changed with that—*no matter what else happens.*" But I cannot deflect. I must get back to August.

She has attested to being in love with this man for three years. However, his definition of love is radically different from hers. It is as though they use the same words but do not speak the same language. "Yvette, I really believe it would be beneficial if you could get August to come with you to at least one of our sessions."

"What? Have you not heard a word I've said? Not now. It's too late for that." I do not believe she is aware of being on her feet. I sit quietly as she discovers that she is in no man's land, neither seated nor completely standing.

I try to rescue her. "We have a lot of time remaining Yvette. Please sit back and relax." Instead, she picks up a mug and walks over to fill it with water as though it was always her intention to do so. She returns and sinks back deep into the chair without taking a sip.

"Yvette, I'd like us to have several more sessions. I can get your insurance carrier to cover them. I know that you're a very goal-oriented person and it would be helpful for you if we devised goals around a calendar, but the truth is that can't be done." I try to inject some warmth into my words. An unfortunate aspect of my practice is consumerism. My patients are customers who, after all, do not have to choose to purchase my services. "Are you aware that I recently published a new book, *Relationship Spheres*?"

"Yes. I looked for it in a few bookstores but couldn't find a copy. But I heard you discussing it on the radio. I'm confident that I fully understand its premise. "So, do you think I inhabit one of August's relationship spheres?"

"Yvette, as I told you during our initial consultation, my principal area of concentration has always been the psychology of the African American urban male. Some say my area is *quack psychology*. Over the years, the greatest demand for my services has come from people exploring environmental causation and their relationship issues."

She nods her understanding and recollection of that conversation, as I continue carefully. "I don't know nor have ever spoken with August, but I saw the two of you working together at Jefferson Sinclair's funeral services. Yes, I was there. I thought you two made a great team. But I don't think August maintains separate, secret relationship spheres.

She wants to take control. "I agree Doctor. I don't think he really cares whether Lydia, Doll, me or anyone else is aware that he has multiple relationships. It's difficult to explain, but I believe he only cares that I care. He only maintains secrecy—believe it or not—to avoid hurting us."

I allow that, since I agree. But I remind Yvette that August has neither denied nor apologized for what most people would consider transgressions. However, before I can move on, she asks, "So then, doesn't that make him a sociopath?"

I disagree. "If he were uncaring, I might be inclined to think so. On the contrary, August's behavior is not sociopathic. I pray you never have a relationship with a true sociopath. Strange though it may seem, August believes his silence, which equates to lies, stems from his compassion. He knows that your socialization guides your views. He knows you can't feel emotionally secure without exclusivity.

"He feels that he is playing your game by your rules. His problem is that he didn't grow up emphasizing monogamy or exclusivity—doesn't know the first thing about it other than what he has seen in movies and on television. Think of him as never moving beyond the teen dating phase. He will indulge the principles of your own socialization, but indulging you is nothing more to him than a dating skill."

Her mouth is agape. She insists on finding a negative label. "So, then he is just immature, right? He has never fully developed into a responsible man. If I walked out of his life right now, he would simply find another date."

"That may be true, essentially. However, it's not as superficial or as simple as that. I think he knows the treasure he has. He just doesn't want it."

"Uh, Doctor?" Yvette looks at me as though trying to make some sort of assessment. I merely shrug. She concludes, "So, what I see is what I get. But just because he was born into a certain environment, his behavior should be acceptable?"

"Yvette, when exactly did I say that? No. His behavior should never be acceptable to anyone who finds such behavior unacceptable. I'm not suggesting that you accept anything."

"Frankly doctor, I think you need to stop tap dancing. My question to you is do you think that I should accept August's engaging in multiple relationships? You aren't stating this clearly but you seem to be suggesting that I should consider settling for a piece of a man—a piece of the cowardly lion or is the tinman who has no heart?"

I say, "I probably would make him the manipulative *man behind the curtain,* actually, Yvette."

"Now you make a good point. On the radio you talked about the need to accommodate an additional personality into my life when I start a new relationship. You said that *each of us must ask ourselves how we feel about the person we must become to make room for a new person.* I knew August was not a factory replacement for David."

She appears to be on the right track, so I simply add, "I know you equate sharing a man to low self-esteem. I think that's at the very crux of this issue—that and the fact that you loved this man."

"That's what I came here for in the beginning Doc. It's what I clearly stated back then as *my problem.* I was unhappy. I was struggling to figure out how to be with this man without doing irreparable damage to my own self-esteem." She glares at me for a long time in silence. She finally drinks from her mug, savoring it as though it contains some aromatic blend of coffee. I think we are ahead of ourselves, but I do not know if I will ever see her again, so I press on.

"Yvette, I have a couple more things before we stop. You say you want my analyses in real time. Okay, here goes. First, I'm not sure how thoroughly you researched prostate surgery, but August will be a very changed man after undergoing a radical prostatectomy.

"An organ in his body closely linked to his manhood, which he sees as his very essence as a person, has been removed. He will be experiencing fundamental changes both physically and mentally. He won't be the same man you knew before. In fact, his multiple-partner days should be over—unless he tries to live a lie. I wouldn't be surprised if he approaches you in a different way. On first blush, you may even find it appealing—*on first blush*."

I pause to permit her to drive for a while, and she does, saying, "I have to decide how I feel about a man slowed down—not by his desire to be monogamous with me—but only because nature limits his capacity to project manhood the only way he knows how."

She takes another sip and looks at me. "And you're wondering if I'll feel empowered by his diminished capacity. Whether I'll have some new feeling of security, even self-esteem, even when he's around other women."

I sum up it all for her. "If you still have an interest in him, I would advise you to be prepared to find out if you really wanted him to become another person—or if you were in love with the person he already was. Oh yes, you'll find out, and you need to be prepared to deal with the answer you get. Yvette, you can never ever get angry with people for the being the way they are or for not being the way you want them to be. And that brings me to a critical question I have for you."

She asks, "And what's that?"

"First, just how long are you going to allow yourself to be haunted by August Caesar's Ghosts? The ghost of Caesar's past, the ghost of Caesar's present, and what will surely be another ghost of Caesar's future? And, *Great Caesar's Ghost*, just how do you plan to serve on a board where you will run interference between Caesar Augustus, the self-made alpha male, and a treacherous old diva, we'll call her *Julia Domna*, who happens to be your gallery's wealthy benefactor? No, Yvette, Edith Sinclair *is not nice*. The

Dalton's and the Rousseau's are all cut from the same cloth. If August—or you on his behalf—ever crosses Edith Dalton Sinclair, she'll cut off what's left between his legs. Trust me on this."

I have committed a few rare violations of personal and professional ethics, but I cannot pull the words back—and neither do I want to. She sits quietly for several minutes and, thankfully, asks no more about it. Instead she asks, "So even if I can't answer your specific question right now, I'm not crazy—August is?"

"Yvette, August is as crazy as a loon. Sticking with our Wizard of Oz analogy, he couldn't find Kansas in the dark with both hands. I don't believe I said that."

"She is insistent. "Then falling for him makes me crazier than him. So, tell me, Walter, why did we waste so much time?" I am quite certain she does not think she is crazy, so I ignore her conclusion. Also, I am aware of her need to have the last word, so I let her have it. I do not answer her loaded question.

Yvette stands abruptly and opens my tripod. She produces a push pin she just happens to have in her purse and pins a plastic-coated business card to my empty poster board. As I look closer, I note the dated color photograph of an attractive woman who runs a real estate office down the street.

"So, this is your friend Lydia. What is this about, Yvette?"

Without comment, she walks slowly to the door, her derriere moving in a snapping motion. Looking back over her shoulder, she laughs at my unprofessional copulative gaze, saying only, "Homework, Walter. I'll see you next Friday at my regular time."

CHAPTER 30

We are a matching set of abstract hourglasses, identical bookends sculpted in illusory motion by the same artist.

I have not yet deleted Yvette's response to my text inviting her over. "Lydia, you must be in great shape. Oh no. I'm okay. Let's keep pushing." Now that reconstruction work is underway on the building that will house her new gallery, Yvette has shown boundless energy and enthusiasm. She and Canuck join me for a run along a winding trail that meanders through a slither of Rock Creek Park.

From there, we head toward my deceased parents' still-vacant house located on the edge of the park. I need to sell it if Sonya cannot or will not buy it. Aaron, who adored his grandparents, will not move into it, preferring instead to pay the high costs of a small space in Old Town.

The park is a long swath of natural greenery, one-mile at its widest, running through the length of the city's northwest quadrant. Many Washingtonians consider the long thousand-acre ecosystem and its popular north-south waterway to be a natural buffer between two cities within a city.

In response to a question from Yvette, I tell her, "There are old affluent Gold Coast neighborhoods stacked along the park's eastern and western borders. For most people who live well to the east of the buffer, neighborhoods just east of the park form the *Gold Coast*—and those neighborhoods west of the park are in another world."

After a visual inspection and airing out the still vacant property, we drink a few bottles of water on the front porch, exchange words with a few longtime residents and, with Canuck leading the way, we walk the same route back to my house.

Spirits are high as we laugh and talk during the easy stroll, occasionally touching, once holding hands. The distance is considerable but not far for two fit women, even two sixty-years old, but afterwards we both need a healthy snack and a soothing hot shower.

Waiting for my hair and a fresh clear coat of nail polish to dry, I lay across my bed wrapped in an oversized terry cloth towel that I have allowed to become partially undone. I am disappointed that Yvette passed on my invitation to join me in the shower, hoping her refusal was not an indication of how we will spend the remainder of the day. When I no longer hear Yvette's shower water running, I lay poised in anticipation, waiting for her to reemerge.

I watch her move about my bedroom bending over to dry off flawlessly shaped legs and dangle jaunt breasts that stubbornly defy gravitational pull. As the cool air blows over her damp body, her nipples extend deliciously at the top of a shapely torso that, even with its sleight pouch, has only a few subtle love handles. The gray hair she has below is much like the swaths that run through her hair and mine.

Her ample derriere remains tight despite a hint of the effects of time. She pretends not to acknowledge my exposed body and my intense interest, but I know better. The nature I now know that we share informs me that the pulse pounding between my legs is the same rhythm that is driving her erogenous tissue to the brink of popping out of its vaginal purse. While I can certainly ramp up my aggression and push her over the proverbial hump, I would rather that she crosses over on her own.

I have left no room for misinterpreting my attraction or my intent. I allow my towel to fall off completely and prop myself up on an elbow to stare directly into her eyes. She stops in midstride to fix her gaze directly on mine. "What?" *What my ass.* My own breasts rise and fall with her deepened breathing, and when I catch her stealing a peek, I avert my eyes momentarily to accommodate her insistence on maintaining the shy facade.

"Lydia, I thought we were going to continue our conversation." While her spoken words are insistent, the tenor of her voice pleads for something other than conversation.

I indulge her, answering matter-of-factly without saying anything much. "So then, let's talk Yvette." I have tried to show patience as we have discussed her need to reconcile her feelings she has about *being there* for August in his *time of need*.

She knows he can—in fact, *prefers to*—take care of his problems by himself. It seems to me that her options are clear. If she will settle down today, we can conduct a non-verbal dialogue that will help her decide what she should do—help her see that she can have it all.

She has all the answers she needs. I saw that when she rang my doorbell this morning wearing a short tennis skirt for a run. When she allowed me to greet her in the foyer with a soulful kiss, I had considered taking her right then and there. But Canuck had been beside himself over finally solving the mystery of the pussy he had been smelling on August for the past three years.

For some reason, Yvette seems personally invested in August's scramble to sell off AJC assets. However, I see no role for her in that exercise and no reason for her to harbor guilt. Inexplicably, she talks as though she has an option to reject Edith Sinclair's generous offer to serve on one of her boards.

She has no such option—unless she wants to watch a lot of gallery-related rehab work come to an abrupt stop. I am learning quickly that Yvette requires help with a considerable load of baggage, much of which *she chooses* to lift and bear.

I have told her that August made us before we even made each other. I have indulged the confusion she feigns when I encourage her to spend as much time with him as she desires—reminding her that his age and condition will limit his grazing range.

But there really remains only one thing to discuss right now. It is our little parlay in body language that begins with the deliciously crisp breeze billowing through my bedroom windows and my desire to be in an inverted embrace. My patience grows thin. She should be using the tip of her tongue to lick a letter of apology all over my wet pocketbook for making me wait.

Nails completely dried, I get out of the bed and walk over to her, encouraged that despite her guarded posture, she has not yet put on a single article of clothing. Rather than trying to sweep her up and overpower her, I take her hand and kiss the palm softly, holding it as I lay my head on her shoulder. She whispers softly. "I know that you just don't understand me, Lydia."

I kiss her softly on her neck. "Oh, but I do, baby. I do understand. But we can deal with all that later." Without moving closer, I kiss her neck again and feel her shudder. Finally, after standing close without embracing for a long time in silence, she gently pulls me closer and I run my hand over her hair in gentle strokes. I slip my free hand around her waist and begin lightly tracing up and down the small of her back to the north slope of her behind.

The motion sends a charge through my own body in anticipation of what I hope is finally about to occur. When I feel her shiver again, I struggle to resist reacting too quickly.

Rather, despite my excruciating need to have more, I maintain the slightest space between us, and as she places her face against mine, I hear her heavier labored breathing. I am losing the ability to be indulgent, unselfish.

I whisper to her that, "I'm through talking for now." I am powerless to further resist kissing her, sucking gently on her upper and bottom lips until she opens her mouth and I feel her tongue venture out.

I give her a long taste of mine, a step toward establishing the connection that I know will meld her body into mine. I push my tongue easily through her pursed lips and probe deeper, expressing my pent-up passion. I sense that she, momentarily, entertains some misguided impulse to push me away, but the opportunity for that senseless behavior has passed.

"I've been wanting to make love to you for a long time, Yvette. To hold you close like this, to kiss you just like this."

Her speech is halting, her message incoherent. "But we haven't really said anything." I ignore her empty protest and kiss her along the length of her neck, blowing softly on the wet surfaces I have created until I hear her gasp and feel her arms encircling my neck. We are on a journey together now, a voyage of exploration and discovery. *There is so much of this world that I want to show you.*

I back her slowly and gently against the wall next to my bed. Like a special gift, Nature has designed both pairs of our nipples to practically press against each other—Yvette's long and firm, mine rounded and flexible, surrounded by fine strands of hair.

I slide one leg in between hers and lean forward until I feel her soft silky mat mesh with my soft coarser grade. I have a surprise for her I hope she can appreciate. As expected, my bulb expands, becoming visible, pulsating fruit pressing into the channel she leaves wide open. Still, I maintain enough composure to limit myself to putting only a hint of gentle pressure on our erogenous surfaces. Still waxing over our skin, I begin a slow grinding motion.

With her upper back supported against the wall, I feel her pushing out to meet me. I open my eyes wide when I discover that she is just as bulbous. We both moan and she calls out my name. I gently nudge her to stoop slightly so that we can commence a dance that allows me to twist in and out. When I place both my palms against the wall next to her shoulders, she responds by reaching around to palm both cheeks of my ass.

We continue twisting to the tunes on disc of classic slow R&B. She follows my lead in submission for a while but the temptation to exert a little more force is overwhelming. Yvette demonstrates some moxie by turning me around against the wall and performing the same motion, leaving wet sticky traces all over my inner thighs.

"Baby, you get as wet as I do." I allow her to pilot for a long time in her own rendition of my slow rhythmic drag. Again, and again, we both become rigid and shudder.

I moan aloud through clinched teeth as a wave radiates through the top of my skull. To her credit, she calmly continues our long sensuous joust by holding on ever so loosely, making just enough contact to enable us to maintain our balance. After a few more minutes, her cry is audible and I hear my name again.

Our bodies press together and meld as our dance becomes a full-bodied slow drag. Then we stand together motionless until I gently push her back onto the mattress, tumble into bed after her, and lock us in a tight, silent embrace.

After a short nap—too short—she awakens me with a kiss. I wonder just what I have unleashed on myself. As my vision clears, I see that her eyes express the hope that we have merely been on a break.

I need more sleep and have no more patience. I flip her over on her stomach and slide my wet tongue deep into her rear cavity. I hear her cry out for help she does not really want until she buries her face in a pillow to muffle her screams. I flip her over onto her back again, and bury my face in her mound of Nubian softness until I can taste her bulb, which is growing once again. I suckle it, listening to her groan upward into the pillow that now covers her face.

I flip her over on her stomach again and, this time, plunge my tongue even deeper. I believe that I have heard the word *stop* several times but it only inspires me to go. I flip her back over and apply enough suction to suck a mouthful of clitoris and some surrounding tissue as though I am trying to reach the chewy center of a lollypop. She wraps her legs around my shoulders to keep me exactly where I am, moaning my name repeatedly as she grabs two handfuls of my hair.

When I finally disengage, I look forward to taking the long blissful nap I crave. However, when I kiss her, the tastes left on my lips and tongue send her into a frenzy. Yvette is all over me with what I can only describe as artistic flair. Perhaps, doing what she knows best, she circles the base of my clit both clockwise and counter. In what seems no time at all, I tremble uncontrollably until an implosion leaves me clawing for a pillow to muffle my screams.

However, all the pillows are on the floor now, so I cry out with no filter. Soon, we are clinging to one another tightly until, finally exhausted, she collapses with me into a long slumber.

CHAPTER 31

"**D**amn AC, that girl makes some good lemonade—with sliced yellow *and* green lemons."

After we have spent an hour catching up, the sound of Shantel back in the kitchen stirring a pitcher brings back memories. "I swear, AC, her lemonade has kept me here for the past ten years. One summer I was all set to move in with a woman closer to my age—a fat little Post Office retiree. I had all my shit to the left of the front door stuffed into four boxes and four hefty bags. But it was hot outside. I stopped to get a cold drink. Shit. That lemonade was so good it made my legs wobble."

I take another sip of cognac and feign losing the ability to stand as AC roars with laughter the way he used to laugh a long time ago when we were running the streets as kids—*if we ever really were kids.*

AC and I were born two years apart on the same day of the month at the same hospital. Our mothers were two young girls who had grown up in this same neighborhood.

Although they both denied it many years ago, some people still swear that Pharaoh is AC's biological father. AC and I are both, I have heard, the spitting images of our mothers, one of whom died in childbirth and the other surrendered her son after birth.

We were inseparable. Then he shipped out overseas without a word to me while I rotted in prison. I never knew when he came home on leave, if ever. I only found out today about his sons.

He never stopped by for a laugh. I received a mysterious cashier's check in the mail years ago—and admit it came in handy. However, prior to today, though I had seen him here and there, I never spoke to him or approached him. Although I once covertly ran a little interference to allow Peaches to take a shot at seducing him, I have not spoken to him or approached him in nearly 45 years.

"AC, the next thing I knew, baby girl was grilling me a sandwich—with ham, turkey *and cheese*. Once she had it in the pan, she pulled me down on the kitchen floor to seal the deal while the sandwich grilled on the stove. The next thing I knew, I smelled my food on the table. Shit, I've been living in this crowded motherfucker ever since."

"What about the woman you were going to leave her for?"

"Come on man. What kind of question is that?" I put AC in a headlock to emphasize the absurdity of such a question. "Look man, I don't plan to die here though. I know you won't believe me, but I saved the check that only you could have sent, the whole 25-large in a credit union account. Shantel and Peaches would drag my ass to the teller window at gunpoint if they knew about it. I'm getting out of here and going into one of those independent living communities for seniors. And the next time I move, they'll be carrying my black ass out of there on a gurney—if not in a body bag."

AC has been warm and cordial toward the entire household but has not had much to say. Even though I complain, I admit that this house has been my happy home. After urban renewal strategies failed in this space designated as DC's southwest quadrant, the local housing authority rebuilt and rehabbed several blocks of row houses and made them available to select families. The lucky public housing residents attended classes in home ownership and maintenance. Peaches had been one of the fortunate few, obtaining a unit that she still shares with Shantel, her three street-smart granddaughters and, unofficially, me.

I remember when this area was for poor blacks and poor whites. Then, they displaced everyone. Families dispersed all over. August and I ran off and lived on the streets until we became Pharaoh's watchdogs. The only rule we ever broke—other than getting arrested—was bringing in teenaged girls whenever they could arrange to be there.

Then, I got the idea we needed a car. We burst into a liquor store brandishing two old rusty pistols. Like a gangster, AC discharged a round through the window. I will never forget the level of cooperation it inspired.

A few days later, the police arrested us in front of the *Ko-Ko Club*. That is where the story gets fuzzy for me. We were both, technically, first offenders. AC was under-aged, so they separated us. No one demanded my release nor inquired about my well-being. Pharaoh disappeared into *Orion's Belt*—and offered no posted bail. I thought we were alone.

In court, my public defender convinced me that an eyewitness had come forward and there was enough evidence to convict us. I signed some documents and hoped for the best. The judge handed down a ten-year sentence anyway. Later I found out that AC's case was in juvenile court. I reached out to him to no avail. Years later, I found out he was in Vietnam.

I cannot resist making comparisons. He has arrived wearing slacks that evidently do not wrinkle, beautiful soft leather slip-ons and a simply designed linen shirt. However, the quality of each item is obvious. I have on nylon activewear, much the same as I would have worn 35 years ago.

I look like a senior version of the young boys who aimlessly patrol our neighborhood. When he walked in, AC handed Shantel his warm weather fedora to put away—which most likely is in Peaches' bedroom. Though I am inside, I have no intention of removing my baseball cap.

"I'm just taking it easy AC. I still get a disability check deposited every month into my credit union account. It's for my back. You know I got this bad back. I don't touch the money because I drive for a limo service. I work under the table and often get more from tips than I make per trip.

"If my passengers want something extra, I know exactly how and where to hook them up. I park a new Cadillac out front every 50K miles, pay a few bills, pay for groceries, hair, nails and lashes, and buy these girls occasional outfits—and I gets to sleep next to that little 35-year old that just rolled through here. I have to hit it more often than I want—more often than I really can." I fall to my knees exaggerating exhaustion.

"You know who you sound like, don't you? Biscuit."

I laugh aloud. "Not weasel assed Biscuit. Come on AC. Is he still alive? How is that police informant bastard still alive?"

August moves closer to me on the sofa as though we are about to become partners in a conspiracy. "That weasel bastard is my son's grandfather."

My voice explodes. "Oh no, AC. Biscuit? Wannabe pimp Biscuit? Fake-assed cab driving Biscuit? Not only did he give us those two rusted out revolvers that night, he was supposed to be our lookout and getaway driver. I never did square that with him—or with you for that matter."

My old friend now has a proper segue to tell me honestly, why he has come here after all these years—even at my invitation. Perhaps he can tell me about that anonymous check the credit union held for two weeks. In addition, perhaps he can explain to me why a private eye made the effort to confirm that AC was with me in the liquor store that night. Most important of all, perhaps he can tell me exactly what happened to him down at juvenile hall.

August's voice starts out just above a whisper. "Would you believe that somebody hired a PI to go way back to that? No, there's nothing more he can do now. It's done and over. I hid the arrest because sticking up a liquor store, even as a minor, was a problem for me. Trying to hide it led to a bigger problem. No. The only people who knew about the robbery were you and Biscuit."

He can now add Shantel to that list, but I cannot see how telling him that would matter now. "AC, you know Biscuit gave up people to the cops. That's why he never did any time. I think he even fingered Pharaoh once. AC, I never knew everything that went down back then. I mean, I knew you got a plea bargain and a deal but I don't know the circumstances."

"What do you mean?" He looks puzzled.

"I mean I don't know why you got a deal and not me. I always assumed it had to do with our ages, but that don't really add up." I have known

August Caesar since he was nine years old, and even after a lifetime hiatus, I still can read his face. He genuinely believes that I already knew what he is about to share with me.

"Smack, after all these years, you don't know? Look man, I'm sorry. I thought you knew and had forgiven me." I simply continue looking at him quietly and patiently waiting for information someone should have shared with me 40 years ago.

He begins slowly. "You already know that Biscuit was driving one of Pharaoh's cars that night. A guard approached him for loitering in the lot across the street from the liquor store. He called the police and they traced the tags and the car back to Pharaoh, who gave up Biscuit in a heartbeat. Then Biscuit fingered us, even though he was only loitering and driving with a fake permit. When they questioned me, I thought they had it all, and I signed the full confession.

"The Army stint was my option, yes—but not my reward. It wasn't a deal. I had already spilled everything to the cops. The sentencing judge, on his own initiative, presented the Army option. I almost jumped out of my seat and ran to Fort Dix. Pharaoh, who was going to freeze my hot ass out after that, found my foster pops and slipped him some cash. He had to clean him up to take him downtown. Smack, pops threw up in the courtroom. The judge almost gave him some time."

I remain silent for a long time. In all honesty, I guess I had always considered AC's release as his reparation for following me down some of those murky paths. I recall that whenever they made him attend school, he took to it as though he had been in class every day all along. Even back then, he did all the counting for us. We almost kept him from the destiny he was naturally inclined to pursue.

The liquor store robbery had been my terrible idea and an irresponsible indiscretion for a grown man like Biscuit to condone. AC was just a kid with no alternative to going along with us. I decide to tell him about my late-night passenger.

"That PI scared me last week the same way they scared you, AC, and I'm an old hand at this shit. He hired my limo for a ride downtown from Dulles. He shook me down like a gangster. He pretended to want to know how you beat the charges when he was only trying to confirm your arrest. Does any of that mean anything to you?"

August looks as though a light has turned on inside his head. "Yes. It does now. Some political hack hired him to look for any kind of dirt he could find in my past. I doubt if I'll ever know who hired him. Once he had you and compared dates, he had it all. He never even talked to me. Somehow, he knew to turn it over to the feds, that it contradicted a statement I attested to on a federal form. I don't know how the hell he knew, how he got a copy of the case or knew where to take it."

I pick up the bottle and refill his glass, as AC continues, "I thought the mess would cost me a lot of money—*my own money*. It did not. Now the local hacks hope this will be enough of an embarrassment to scare me away from running from office. Funny thing is, I never wanted to. All they really had to do was talk to me."

AC is trying to downplay the whole affair, but this ordeal clearly has been staggering for him. I keep the onus on Biscuit. "Do you think the PI got to Biscuit? I do too. Biscuit must be the one who gave us up. Somebody ought to shoot his ass on GP—you know just for old time's sake."

The door swings open and Shantel's three daughters return from admiring Sonny's sports car. They linger in the front room, curious about the father of this stylish boy outside polishing an expensive red convertible. Their hairstyles, makeup and form fitting jeans—stuffed with their own oversized third-generation peaches—make the three teenaged girls indistinguishable from adult women. They quiz AC for information to reconcile against what Sonny has told them.

Then, Peaches walks in, sits down on AC's knee and shoos the girls back outside. Curiously, Shantel has had very little to say, staying upstairs in the bedroom or back the kitchen. I am certain the fans can smell her gumbo in Nationals' Park. Peaches is wearing a figure-hugging sundress. As she jokes with AC, she bounces around and giggles until her song plays on the radio. Then, her movements start to resemble a lap dance.

"Oh yeah, player. That's why they call me Peaches. It's Estelle, but don't you dare call me that. That was just some Creole-Bayou type shit my mama came up with."

Even at fifty, I have seen Peaches bring out the lust in men. August may be sending her mixed signals. He accepted her invitation to stay awhile after Sonny leaves on the condition that I drive him home.

I agreed to take him home whenever he was ready, *including in the morning if that's his preference.* When he did not rule out that possibility, she had every reason to feel confident. *"Eat some more gumbo, player. It'll get your strength back up—put some solid lead in your pencil."*

After watching Shantel move around in her dress all day, I may not be down here to run interference for him later tonight. I laugh as Peaches attempts to stand up but loses her balance, tumbling hands-first back into his lap. After she *finally gets up*, she makes her way upstairs—but August does not accept her obvious invitation to follow. *"So, if I want to show you my new dress, I got to come all the way back down here?"* Her next attempt will not be as subtle.

Watching him fail to answer the call of duty begs a question for my old friend. "So, you had the surgery in New York? You know, even at my age, I don't know a thing about prostate cancer and don't know anyone—except now you—who's had the surgery. You seem to be getting around just fine, even though I notice you're riding shotgun and sipping light."

He answers simply, "I wanted the best chance to come out of it with my mojo intact. Everything worked out fine but I still have a way to go."

When the kitchen abruptly goes completely silent, I quickly change the subject. "But, fuck all that. Who shot you, man?"

"Smack this is the first time I've been able to speak freely about it. The detectives have just been going through the motions—certain I intend to take matters into my own hands. I was just picking up my Chinese food like I've done a thousand times before—just like dozens of other people I know who have been going there all their lives. I run into people I know all the time."

"Yeah, I go to a place right around here. But I've been out that way too. That pepper steak they got is the bomb."

"I saw the car sitting out there with the motor running. I saw the window opening but kept walking toward my car. As I passed the window, I expected to hear a greeting but instead saw and felt the heat from the flash. I felt the round tear through my right side. But the punk didn't know it would light up his face. A corner of the parking lot lit up like a night game."

I remember Pharaoh always said it was a detail overlooked by amateurs and shooters driven by emotions. However, August can tell from my face that there is only one piece of information that has shocked me. "Yeah, Smack. I said he."

"So, you do know him? Why would he shoot you?" He shrugs. "Not over a woman? No? Then it must have been over money? Bingo, I can see it on your face—*his money*, huh? Okay then, over what he *thought was his money*. So, you know where we can find him?"

"No can do, Smack—no payback required. I can't say more, other than the boy's greed and insecurity temporarily rendered him mentally unstable. Just the notion of me having a little control over something he saw as his pushed him over the edge—only to lose his nerve at the last second. He could have lost his freedom."

"So that's it? You ain't going to take care of this? Then you must be planning to bribe his ass. There must be a piece of change in it for you then—right?"

"I'll just say he's worth a hell of a lot more to me out of jail. Hell, he could get a whole team of lawyers to make sure he never did any real time. Plus, he's the relative of a powerful friend."

"Oh, the people at the funeral? I could smell the money through the TV set. You know, I was wondering if you'd be okay with all this shit going down."

"I'm good. I've been scared to spend money for the last five years."

I am certain that Peaches and Shantel are hatching a plan to isolate AC. I am about to warn him when the front door opens again and Shantel's oldest daughter walks in. She calls to her mother. "Can I go for a ride with Sonny?"

We both laugh. AC jumps up and goes outside to counsel to his son. She is a teenaged girl who, despite having her mother's body, is only 17—over the city's legal age of consent but still too young for Sonny. However, I laugh, knowing that he should be protecting little Sonny from LaToya who has been on dates with older men. When AC opens the door to come back inside, I catch a glimpse of Sonny's car pulling away from the curb. "What's that the Book says about the sins of the father AC?"

"What?"

"Never mind, so what's next for you?"

"Would you believe a road trip? Sonny and I are going to put some miles on my SUV. We're driving out to see my people near Oakland, and stopping at points of interest in between. Depending on how things go there, either my son will be flying back alone for the grand opening of *Sonny's Barbershop & Hair Salon* or we'll be driving back together. I need to try to reconnect with my family, Smack. If all goes well, I'll stay out there a month and give one of my grandsons the truck as a belated graduation present."

"And come back to handle that Renaissance thing, huh?"

"Yeah. By the way, do you like making that airport run?"

"Hell no, man."

"I know you don't want an office gig. What if I asked you to be our lead driver—put you in charge of the two other drivers we budgeted?"

I prefer to speak plainly. "AC, you mean *your chauffer*. Hell yes, but I answer only to you. Who else is going to watch your back? By the way, what's up with you and Peaches tonight?"

"There ain't a damn thing up. I tried to explain that to her. There was a time when I'd be upstairs right now, bending her over."

"I know that's right. I think she needs a *good old school drilling* round about now. So, then you can't anymore—I mean, like you used to?"

"Hell, Smack, that decline started years ago. Oh, I can pop a pill and stand on deck. I know Peaches probably still got *the bomb*. But I think I need to slow it all down and just try to square things up with Doll."

"Oh, really? *With Biscuit's daughter?* Can I ask why?"

AC looks down reflectively, as though what he is about to say may be news for both of us. "Mainly because, except for Biscuit's trifling ass, her family is *my family*—the only real one I have left here, other than you. That was clear in the hospital. Getting closer to Sonny has pulled us all closer together. Plus, I'm not a young man anymore, Smack. You must have the secret to the *fountain of youth*—still drinking *yack* and smoking *blunts*."

"Well, just so you know, I can still deliver the meat." I say loud enough to reach the kitchen.

AC smiles at my announcement. However, his description of Biscuit's daughter suggests to me that rational appeals will not get the job done. He continues to talk like an old man. "Well, I hope you never find out how it feels to need help wiping your own black ass. That shit will make you stop and think—no pun intended."

I need to change the subject. Knowing that he needs a ride, I inform him, "I'm going to have to get my swerve on upstairs tonight. So, me and Shantel will be slipping upstairs early. That gumbo is always better the next day. And you already know Peaches has a different plan."

He immediately interjects, "Then she'll have to find another man."

I do not like the sound of that, and tell him, "AC, I'm not trying to hear about this for the next two years. Where you gone sleep tonight? Come on man, cowboy the fuck up. I got all the pills. Which color do you use?"

CHAPTER 32

U sing a hotel's landline phone, I dial the *burner* mobile phone number given to me by the investigator known simply as *Ed*. He is expecting my call and picks up after the first ring. "Hello Adele. Yes, I'm all done. No, it was almost too easy."

Ed's voice booms in clearly through the tabletop speaker. I adjust the volume for my breakfast meeting guests, two old friends with very different styles of brokering the considerable power they each wield.

We have been eating breakfast in the private dining room of a quiet little hotel off the beaten path. Ed is aware that one guest anxiously awaits the full report he has summarized for me. The other guest is an unexpected meeting participant.

I give him a vague heads-up. "Ed, I've got *a couple of people here* with me awaiting your report. First, I'm curious—how many leads did you get to cooperate with you?"

They appear startled by the hearty laugh I have grown accustomed to hearing. "Almost everybody gave me something on somebody else. What a cast of characters. I almost did it for free. I said *almost*. The only ones who clamped shut were old Miss Jackson and that older fellow from California—they just laughed in my face."

I ask what is for me the most critical question now that our investigation has closed. "Do you think anyone can tie you to us—back to me?" Ed has acknowledged that the collateral damage from this assignment exceeded our requirements and expectations. However, he has not yet explained, to my satisfaction, his overzealous pursuit of several sources.

He is serious again, turning on the professionalism that, until now, cemented his status as my private investigator of choice—the ex-Marine military policeman I have engaged whenever success and secrecy were of equal importance. "Not a chance. Yeah, my man AC, or *Afro Cool*, will be wondering about it for a long time." Ed pauses to laugh derisively at his own joke. "I don't think anyone even asked my name—so many skeletons and demons in so many closets."

My unexpected guest surprises me by interjecting his own specific question about August's son—who we agreed was off limits. "What about the boy—*Sonny*? Was there anything there?"

Ed clears his throat. "I'm sorry. To whom am I speaking?" After I introduce my popular guest, Ed continues. "Oh, please accept my apologies, sir. I had no idea you'd be listening in this morning. No, there's nothing on Sonny—yet. Not even a reefer beef or an overdue parking ticket. He's just a spoiled little shit." I detect disappointment.

I hold my tongue as Ed continues. "But I had a ball with the one they call *Smack*. Except for an old conviction and time served, plus an unregistered pistol, Smack is actually pretty clean."

Much to my surprise, my unexpected guest takes out a note pad, after having professed to be at this meeting only *to visit with an old friend*. He asks, "Now, who's that again, Ed?" A hand taps my arm gently, signaling me to allow Ron some latitude.

Ed says, "His name's Russell Adkins, *AKA Smack*—yes just like the drug. He's an old-school roughrider—*all bullshit aside*. I got his name from *an invisible man* impersonating a dead cab driver—put him right next to Caesar in the liquor store. Funny thing, Smack's girlfriend was dying to give me everything she knew on Caesar. It felt like vengeance."

"Vengeance you say, Ed. Really?" I am intrigued to hear a term that describes the theory that has been replaying in my mind.

Ed says, "Speaking of vengeance, Caesar's girlfriend's daughter—the detective—had the actual smoking gun, and handed it over cheerfully. Of course, I destroyed it."

Yeah, after you screwed him with it. I used a huge chit to find out if there was an official record to confirm a rumor I had heard after August's radio interview. I used an even bigger chit to implicate Detective Sergeant JoAnne Saxton in the record's disappearance.

Ed adds, "She had it, but I doubt if she was the one who deleted the file—nothing to gain by that. But she was planning to blackmail AC herself. What are the odds? Yes, she was a concern, at first, but I don't sense that anymore."

I know who ordered the detective's commander to delete the file. Now that she's on the fast track to lieutenant, she is calm, and seems to have cleared her conscience. "Was there anything else?" My voice sounds harsh. I am annoyed with Ed for not simply delivering the printout to me, which would have ended his work on this job. Until just now, I had wondered who had hindered my ability to manage a trusted asset.

Ed continues, "Oh, yes. You asked how much this incident hurt Caesar financially." It is an issue that falls outside my own scope, but I need to know. Ed continues, "Not much really. He didn't lose much on the contract they took from him. He was not on the list of finalists for the new larger deal. He's a rare breed, a street thug with no property liens, personal or business debt—must've been living on a shoestring. He also has retirement income."

August's personal income is none of our business. I have never intended to cripple anyone financially. However, I have no illusions about the negative impact Ed's work will have on his reputation as a contractor.

However, Ed is still talking. "He can count on investments, annuities and the like." Again, I hear disappointment. "Then there's his new gig with the old lady." A hand waves off my impulse to admonish Ed's insolence.

I end it. "So long, Ed. Thanks. Yes, I know this phone number will no longer be available." Late last night, a brown envelope containing cash slid under his hotel room door last night. He does not yet know that I will not engage him again. "Drive safely on the turnpike."

After hanging up, I look across the table at my two companions, who both look back at me in silence. I begin, trying to mask my displeasure. "He should have shared he intel with me—not just hand it over to the Feds. I can't help but wonder how he even knew the intel was actionable, or how?" I ask the question rhetorically, but they both sense my suspicions and dissatisfaction. "Of course, we won't be working together again."

Ron speaks again, further raising my suspicions. "Never say never, Adele. And don't worry. August and his family won't be missing any meals."

His words are troubling, suggesting, as they do that, he has a right to determine how much money August needs. He continues, "But, if he gets any more ideas about launching a campaign, we'll just point our reporter in the right direction. Hey, Ed didn't shoot Caesar, did he?" I ignore the question and the devious smile that flashes across his face. Much to my chagrin, he is still talking. "What's this I hear about him continuing at Renaissance Partners? Is that still on the table?"

Although he directs the question to my client, I respond for her. "Who cares? Let him have that. Look, everyone respected Jeff Sinclair. Just knowing of his interest will increase funding for fine arts education next year. Look, I fix problems. I don't leave trails of blood in my wake." We sit in silence a moment longer.

Finally he says, "Okay. If no one else thinks we should proceed further." He looks at his friend. "DC is a very forgiving town. The non-profit could still be a springboard—neighborhood revitalization projects are popular." Everyone knows that our guest has no qualms about drawing blood or leaving his fingerprints, and mine, at the scenes. We both turn to the older woman dressed in a beautiful black two-piece suit and an understated but stylish matching hat.

She speaks for the first time since Ed took my call. "I'm fine with this outcome as it stands. This business has concluded. We'll not inconvenience Mister Caesar further."

After she speaks, her old friend turns to look directly into my eyes. I can still see genuine concern. In fact, I see fear. "Do you really think he would've been a viable political threat to anyone—I mean to *anyone currently on or running for the council?*"

It is an odd question coming from a man of few allegiances. Several activists have asked me the same question, but their interests have been obvious.

I take the opportunity to rattle his cage. "Well, you have to admit that he's got all the right gifts. After his radio interview, callers blew up WDMV's switchboard and my cell trying to find out if he was running. A dozen organizers sent me text messages. Plus, Jay Spencer would never, regardless of when he committed, go back on the promise he made—so August still has some pretty strong support." I want to rub it in.

The smell of fear becomes a stench. For the first time, I think I detect signs of insomnia. I do not understand why a politician of his stature would worry about August Caesar. Seemingly unable to adjourn, he asks, "So, do we know what he really wants—I mean ultimately?"

"You mean, other than a loose shoe, a tight pussy and a warm place to shit?" He appears startled by such language from one of the city's most respected matriarchs. I am not. I want to laugh, but I see no trace of a smile on the aging woman's stern face. I think she is ready to adjourn.

I break the awkward silence. "Okay. Okay. Then I guess I'll see you at the next pain-in-the-ass town hall meeting, Congressman."

"Don't remind me, Adele. Thanks for inviting me to visit with my old friend."

Visit—visit, my ass. "Oh, don't mention it." I say, shaking the hand he extends. He holds mine for a long moment, looking into my eyes in a way that suggests that there is something going on I do not know about.

After the two of them embrace and DC's Delegate to the House of Representatives has left, I turn to embrace the woman who taught me everything I know—especially about never revealing who or how much I know. "Mrs. Sinclair, is your driver meeting you downstairs?"

She waits until the elevator door opens and closes out in the lobby. "Yes, Russell should be right downstairs now. So, thank you, dear. Don't feel bad for August. He's better off than anyone knows. He was going to dump that security guard business anyway. However, do worry about Ron—there's something about hush money. The Speaker advised him not to seek reelection."

"Who'll you run in the next cycle?"

"Oh, you'll know that before anyone else does. Adele, just so you know, I really don't care what else August does now. We just didn't need another *short-cutter* running amok with his pants down in the District Building right now. But, if he ever finds out who was behind this, he could be very difficult. Do you understand?"

"Yes ma'am. I absolutely understand."

"I love this little hideaway. Everything was so lovely here this morning, as always. Tip generously. I'll be at your son's new church next Sunday."

"Yes ma'am. Thank you."

She stops and turns back to face me. "Funny thing. All this, and August never once mentioned to me anything about running for office—not even once. Maybe all we did was free him to do Jefferson's real bidding."

"Do you still have confidence in your person on the board?" I ask.

"I don't know. She's distracted lately. She just discovered that her 35-year old daughter's a lesbian, even though the child has never brought a fella home in her life. And guess who just left the girl standing at the alter—the new executive director August hired for Renaissance."

"Oh my God." I take step back.

"I know. But tell me, Adele, do you feel certain my husband was sincere about the campaign? I keep smelling red herring."

I ask, "You think Jeff had time to school August?"

"*School August?* So then, you also plan to keep on underestimating him?" Mrs. Sinclair is pensive for a moment, then laughs—perhaps at her own expense. "Well, I know this is like the pot calling the kettle black, but that would be an underhanded thing for my husband to have done to me." She laughs again, this time from deep within, and asks, "But then, you know what?"

"What's that, ma'am?"

"Old Jamaicans have a saying about hurricane season. *June, it's too soon. July, we'll get by—but August, if we must.* You want to know something else?"

"What's that ma'am?"

"That crazy old man died popping that thing into my behind. I swear, I feel it every time I say or hear his name—*just as he predicted I would.*"